WHERE LOVE IS PLANTED

A MERISIDE ROMANCE - BOOK 1

DAWN KINZER

This story is a work of fiction and the product of the author's imagination.

Cover design by Lynnette Bonner of Indie Cover Design
https://www.indiecoverdesign.com

Images©

https://www.bigstock.com/Photo ID 444554282/model
https://www.istockphoto.com/Photo ID 483348551/prisoner
https://www.bigstockphoto.com/Photo ID 1305772852/
potting a red daisy in dirt
https://www.depositphoto.com/Photo ID 142136520/spring

Where Love is Planted/ Dawn Kinzer.1st ed.

ISBN: 978-1-7367770-4-6

To Dad . . .

You offered the gifts of grace and unconditional love.
You taught me what it felt like to be seen and heard—
and how important it is to take time to listen.
You've always had my back,
and so much of you has formed so much of me.

Let us not become weary in doing good,
for at the proper time we will reap a harvest
if we do not give up. ~ Galatians 6:9

One

On a beautiful day like this, Beth Miller could almost forget that one, swift irreversible moment when her life and the lives of others had been forever changed.

Her light sweater and jacket shielded her from the slight chill lingering in the late March air. She stretched out on the bench beneath the cherry tree that stood between her studio apartment and Agatha Sharp's craftsman-style home. Beth crossed her arms and tucked them under her head. Sunshine broke through the pink canopy above, and she tilted her head to embrace the warmth. There was time to relax before heading to the cemetery.

Two years to the day. Her throat clogged, and a hot tear escaped. Those darn emotions. Rushing to the surface again. Just when she thought they'd been restrained.

Yet . . . God had sent a reminder with those caressing, golden rays from heaven that he hadn't forgotten her pain. And he was still there, walking beside her. Even in those moments when she didn't feel him or had forgotten how much she needed his presence.

Faint scents, barely detectable, heightened her senses. The hyacinths were close to blooming, and soon the garden would be filled with their lovely smell. Daffodils also displayed a strong, cheerful appearance, but tulips weren't revealing their colorful petals yet. Later in the spring, lilacs would showcase lovely blossoms. Of all the flowers, they were her favorite, and there were so many varieties to choose from—blue, lavender, magenta, pink, purple, white, and yellow. Maybe one day, she'd plant a lilac bush in each hue in her own garden.

Beth inhaled a whiff of salty air, a reminder of how close she was to the Sound. Living in a Washington port town with access to both the Olympic Mountains and the Pacific Ocean was difficult to give up, hence she'd attended a college less than a five-hour drive from home.

Driven and goal-oriented, she didn't want any success at the expense of her family, but God had placed desires in her heart. Why would he give her those dreams if they were to be kept in sight but never within reach?

Lord, I don't want to complain. I really don't. You've given me so much.

She could continue working at the family business and still find ways to feed her passion, but what she was able to accomplish there wasn't at the level she wanted to achieve. Was there something God required of her before she fulfilled her calling? Sure, she had flaws, like always wanting to feel in control. But she was working on that.

Unfortunately, there was another step to complete before becoming a horticultural therapist. Beth had been close to achieving it, but following the loss of her dad and brother, the only choice she could make was to leave her internship, come home, and be with her grieving family.

Her brother had been her best friend. He'd trusted Beth—depended on her like she him—and she'd made that promise. One she strived to keep. Liam had begged her to take care of Mom, Harmony, and Kaylee. But too often, she fell short. And the secret she kept from her family? It burdened her with guilt, but the facts carried potential to cause more hurt. So she'd buried the truth within her heart.

Now, two years later, at the age of twenty-nine, she still hadn't found a way to finish that last requirement for professional certification. And she sometimes struggled with feeling like a failure, professionally and personally.

Dad, I miss you. You always knew what to do.

She was almost four when her father had taken her on a daddy-daughter date while Mom stayed home with toddler Liam. They'd gotten ice cream before strolling the local piers, and because one structure had no railings, Dad had taken a firm hold of Beth's hand. But when a conversation with several fishermen lasted too long, she'd grown impatient and slipped from his grasp.

Not paying attention to her surroundings, she'd backed too close to the wooden floor's edge and toppled into the cold water. As Beth sank slowly into the depths, she felt no fear, only peace.

Then with a *whoosh*, her dad's strong arms grabbed her and carried her to the surface. As soon as she was pulled from the water, a fisherman wrapped a warm blanket around Beth's shoulders. She felt perfectly calm and didn't even cry, but her father was shaken and insisted they return home.

After that experience on the pier, Beth trusted her dad to be there when needed. Until that painful day when he wasn't and never would be again.

The soft glow of light filtering through her closed eyelids was suddenly snuffed out, and she shivered as darkness blocked the sun's heat. Beth opened her eyes with a squint. A cloud didn't hinder the soothing rays—a man towered over her. She bolted up and sat rubbing her eyes, trying to focus on the intruder.

"I didn't mean to startle you." The guy sounded sincere, but he didn't back off. Instead, he merely changed his stance and hung his hands on slacked hips.

"Okay . . . I believe you, but it was little unsettling being snuck up on like that." Beth did a quick study. Tall, dark, good-looking. An older version of the teenager in the photographs Agatha had shown Beth. The elderly woman had mentioned he'd turned thirty-two earlier this year. "You're Agatha's nephew, Tyler."

He stroked his well-trimmed dark beard. "Great-nephew. And you're . . . Aunt Agatha's renter, Beth. Did I get the name right?"

Renter. She nodded and smiled through gritted teeth. Better set him straight from the get-go. "Yeah, I live in the studio apartment. Your aunt and I have become close friends." Beth cherished any time spent with Agatha. The woman was talented, kind, and wise. "We didn't expect you until the beginning of the month."

"I'm not officially on the clock until a week from Monday, but I decided to come early and get settled in. Get the lay of the land. Called Aunt Agatha last night, and she gave the okay."

"You've been hired to work at the women's prison?" Since it was only a twenty-minute drive from Meriside, other residents of the town were also employed at the facility.

"Yep. I'm a social worker." He smiled. "My job is to help inmates adapt while there and prepare for life after."

Beth winced. She once held great compassion for the incarcerated, but it was difficult to feel the same after being personally impacted by someone who had broken the law. "How does that work? A man in that role?" Her tone sounded more caustic than intended, and his eyes narrowed.

"Similar to male guards and wardens. Or female wardens and guards hired at penitentiaries for men. If employees stick to their jobs and do them well, gender isn't an issue." He shrugged. "But it can make some situations more complicated if boundaries are crossed."

"I see you two have already met." Agatha moved down the back steps of her house gracefully, a navy wool shawl draped over her and two forest-green ceramic mugs in her hands. She wore her silver hair in a long side braid that rested in front, over her right shoulder.

An artist and retired art teacher, Agatha lived in color. The design on her flowing full-length bohemian-style dress blended muted shades of the rainbow, and her camel-colored boots peeked from beneath. "Beth, I saw you out here and thought we might enjoy a bit of jasmine tea together." Agatha handed one mug to her and extended the other to her nephew. "Ty, would you like some? There's more hot water. I can make myself another cup in a jiffy."

"Thanks, but I have errands to run, including the grocery store. I promised you lasagna." He placed his hand on his aunt's shoulder. "I'll be back in an hour or so." Tyler tilted his head toward Beth. "See you around."

"Yeah, see you," she called after him, attempting to sound cheery for Agatha, despite her annoyance at his assumption he could make his handsome self at home and treat Beth like she only represented income to Agatha.

Tyler ambled down the drive, and Agatha sat next to Beth and winked. "Don't let him get under your skin." She lifted her cup to her lips and sipped.

"I—I did no such thing." Beth's face heated. "He was a tad rude, but he's your nephew, so I'll be nice."

"I'm sorry to hear he made a bad first impression. He's really a special soul, that one, but he's been through some hard times. Ty—" Agatha shook her head. "Never mind."

They sat in silence for a moment, and Beth savored the tea's sweet, floral taste and her friend's company. She hadn't missed the resemblances between aunt and nephew. Both stood tall and walked with confidence. Their eyes shared the same lovely sea-green shade.

The older woman cleared her throat and held her cup on her lap. "Still going to the cemetery today?"

Beth nodded. "I'll meet Mom, Harmony, and Kaylee there at four. Then we'll get takeout from Jake's and have a quiet evening at Mom's."

Agatha reached over and grasped Beth's hand. "I know the loss stays with you, but I promise, time does help heal."

"People always say that. But how much time?" Beth sighed. "It's been two years since that senseless accident. Two years Mom has lived without a husband at her side, and Harmony and I have gone without our dad's love and advice. Two years we've missed our brother's smile and sense of humor—and Kaylee has grieved her husband. Dad and Liam weren't even at fault, yet we've all suffered such loss."

"What happened wasn't fair. Yet, we must go on and adapt. Life constantly changes." Agatha gave Beth's hand a quick squeeze, then let go. "And when we ask in faith, God gives us the strength."

Beth managed a weak smile. "There's been no shortage of prayers for strength."

WHERE LOVE IS PLANTED | 11

"I'm glad you have family who supports each other." Agatha brushed a fallen leaf from her lap. "You've sacrificed a lot to be their rock."

"I had no choice."

"Of course you did. But you chose to put their needs ahead of your own. And I love and respect you for that." Agatha wet her lips, then turned her head. Beth followed her gaze to watch a hummingbird land on a nearby feeder filled with clear sugar water.

The garden attracted birds throughout the year, and it wasn't unusual to see hummingbirds in March. With food available, the small, delicate winged creatures stuck around through the winter.

"Family is important." The gentle woman faced Beth. "Because I never married and had children of my own, I gave time, energy, and love to my students. That's why I continued to teach for so long, even though my friends retired much earlier and encouraged me to do the same."

Agatha set her tea on the bench. "For a while, Ty's father helped fill that void for me. I raised Richard during his teen years after his parents were killed, much like your brother and father. Of course, it was still a different situation. Their accident was due to icy Minnesota roads.

"Richard had a hard time adjusting from life in the Midwest to living in Seattle. But it also gave him a heart for those who struggled." Agatha crossed one leg over the other, then straightened the fabric draped over her knee. "You see a lot in the inner city, but instead of becoming an angry kid, he learned compassion. And he made friends in school who didn't have the kind of life he'd grown accustomed to. It opened his eyes to another world, and when he went into ministry, he decided to become a chaplain in the air force."

"Where is he now?"

"He's been transferred to Germany for his remaining years in the service."

This was all new information. Beth had certainly leaned on her friend and poured her heart out. She wanted Agatha to feel she could do the same. "Why haven't you mentioned this before?"

"Even though I enjoyed those years with Richard, our relationship has also brought some pain." Her forehead wrinkled. "As I've aged, he's taken it upon himself to check in on me religiously, and that brings some comfort. But there were years when I rarely heard from him. His wife is a lovely woman, but I think she felt threatened by my relationship with him. I believe she saw me as a stand-in mother-in-law and felt the need to keep some distance."

"That's sad. It could have been so different."

"Well, it certainly wasn't what I'd hoped for. But even though we can respect and care about each other, not all Christians *like* each other. People are still human." Agatha cocked her head and smiled mischievously. "Richard's wife is very traditional, while I'm a bit more of a free spirit."

Beth chuckled. "That you are." She drained her tea and set her empty mug on the bench. "Did you ever spend time with them? Holidays?"

"Several times I traveled to wherever they were stationed and spent Christmas with them. But I always stayed at a hotel. It was easier that way." Agatha shrugged. "And because Richard was in the military and they moved around a great deal, I never got to spend much time with Ty. When he was younger, he'd come for occasional visits with his father, and I treasured those days. That's why I'm so thrilled he's here now. I get another chance at knowing my great-nephew."

Ty was fortunate to have someone like Agatha in his life. She'd certainly become important to Beth. Since Beth's closest childhood friends had all moved away from Meriside, Agatha had become Beth's confidante. Someone to talk to when she couldn't share her heart with her mom or sister for fear of causing them distress. Agatha was right. Beth had to be their rock, and because of that, she'd never been as vulnerable with them as her mom and Harmony had been with each other.

Beth shouldn't be selfish. Agatha deserved the blessing of having time with family, and it was clear that Tyler's arrival meant much to her. It was just that Beth and Agatha had grown a lovely friendship.

Would Tyler's presence change that? Beth couldn't take another loss. Not just yet. And what was Agatha leaving out when she mentioned Ty had been through hard times?

Two

T he aroma of Italian cooking lingered in the air. Tyler eyed the remaining lasagna in the pan. Enough for the entire neighborhood. Oh, well, leftovers were even better, and he could put a couple of containers in the freezer for easy meals later.

"Thank you, Ty." Sitting across the dining room table from him, Agatha dabbed the corner of her mouth with a napkin. "I don't cook much for myself anymore, and this was a real treat."

"You're welcome. I enjoyed spending time in a kitchen again." The large room with tall ceilings practically echoed given all its space.

It felt awesome to be in a home again, instead of cramped in his former one-bedroom apartment with walls so thin he could hear his neighbors breathing. Maybe that was an exaggeration, but he could hear plenty, and none of it pleasant. The couple to his right fought constantly, the neighbor to his left kept his TV on full blast past midnight, and the guy living above him made enough noise, you'd think an elephant had taken residence instead of a human. And the closed-in place had potential to bring on PTSD after what he'd experienced in the past.

"Are you sure it's okay I stay with you for a while?"

"Ty, of course. You're welcome here as long as you want. I enjoy the company. The house is way too big for me, but I bought it because of the sunroom. If I had my druthers, you'd move in permanently, but I understand a young man needing his own space." Agatha sipped her ice water. "You've indicated you may not stay long in the area. Are you taking this job on a trial basis?"

"Not exactly." Ty drummed his fingers on the table, thinking for a moment as to how to explain his situation. "There's a position at a men's penitentiary in Colorado where I served time that will be available in one to two years. I was told by a friend that the director of social services will be retiring. My buddy Brandon lives in Canon City, and that job could be my opportunity to join him there."

"I remember him. He's been a good friend."

"I don't know where I'd be now if it wasn't for him." But he'd probably be focused on himself instead of helping others. Ty leaned forward. "Brandon and his brother are working with his dad's construction company, and the boys are in line to take over the business when Mr. Willcox retires."

Agatha had a heart for young people, and he could trust her to understand his ambitions. "But Brandon and I want to create a program for at-risk kids. My experience as both a convict and a social worker in the system will help us provide better assistance to young people who are heading to prison or who are getting out of juvie. We might also find ways to work with boys and girls whose parents are in the corrections system."

"That sounds exciting—and admirable." Agatha tilted her head, and her eyebrows furrowed. "Your dad mentioned you were unhappy in Arizona, but if it may only take a year to get your dream job, why not stay at the penitentiary where you were working until the job in Colorado opens up?"

"My work at that prison prepared me in a lot of ways for the position in Colorado. But I didn't like the heat and living in the desert. Maybe I could have learned to handle the 110 temps, but I disagreed with the tactics used by my supervisor. And the man wasn't open to my suggestions."

Ty shrugged. "My supervisor blocked every change and new program I tried to implement, those that I was convinced would help and motivate the inmates to do better—*be* better." He'd wanted to accomplish so much more there but had felt shackled when it came to making any decisions.

"I heard about potential employment here and decided to check it out. When I apply for the position in Colorado, I'll be competing with other strong candidates—people who will have far more experience than I do. So I can't base all of my decisions on that job and assume I'll get it." He picked up his unused knife and laid it on his empty plate.

"I still might not have considered working with women prisoners, but after I was reprimanded for trying to help an unpopular inmate in a tough situation, I decided to apply for the position and get my license to work in Washington State." Ty grinned. "I'll get additional experience, and the bonus will be spending time with you."

Agatha folded her hands and laid them on the table. "I hope your father didn't push you into moving here so you could keep an eye on me while he's in Germany."

Ty laughed. "Dad encouraged me, but I make my own decisions." He reached over and covered her hands with both of his. "Look, I know better, and Dad's no fool. Agatha Sharp doesn't need a caretaker. If anything, Dad was probably hoping you'd look after *me*—just like you took care of him all those years."

An escaping tear ran down her soft, wrinkled face, but a warm smile grew at the same time. Had his words touched her that much?

"I was up-front during the interview at the prison here that I could only commit to a year and see how it went. They were desperate to fill the position, so they took that risk. But if things don't pan out the way I hope they will, and I don't find work in Colorado within two years, I might stick around longer."

She raised his hands to her lips and gave them a gentle kiss. "I'm in no hurry to see you go."

"In the meantime, Auntie, I know we talked about me living with you for a month. But if you're open to it, and it's not inconvenient, I may need to stay longer. And I insist on paying rent and helping with household expenses."

"You're my guest. You're family. I'm not taking your money."

"That's the deal. No compromise on this."

"Okay." She gave him a sly grin. "But as your landlord, I determine the fee."

Ty hung and shook his head, smiling. Then he faced her again and nodded. "You win this round."

"I'll let you know the terms and have you sign on a dotted line."

"If we're doing this, you should know what I have in mind. There's a small place I spotted in the listings with a great view of the water, but it's for purchase, not rent, and it needs some fixing and updating. I'm not an apartment kind of guy. I need more space and privacy after being in prison. But I'm handy.

I could make some necessary changes now and then remodel during the coming months. I want the house ready to sell when the time comes to move on."

On his income alone, he'd never have saved enough money by now for the down payment plus renovations, but his maternal grandfather had set up a trust fund after Ty was born, and he'd wisely not given access to the funds until his grandson turned thirty. Grandad might have changed the age to forty if he'd been alive to witness Ty's stint behind bars.

"You could still live here while working on the place. It would give you some reprieve. With flipping a house, you never know what you're going to run into. You could end up with more challenges than anticipated."

"Thanks. I appreciate the offer." Ty stood and reached for Agatha's plate, but she playfully pushed his hands away.

"You prepared the meal. I'll clean up." She pushed her chair away from the table. "From what I can see, you didn't leave much of a mess for me to take care of anyway."

"I clean as I go. A habit I picked up as a kid." He slid into his seat and leaned back. "Life with a military dad and a finicky mom."

"Your dad wasn't always so rigid—at least not while he lived with me. I wouldn't allow it." She winked. "It's important at times to keep your feet on the ground and be disciplined, but we also need freedom to spread our wings and soar. And trust me, there were times when your dad cut loose—with safe and healthy opportunities, of course. I wouldn't have it any other way. I think your mom was brought up in an environment where there wasn't room for imperfection or failure."

"I didn't get the chance to spend time with any of my grandparents, so I'll never know for sure. Mom doesn't talk about her parents."

"Your paternal grandparents would have loved you dearly. My brother was my protector and friend, and he had a wonderful sense of humor. I have plenty of stories to share."

"And I'd love to hear them." His aunt was so different from his parents, but he already felt connected to her. Time with Agatha would be good for him—in many ways.

She cleared the table of dishes, and he followed her into the kitchen with the leftover lasagna.

"Selfishly, I wanted to spend your first night here alone with you. Help you get settled in." Agatha set the plates down and leaned her hip against the counter. "But if you don't mind, I'd like to invite Beth to have dinner with us soon."

Was his aunt playing matchmaker? He'd been in town less than twenty-four hours. "I don't know, Auntie. I'm just starting a new job. And if I buy that house, any free time will be devoted to fixing it up."

"Balance is important, and it will be good for you to meet a variety of people outside of work." She tilted her head and gave him a knowing look. "I'm not asking you to date her."

"Good." Maybe she *wasn't* trying to set them up.

"Beth is a dear friend, and a casual dinner could be an opportunity for you to know her a little better. I'll even let you show off more of your culinary skills."

"Sure. I guess I can be open to sharing a neighborly meal." So Beth and Agatha were tight. That explained why the cute brunette had bristled when he'd referred to her as the renter.

While his aunt focused on dishing out portions of food into containers and loading the dishwasher, Ty wandered into the heated sunporch with three walls of windows where he caught the remaining pink and purple sky, the setting sun no longer visible. One side of the room gave him a water view over tall evergreens, if even just a glimpse of the blue body, while the other two faced the gardens. Agatha had set up her art studio in the room, and the watercolor propped on her easel caught his attention. *Wow* . . .

He sensed her presence. "Auntie, I always knew you were an artist, but this ... this is something else."

She poked him gently in the ribs. "I hope you mean by 'something else' that it's not a monstrosity."

"Far from it! I don't know anything about painting, but I do know what I like, and I *love* this. Everything about it draws me in and makes me want to spend time there." He glanced out the window to his right. "It's your garden."

"When in full bloom." She gave a contented sigh. "You may not know much about art, but I know *nothing* about keeping plants and flowers alive. When I bought this place, I tried to revive the barren gardens. Unfortunately, my feeble attempts were epic fails.

"But several years ago, when I renovated the massive shed in back into living space, Beth moved in and worked her magic. She plants everything with love. Soon the yard will be teeming with spring flowers, and that area will become a calm oasis filled with color, birds, honeybees, and butterflies."

"Sounds peaceful." Ty moved to face the windowless wall and a framed painting of puffy, heart-shaped pink flowers dangling from long stems. "And these?"

Agatha stepped next to him. "Bleeding hearts. Placed in the rock garden beneath the cedar tree out there. They'll bloom later in April and attract the hummingbirds."

"Nice."

"Oh, they're much more than *nice*." Agatha's eyes twinkled

with delight and wisdom. "Pink bleeding heart flowers symbolize kindness, love, and romance. The pink and white blossoms may also signify unrequited love or a broken heart."

"Got it. Mushy stuff." He wrapped one arm around his aunt's thin shoulders and gave her a gentle side hug.

She peered up at him. "Yes—and no. Beth also taught me that in some cultures, the flowers represent compassion and the ability to speak freely about emotions. My hope for you, Ty, is that you find both here."

"Thanks, Auntie."

"You're welcome. I mean it." Her eyes filled with understanding. "I also meant what I said earlier. I'd like you to get to know Beth, especially since you'll be living on the same property. She's a lovely young woman and one of the most unselfish people I've ever met."

He should have been warmer to his aunt's friend, but if he were honest with himself, he'd been a bit taken aback when face-to-face with the gorgeous woman. Her short, dark brown waves had a tousled look, as though she'd just gotten out of bed and hadn't bothered to brush her hair. And her chocolate-brown eyes had studied him like she'd been peering through a microscope at an unwanted insect she'd found in her garden. She'd rattled him, so he'd tried to act nonchalantly. Perhaps he'd come across too cool. Not good, considering Agatha's request.

He'd be friendlier for his aunt's sake, but with Agatha's glowing description, he was sure to be in dangerous territory of liking Beth too much. Ty wasn't sticking around forever. And for now, he needed to focus on his job, the promise he'd made to Brandon, and moving on with his life.

Maybe it wasn't his assumption about her relationship to

his aunt earlier that day that had helped create Beth's chilly reception in return. "Auntie, I need to ask you a question."

"Sure, Ty."

"Did you ever mention anything about my history to Beth?"

"No, honey. That's your story to tell."

He'd changed, grown, worked hard to prove himself, but even kind people could be tempted to judge, so he'd kept those dark days private, unless it was necessary to expose them. There was no reason to share them now, was there? So why was he fighting the urge to confess his sins to a woman he'd only just met?

Three

T heir town's name, Meriside, meant *beside the sea.* Friday brought gray skies, a cool ocean breeze, and choppy waters, typical of late March here. Hot coffee would be welcomed on such a day.

Beth juggled a tray carrying three lattes—one hazelnut and cinnamon decaf, one unflavored with an extra shot of espresso, and the last made with soy milk—as she opened the door to the family's business. Sure, in their kitchenette, they had a handy-dandy machine that made single cups in no time, but she enjoyed treating loved ones to their favorite drinks.

She inhaled the pleasing fragrances filling the room. With Easter only two weeks away, the shop showcased white lilies, daffodils, hyacinths, and a variety of tulips. Although Your Secret Garden operated greenhouses for starting and growing many plants, the space wasn't used for forcing bulbs into blooming. Because customers expected certain varieties of flowers to be on hand for the holiday, they were shipped in from various growers.

They'd chosen the name, Your Secret Garden, because adding *your* felt more personal. Her family had agreed to provide a place where people might find what they needed to create their own oasis, however small it might be. Even one blooming plant in a tiny space where someone could retreat had potential to bring respite from this crazy world.

Beth believed every human being grew a secret garden within. A beautiful part of themselves that might or might not always be shared with others. Their dreams, creativity, and deepest thoughts were stored there.

Mom was busy with a favorite customer, Mrs. Warner, showing off a lovely floral arrangement that included white roses and pink cherry blossoms. Beth caught her mother's eye, and tilting her head toward the tray she'd laid on the counter, hinted a drink would be waiting for her.

Harmony was pouring through a catalog, seeking treasures for the gift shop. She tried to cover the walls and stock the shelves with pieces created by local artists but filled the gaps from other sources.

Beth resembled their mother, Candace Miller, with short dark hair and brown eyes. And Liam—well, her handsome brother could have been Beth's twin had they not been born eighteen months apart. But with her bright red hair and blue eyes the shade of forget-me-nots, Harmony was the image of their deceased father, and Beth loved her even more for it.

"Morning, Sis. Have you discovered any more potential good sellers?"

Harmony closed the book, picked up a tablet next to her, and displayed a list of ten items. "I like these, but I want to run them by Mom first before putting in an order. We're moving into another busy season, so I want to be prepared. As soon as spring arrives, people get the urge to make changes to their décor."

Beth removed the more potent drink from the carrier and set it next to a plate of snickerdoodle cookies. Their sister-in-law Kaylee had thrown herself into baking lately, and these must be her latest batch of tempting goodies. She did have a knack for whipping up delicious treats.

"Ohhh, thank you!" Harmony grinned, then took a long sip of the strong coffee as though wanting to savor every drop. "Anything to do with Easter has been selling like crazy. If that continues for the next few weeks, I might not have to worry about having holiday items left over."

"The garden center and nursery are getting into full swing too."

"Mom said you asked for a family meeting with Michelle."

"Yeah, we all need to chat." Beth rubbed her right temple. Their accountant had popped into the shop the day before, asking to speak to her.

Beth had suspected then by Michelle's worried expression that finances weren't as healthy as she'd hoped. Harmony was great at managing the gift shop and helping their mother with floral arrangements, and Beth was knowledgeable about indoor and outdoor plants, but Dad and Liam had the savvy needed to run the multifaceted business. And Liam's widow— Kaylee? Her interest in Your Secret Garden had waned even more after Liam's death, and they'd given her time and space to grieve.

"We have enough funds to hire seasonal help for the next few months, but I don't know if we'll be able to afford additional employees through the entire summer." She'd felt good about providing responsible high school students with summer jobs, and some adults had been regulars for years. Beth hated the thought of scaling back, but what else could they do if they couldn't pay them?

Her mom placed Mrs. Warner's purchase in a sturdy box for transporting the floral arrangement, opened the door for the woman, and wished her a good day. She strolled over to her daughters, smiling.

"Millie is so kind. She's taking that arrangement to a friend who had surgery and will be homebound for some time. She's always doing sweet things for people." Mom leaned against the counter. "My daughters are much like her." She picked up the unclaimed coffee cup and gave it a slight tilt toward Beth. "Thank you."

"You're welcome." Beth took a deep breath. "So, Mom, we need to set up a time to meet with Michelle."

Her mother's smile faded. "How bad is it?"

"We may need to make some adjustments, but we'll figure it out. We always do, right?" Beth tried to sound reassuring. "We'll come up with a plan." She'd do whatever necessary to take care of her family. They depended on her now more than ever.

"I just—I just don't want to feel like I've let your dad and brother down. They worked so hard to build up the business, but without them . . ." Mom grimaced. "Even with loyal customers sticking with us, we can't compete with a national chain. Since that huge store opened last year, people have gone there in droves to get supplies for house and garden projects. The huge parking lot is always full, and with trucks hauling in plants once a week, people can get much of what they need at a discount compared to what we can sell our products for."

Harmony shrugged as though there wasn't any reason to feel concerned. "We could secretly deliver vast amounts of spider mites, fungus gnats, and aphids to their plant population."

"What?" Mom said as she slammed her coffee cup on the counter and several drops flew out the lid's drinking hole.

WHERE LOVE IS PLANTED | 27

"Harmony!"

"Just kidding!" Harmony raised her hands as though surrendering. "Don't worry. We'll make Dad and Liam proud. I promise." You'd think she'd live up to her name and be a peacemaker. But no, she was more of a firecracker with a sense of humor.

Beth often appreciated her younger sister's positive attitude, but other times, it was annoying. She took too much for granted and assumed her every whim would eventually be satisfied. Even now, it didn't sound like she was taking their financial issues seriously.

"I just want the best for you girls—and for Kaylee." Mom sighed. "And Beth, sometimes I feel bad because you've sacrificed so much. First leaving school to help care for me when I had cancer and then giving up your internship after the accident to help here. I know God is faithful, and he'll take care of us, but I sometimes wonder how this all fits into his plan for your life."

"I've asked that question many times, but I haven't gotten any answers—yet." Beth smiled. "In the meantime, I can still share my connection to nature. I'll find a way to complete my internship someday." It might be time to change the direction this heavy conversation was headed. She gripped the paper coffee cup in her hands a bit tighter. "I have something new to run by you."

Harmony perked up. "Do tell, Sister!"

"You remember the house I fell in love with many years ago?"

"No . . ." Her mom's eyes squinted. "When were you interested in a house?"

"Are you talking about the place Jody's grandparents lived

in?" Harmony sounded surprised. "You still hanging out up there?"

"When I need to think, pray, get some clarity. The view is breathtaking."

Mom smiled as though reliving a memory. "You always enjoyed time with Jody and her grandparents."

"I did." Warm feelings washed over Beth. "The Hudsons were kind, loving people, and not having any grandparents of my own, they filled that role for me as a kid."

"I was grateful older people embraced you girls the way they did. Harmony was attached to our neighbor, Mrs. Landon, until she took her last breath." Mom raised her drink to her lips but set it down before taking a sip. "Mrs. Hudson has been gone for some time, and didn't Mr. Hudson pass away in the nursing home years ago?"

"Almost three now. Jody hated seeing her grandpa move to a facility, but the family had no choice. And then her dad got a job transfer to Chicago soon after. They hoped to keep the house in the family, so they leased it out, but the renters moved out over a year ago. With Jody teaching in Italy and her parents living in the Midwest, no one has been around to take care of the place."

Better get on with her announcement. Beth took a deep breath. "Jody loves her job, and she may have found her forever person, so she's decided to settle down in Italy. Two weeks ago, her family decided to sell the place, and they've chosen a real estate agent." She took a deep breath. Might as well spit it out. "I'm thinking about putting in an offer."

"That old dump?" Harmony shielded her face with her coffee cup. "Sorry. You love that spot, but . . ."

"I realize the house needs a lot of work." Beth's shoulders

dropped. "But the bones are good, and with some TLC, it could be cute." If she could afford to make the changes. A mortgage might be doable, but repairs could be costly.

Two women walked into the shop and headed straight for the display case containing freshly cut flowers.

"I need to help these ladies, but I'd like to hear more later." Mom took a sip of her coffee, then set it out of sight before greeting the customers.

Harmony leaned forward across the counter. "That doesn't mean *I'm* done talking about it."

It wasn't practical or the best timing to think about buying a house right now with the family business struggling. But she could dream, couldn't she?

"I thought you were happy living at Agatha's and that you'd developed a sweet friendship with her. But if things have soured for some reason, you could always move back in with Mom and me. There's far more space than what the two of us need. You can even have your old room back." Harmony gave Beth a gentle punch on the arm. "It could be fun!"

"It's wonderful staying on her property, and Agatha has been amazing, allowing me to create her gardens." Beth gave her sister a teasing smile. "As much as I appreciate your willingness to spend even more time with me, I need my own space."

Beth hesitated. How vulnerable should she be with her sister right now? "The studio apartment has been great. It's small, cozy, and easy to maintain. But I'm approaching thirty, and I wonder if it's time to have a place of my own."

"Why the rush? Why do you feel that a birthday needs to define when you purchase a home?"

"I wouldn't have considered buying even a small condo

right now, especially with the financial future of this place being uncertain, but I have a special attachment to the Hudson house. And I might never get another chance to claim it as my own."

It was more than the childhood memories created there. Some kids had spiritual breakthroughs—encounters with God—at church camp. Beth experienced her own one summer night at the property while sleeping under the stars.

She traced a long, black mark on the counter with her finger. "There's another good reason to consider the purchase. Agatha has been both friend and mentor, but now that her great-nephew has moved in . . ."

Harmony nodded. "You're afraid of having to share time with her."

"Jealous thoughts have niggled me, but I don't want to hold on to them. Agatha deserves to spend time with him, and I shouldn't stand in the way of that. She's missed out on so much family time already because of distance and various dynamics," Beth said, lowering her voice, not wanting the two women picking flowers for a bouquet with her mother to overhear. "I'm willing to sacrifice anything for that sweet woman."

Agatha had also mentioned that Ty had experienced some hard times. Beth didn't know what that entailed, and it wasn't her business, but maybe he needed his aunt even more than Beth did. "If I moved out, he could have the apartment."

"Has Agatha hinted that she'd like you to leave?"

"No, not at all. But last night, I walked by the kitchen window and heard laughing, so I peeked in. They were cooking, and they just seemed so . . . happy together. It made me wonder if it's time to act like a grown-up and take on responsibility for my own home. And then when I got Jody's email later about the house, I took it as a possible sign."

"Hmm . . ." Harmony had that all-knowing expression on her face. The one that said she'd solved a mystery.

"What?"

"This nephew . . . what's his name?"

"Tyler Sharp, but Agatha calls him Ty."

"Cute."

"I guess the nickname is cute enough."

"That's not what I meant." Harmony raised her eyebrows, then cocked her head, as if waiting for a confession she didn't need but wanted to hear regardless.

"Okay, the guy is attractive—handsome in a rugged, yet intelligent kind of way."

"And maybe caring and sensitive, considering he spends time with an elderly aunt in the kitchen. And by choice, it seems."

"There's one serious drawback—a deal-breaker."

"I can't imagine any at this point."

"Harmony, he was just hired as a social worker for the inmates at the women's penitentiary. God forgive me, but you know how difficult it would be for me to get involved with someone whose job is to help the incarcerated live better lives. I may have forgiven, but I haven't forgotten."

"It's been two years, Beth. Grieving takes time—healing takes time. We all need to face it at our own pace and give each other grace while we work through our stuff. But at some point, we need to move on. Dad and Liam would have wanted us to live as fully and peacefully as possible."

Her sister had lost a brother and father just as Beth had. How could Harmony, six years younger, be so much further ahead in her healing than Beth? Why was Harmony acting like she had grief all figured out? Had she sincerely dealt with her tremendous heartache, or had she buried her sorrow? Would deep hurt someday reveal itself in some ugly, unexpected way? Or was Beth still struggling because of holding on too tightly and the secret she still carried?

Four

M any people looked forward to Friday because they hated their jobs, but these past two weeks, Ty had experienced rewarding and uplifting moments. And they weren't only due to the positive effects mid-April spring weather had on him, so he felt grateful.

He'd taken over facilitating several educational programs with the prisoners. One he administered in a group setting, but he was also focusing on tailoring several to individuals who required more direct attention. Ty was convinced that learning was key to self-esteem and prisoners believing they could find opportunities on the outside.

While he wasn't a therapist, he was trained to help lead group sessions for inmates who suffered from mental illness or drug addictions. A meeting with seven prisoners earlier that day had gone well, and a woman who had gone through detox only a week ago spoke for the first time. She spouted nasty, colorful words, but at least she'd shared instead of letting her ugly thoughts and hurt feelings fester inside. Ty was used to seeing anger and hearing foul language. He could deal with it. Progress came in a variety of ways.

The days sped by as he acclimated to his new role in the women's prison and worked on getting up to speed with case files. His office felt a bit tight, but he'd made do with the space.

With no plans for the weekend, Ty was tempted to stay late and hibernate in his office. He could read through additional records and become more familiar with the inmates assigned to him. But he'd make that decision after his last appointment. It was still early in the day, and anything could happen in the coming hours. Not that he was all work and no play. He looked forward to getting out on some hiking trails soon and exploring. And it wouldn't hurt to feel more grounded in other areas as well.

That included attending worship services on a regular basis again. He needed that weekly plug-in with other believers to strengthen him for the week ahead. He'd enjoyed the Easter service at Agatha's church last weekend and planned to go with her again this Sunday.

It wasn't a surprise to see Beth there as his aunt had mentioned her family were members, but it was the first time he'd met Candace, Harmony, and Kaylee. All seemed like nice people, and they'd invited him and Agatha for brunch following the service, but he'd declined.

His parents had asked to video chat, and since they were overseas, it was a little more complicated to work around the different time zones and connect. He appreciated the Millers' invitation, but he didn't want to disappoint his parents. He'd encouraged Agatha to join the women, and she'd returned with containers filled with food. Ty rewarded himself with the meal after surviving his parents' interrogation as to how he was doing with the new job, living with Agatha, and if his aunt was really as well as she claimed.

Tyler flipped through some documents, then set them aside, except for one—Teresa Sampson. A rap sounded, and his focus moved from the paperwork to his open door.

"Sharp, your appointment is here." The stocky female guard ushered in a thin woman with short light brown hair and colorful tattoos covering her left arm.

"Thanks, Officer Kade." Ty stood and motioned for the inmate to take the chair in front of his desk. "Teresa, please make yourself comfortable."

The woman studied him for a moment, then relented and dropped into the seat, slumped and appearing defeated.

Ty left the door partially open and noted the officer remained outside. Not that he expected any trouble, but anyone working in a penitentiary was aware that situations were unpredictable. Anger and frustration sometimes exploded when least expected, and it didn't hurt to have another pair of hands to help control volatile situations.

"I'm Mr. Sharp. And as the new social worker assigned to your case, I wanted to spend a few minutes getting to know you." He sat on the opposite side of the desk and opened her file. "Quite a history here. Breaking and entering, multiple thefts, public disturbances under the influence, and using a knife to threaten a neighbor."

Teresa shifted in her seat, and her gaze dropped to the floor. "I'm not proud of those things, but that was before," she said in a quiet yet defensive tone.

"Before . . .?"

Her head jerked up, and her hazel eyes pierced his with a look that said he should know what she meant. "Before I sobered up." She didn't add "you moron," but Ty heard the implication in her voice.

He didn't react to her abrasiveness. This was tame compared to what he'd experienced in the past. Trust and respect didn't come quickly in the system, but he had plenty of time—and so did she.

He laid his arms on the desk, leaned forward, and caught her eyes with his. "How can I help?" He already knew the answer, but Ty wanted Teresa to acknowledge her heartfelt desires.

"You want to help *me*?" She sounded skeptical.

"Yes."

Her shoulders visibly relaxed, but she sat silent for a moment. "I need to see my kids."

"You have two, right? A boy and a girl."

"Yeah." Teresa sat up a bit straighter. "Matthew is six, and Kelly is four."

According to records, Teresa was twenty-three. She'd gotten pregnant at sixteen, become a mom at seventeen, and had left high school without graduating or getting her GED. Something Ty hoped to help her remedy. And then she'd married the baby's father after turning eighteen. Some teens made it in those situations—most often with family support. Even then, people didn't always make the best decisions.

"My ex—he's dead. Died almost three years ago from an overdose. Before I was put in here." Teresa fidgeted and shifted her position in the chair again. "That's what kind of put me over the edge, you know?"

"I can imagine that was tough."

"When I got in trouble and was sentenced, my ex's parents got custody. My folks are all gone. I don't have any other family. So I'm glad my kids got a good home to live in—not foster care. My in-laws are good people. But I got a right to see my children, and their grandparents won't bring them here."

"How long has it been since you've had contact with Kelly

and Matthew?"

"Over a year. Not since I got incarcerated. Kelly had her third birthday when I last saw her. I don't know if she remembers me or if Matthew even knows I'm alive." Teresa sniffed loudly and swiped her hand under her nose. "I send letters, but I don't know if they get them."

Ty heard tremendous pain in her voice.

"I told my in-laws . . . I've gone through drug counseling, I go to group sessions regularly, and I'm staying clean. I've begged them to let me talk to Kelly and Matt, and they've refused. But I'm their mom! *I'm* their mom! They have no right!" Teresa's eyes filled with tears as her volume escalated. "And now the grandparents won't take my calls. How am I supposed to know if my kids are okay?"

Communication with the outside could be tricky. Inmates were allowed to make outgoing calls but only during designated times, and phones were programed to limit the time to twenty minutes. Under no circumstances were incoming calls allowed, and in most prisons, cell phones were considered contraband. Although some prisoners managed to use prepaid accounts funded by friends or family, many relied on their collect calls being accepted.

"I can't promise that I can fix this, Teresa." *God, help me do right by this family.* "But I'll talk to other staff members who are familiar with your status here. Get their recommendations and see how they'd feel about arranging a meeting with you and the grandparents first before we bring in Kelly and Matthew."

"You will?" Was that a hint of hope in her voice?

Ty attempted a confident smile. "I'll do whatever I can." He glanced at his watch. "Our time is up for today. You're

needed in the kitchen, and I have a team meeting." He handed
Teresa off to the guard, grabbed his things, locked his door,
and headed down the hall to a large room.

Several nature photos hung on the concrete walls. Sun
shone through the two windows, making the area feel more
welcoming than his plain office. First to arrive, Ty dropped
his laptop and stack of case files on the long table and slid
onto a cold, metal folding chair.

Others soon strolled in and found places at the table, some
offering a nod or a greeting. These group discussions involved
correctional officers, administrative and management per-
sonnel, and support staff. The players covering mental health
included a psychiatrist, a psychologist, and a correctional
mental health counselor.

Several social workers entered. Max Waters, his supervisor,
was a stocky, balding man who Ty had shared almost daily
conversations with over the past two weeks. Tyler had met the
other social worker, Sharon Lane, earlier that week during a
smaller gathering. Gray-haired and slender with clear blue
eyes, she'd worked for many years in the penal system.

The larger team's focus wasn't limited to what happened
in prison. Their roles also involved helping former inmates
with reentry into communities, with the hope that they would
be successful in creating a productive life for themselves and
would avoid making the same—or new—mistakes and end up
back here.

Community-based services such as housing, healthcare,
care management, mental health and substance-use treatment, as well as education and employment—it didn't matter
the penitentiary or the climate toward ex-cons in the local
area, there was always a need to improve access to those services

in the facility and in the community. Ty had faced those challenges before, and he didn't expect it to be any different here.

Two hours later, they wrapped up their discussions, and Ty's stomach rumbled. The two cups of coffee he'd downed during the long session hadn't been enough to stave off hunger. He should have grabbed one of the pastries offered before the meeting started.

Ty glanced at the empty platter—too late. Good thing he'd thrown a box of wheat crackers, an apple, and a banana into his backpack that morning. One of these days, he'd take time to make a sandwich. Maybe he could bring in a small refrigerator for his office. One more thing to add to his list of to-dos.

Max approached and leaned against the table. "Tyler, you got a minute?"

"Sure."

The room was soon vacated except for the two of them. His supervisor pulled out a chair and sat next to Ty. "I'm glad you spoke up today about Teresa and wanting to mediate with her in-laws. Like I said during the meeting . . . I agree it's important for her to have hope for a better future, and part of that involves having access to her children, whether she ever gains custody of them again or not. I think you came up with some good ideas on how to approach the grandparents."

"Thanks. I appreciate your support in this." Ty felt a *but* coming.

"But . . ."

Yep, there it was.

"Just a reminder to always be mindful about boundaries."

"You're worried I've overstepped?" Ty would rather have a straight, honest conversation if there were any problems than have someone be vague, especially his boss.

"No, I'm not concerned at this point. But it's clear you're passionate about making a difference in these women's lives, and that rang clear even more when you were sharing Teresa's situation."

Ty nodded. "I get it. We can't give the impression, especially when working with the opposite sex, that we're getting personally involved."

"Right." Max leaned back, relaxed, with one leg perched on the other. "The inmates need to *trust* you but not *fall* for you. You're a good-looking guy." He chuckled. "That observation comes from the women housed here. They're not afraid to speak their minds—and loudly."

Ty didn't embarrass easily, but heat crawled from his neck into his face at the thought of prisoners talking about him, assessing his appearance. He mentally shook it off. Women guards dealt with nasty stuff from not only the men held in correctional facilities but also their male counterparts all the time. How did those female officers handle it without losing their cool?

"Those kinds of situations—*relationships*—only complicate things and make it even more difficult for us to serve them well."

"So be empathetic, yet impartial." Ty always kept that in the forefront.

"You come to us with history as an inmate yourself, so you understand the culture. And you also came highly recommended by people who worked with you at the penitentiary in Arizona. So, don't take offense. I'm reminding myself as much as I'm holding you accountable."

"I appreciate a straight shooter."

"Good. So do I, so don't hesitate to come to me with any concerns. It's critical for corrections social workers to set and maintain boundaries with the prisoners. It's important from a personal as well as ethical standpoint. While we're here to serve them, there are limits on the type of help that can be given as well as when it *should* be given."

Ty wasn't attracted to Teresa, so he wasn't worried about his feelings, but the fact that children were involved did make him feel more vulnerable. If anyone could tug on his heart, it was a kid. "In Teresa's case, she's requesting visitations to rekindle relationships with her children. Trust me, my focus will be facilitating meetings first with the grandparents and then hopefully with the kids."

"Good." Max stood and shoved his chair close to the table. "And how are *you* doing—outside of this building? Feeling settled in yet?"

"I'm getting there. For now, I'm comfortable at my aunt's. She's a gracious host, but I'm still looking for a place of my own."

"Nice that you have family around. This job is stressful. Maintaining a healthy lifestyle helps avoid burnout, which ultimately benefits the inmates. It's not selfish to take time out for yourself." Max grinned and pointed a finger at Ty, as if to make his point even stronger. "Remember that."

Max was a good guy, and Tyler was fortunate to have the man in his corner. "I will. Thanks, boss."

Tyler hiked back to his office and opened his backpack. According to the day's schedule, he had less than twenty minutes to down a banana and a few crackers before his next appointment. He settled in and opened his laptop to feed his fantasy. Hadn't Max just encouraged him to take mental health breaks?

The page opened, and the screen displayed photos of a house situated on a hill, overlooking a large body of water in the distance. The building needed a lot of work, but Ty had picked up some skills while working summers during high school with Brandon, his brother, and his dad on construction sites. There were jobs he'd have to hire out—like electrical and plumbing—to make sure everything was up to code. But he'd handle what he could of the renovation himself.

Two nights ago, he'd toured the property with a Realtor and put in an offer. Now all he could do was wait and see if it was accepted.

Five

"Unbelievable." Beth hung up and stuffed her phone into her back jeans pocket. She opened the bag of soil sitting on the potting bench and scooped out enough to fill the bottom of the blue ceramic container before her.

"What's up?" Harmony set a wooden box near Beth and leaned against the bench. They'd fill the weathered rectangular form with lovely ivy and display it in the gift shop. "You didn't sound too pleased with how that conversation ended."

Beth sighed and thrust her trowel into the pot. "The Hudson house has a potential buyer, and he's already put in a good offer." She brushed hair to the side that had fallen across her right eye. "I thought I'd have more time to figure out how I could come up with enough money for a down payment and the financing to buy it myself." She groaned. "That's not all. The agent told me the guy isn't from around here, and he plans to flip the house after it's renovated."

"And that's a bad thing because . . .?"

"I'd feel better if it was sold to someone who loves the property as much as I do. Someone who would appreciate it for what it has to offer now as well as what it could be." Beth shook her head. "If Jody knew how much I wanted her grandparents' place, she'd talk to her dad on my behalf. But using our friendship to hinder the sale wouldn't be right. I'm not that kind of person."

Harmony's eyes sparkled. "Funny how it depends on your perspective."

"I don't see anything humorous about this." How could her sister be so insensitive? She knew how much that house meant to Beth.

"Think about it!" Harmony smacked the side of her own head with one hand, but not hard enough to cause pain. "You just said you don't have the funds available to purchase your dream home. And you've acknowledged that you don't have the resources or know-how needed to fix up the place."

"Right . . ."

"So if the place is sold now, what's to stop you from making a plan to put in an offer once it's gone on the market again—with all of your remodeling problems solved? From *my* perspective, it could be a win."

"Regardless, there are still a lot of *ifs*, and my getting the house wouldn't be guaranteed." Beth chewed on her lower lip. "But I suppose that could be a possibility."

"Oh, good grief! When did you become such a pessimist?"

Beth made an ugly face at her sister. "It's not that I'm focusing on the negative, but we've dealt with a lot of blows these past years."

"I know. Mom's cancer—then losing Dad and Liam. Life is never going to be the same."

"Look . . . I don't want to dwell on the painful experiences or the disappointments. Some of my decisions have hindered my progress toward my goals, but I wouldn't go back and take a different path. It's just that some days, it's hard to trust things will work out for me."

"'Now faith is confidence in what we hope for and

assurance about what we do not see.'"

"Hebrews eleven, one." Beth tilted her head and smiled. "One of Dad's favorite verses."

Harmony did a quiet drumroll on the bench with her hands. "You're officially off the clock at four. Instead of staying late like you have been for too many nights . . ." She put her hand up to quiet Beth before she could say a word. "Just hear me out. It's Saturday. Take a break from this place and spend some time at the property before a new owner takes possession. I'm sure the Hudson family wouldn't mind you enjoying another visit before the key is turned over."

Beth grinned. "They did give me permission to hang out there anytime."

Beth drove up the hill, turned left at the sign with *Hudson* carved into aged wood, and headed down the winding driveway through the canopy of trees—maple, alder, and cottonwood mixed in with cedar, Douglas fir, and hemlock. She reached the clearing and parked her blue Kia next to a familiar white Toyota truck—Tyler Sharp's.

What's he doing trespassing on private property?

She'd leave her purse in the car but take her cell. Beth got out and slipped her keys in one coat pocket and her phone in another. An army of evergreens stood straight and tall as if protecting the lot. Untended, invasive wild blackberry bushes had taken over one side of the yard, but that meant easy picking later in the summer—if one could evade the sharp thorns. Mrs. Hudson had enlisted Jody's and Beth's help many times in baking delicious berry pies, muffins, and cobblers. And in doing so, Jody's grandmother had also created sweet memories.

Beth's eyes darted from one area to the next as she ambled toward the large porch on the back side of the house with the water view. No sign of Ty. The place felt as deserted as when she'd last come up here, but the wide porch steps appeared even more worn and damaged. Several boards had broken through. From curious animals exploring the abandoned building? No matter. She hadn't used that entrance and gone inside in years, and she hadn't planned on trying today.

The mid-April sun had lowered but wouldn't completely disappear for another hour, closer to eight o'clock. She shielded her eyes from the blinding glare as she gazed at the sparkling seascape below, where a ferry headed toward Seattle. Seagulls called in the distance, the Olympic Mountains rose beyond the Sound, and the faint scent of saltwater wafted in the air.

"Beth?"

She lowered her hand, turned, and looked up. Six feet plus tall and standing on the porch, he towered over her. Beth could have been staring at a statue of some dude on a pedestal, but he wasn't a hero—to her, anyway. His black sweatshirt's sleeves were pushed up on muscular but lean arms, and one hand grasped a small notebook and pen at his side.

"Hi, Tyler."

He gave her a small smile, but his eyebrows knit together. "What are you doing here?" Was he happy to see her or perplexed by her presence? And what purpose did he have for showing up at her sacred place?

"I'm a friend of the owners and have permission." Beth pointed to the paper he grasped. "What are *you* doing here?"

Ty lifted the pad and tilted his head in its direction. "Ahh . . . taking notes."

"Whyyy?" she asked, raising her eyebrows.

"Becaaause I'm buying the place," he said slowly, "and I'm making a list of things that need updating."

Beth's heart skipped a beat, and she stepped back. "Are you sure?"

He dropped his arm to his side. "Am I sure I'm the new owner? Or that the place requires fixing?"

"I just talked to the Realtor earlier today, and she said an offer had been made but nothing about it being accepted."

"I only got word a couple of hours ago. If everything goes according to plan, and it will, the deal will close in four weeks." Ty tapped the notebook on his thigh several times. "Is there something I should know? Reasons to pull my offer?"

She couldn't lie. "No," she said abruptly. *Why him, Lord? Of all the people to have this sanctuary, why Tyler?* He'd already moved in with Agatha and disrupted Beth's relationship with the older woman. Now this house? Why was everything she held dear taken from her?

"I'm confused." Ty maneuvered his way down the rotten steps. "Have I done something that's upset you?" He sounded sincere in his concern.

"No—not at all." Now she'd told a fib.

"Okay. Then why the gloomy face?"

He was being nice, and she was being selfish and overly sensitive. *Get a grip, Beth.* It wasn't like he'd done anything to intentionally cause her hurt or disappointment. "The truth is . . . I've fantasized about buying this place. My best friend's parents are the current owners. Her grandparents lived here for years before they passed away, and I have many fond memories of time spent with them."

Do not get teary now. Beth sucked in her emotions. "The family rented it out for a while, but the tenants abused the home, so they were asked to leave. It's sat empty since that couple moved out, but the Hudsons couldn't bring themselves to sell until now."

Tyler stood quiet, focused and listening.

Beth surveyed the area and inhaled a deep breath. "Anyway, the timing wasn't right for me to put in an offer, and the home needs and deserves some TLC at this point. But I heard the potential buyer was planning to renovate and then sell." She turned and looked him in the eyes. "Is that true?"

"That's my hope, but I won't sell for a year, maybe two."

So he didn't intend on just making some quick cosmetic fixes before turning around and putting it back on the market. Beth breathed a bit easier. She'd have more time to come up with a financial plan, and hopefully any renovations done now wouldn't need to be revised. There were plenty of horror stories about contractors with little integrity who charged high fees and produced devastating results.

"Working construction off and on, I picked up enough skills that I can make some changes myself, but the rest I'll contract out. Everything will be done right. I guarantee it." Tyler stroked his beard in a thoughtful gesture. "And since you have a vested interest in the final outcome . . ."

"As a *future* potential buyer . . ." Was this conversation leading to more disappointment or to possibility?

"Would you be willing to brainstorm with Agatha and give some input on the interior?"

Was he just trying to placate her? For all he knew, Beth's opinions could be far different from his own. "Your aunt is an artist. I'm sure she has a better sense of design and what works together."

"Oh, sure. And she's agreed to look, but aside from color palettes, she doesn't feel confident in knowing what younger generations might prefer in flooring, countertops, tile work, lighting. I know what's important to guys, but the place needs to attract women too."

"It would be fun to create something with Agatha." That part of the project felt appealing.

"Right!" Tyler grinned. "Within budget, of course. I can't go crazy with money. I'd pay you both for your time, but I couldn't promise much."

Not that she wasn't already busy enough at Your Secret Garden, and she planned to contact her school advisor again with the hope of finding another internship. They weren't plentiful, and she couldn't completely abandon her mom and sister. They still needed help running the business, so any internship would have to be within a drivable distance. But how could she refuse a role in restoring the home? That was the next best thing to being able to buy the house herself.

"I'm not a professional designer, and you have no idea of my style, so you could be taking a huge risk."

"I trust you." The corners of his lips turned up into a good-natured smile. "Agatha wouldn't have anyone living on her property who didn't have good taste."

A spark of excitement ignited within Beth. Instead of fighting the idea, maybe this was just what she needed—a creative outlet to take her mind off what she couldn't control.

"I would love that, Ty. *Really.* Even if this house never becomes my own, it will feel satisfying to leave a final imprint. But no monetary payment is necessary. Seeing this place brought back to life will be reward enough."

"All right then. I appreciate the offer." His stance relaxed, and his eyes shone with pleasure. "But if you're also willing to help with landscaping, I'll sign a contract with you for that part of the work. It's only fair."

The area in front of the porch could use some sprucing up. Ideas began to flow through Beth's brain for the entire yard, including a large patio. Blooming plants in a rainbow of colors—perhaps a pergola. *Shut it down for now, Beth. Remember—budget.* "Our business doesn't usually get involved in landscape design, but I'd be willing to give it a try, if you are."

He held out his hand for a shake. "It's a deal, and from Agatha's rave reviews of what you created in her gardens, I have complete confidence in you." Ty's strong hand grasped hers, and his warm touch radiated through her body. "I don't need anything elaborate. Just attractive—with low maintenance."

Beth resisted the surprising urge to remain in his hold, and she slowly withdrew her fingers from his. "I'll head home so you can get back to your list."

"Wait." Tyler pointed toward the stone firepit. "I was planning to start a fire, watch the sunset, enjoy the stars. The view is amazing from up here."

"It is . . ."

"Then stay awhile." Ty made a gesture toward his vehicle. "I stashed wood and camping chairs in the back of my truck, and Agatha sent a thermos of hot coffee and way too many brownies for me to consume myself. But if I go home with leftovers, I might hurt her feelings."

Beth hesitated. She didn't want to give a hasty answer and then regret it later. It was one thing to bring in plants and make the property more appealing. She'd agreed to that responsibility because it meant more income for her family. And it would be fun to work with Agatha and try her hand at interior design. But enjoying a fire and a beautiful evening with Tyler felt more personal than talking about wall colors and backsplashes.

Still, didn't she owe Agatha some kindness toward her nephew? Wouldn't it be the right thing to stay? At this point, it would make sense to learn more about him, especially since they'd be working on the house together.

"C'mon, Beth. Help a guy out. Keep me company, protect me from any cougars or coyotes, and indulge in some chocolate." He shifted his stance. "What do you say?"

"Hmm . . . and the bears?"

Six

B eth sat in the green nylon camping chair, listening to the crackling fire and sipping hot coffee. Good thing she always carried travel mugs in her car. Not expecting guests, Tyler had brought only one with him.

He poked at the burning wood with a long stick, and bright sparks soared into the charcoal-colored sky. "Agatha's brownies are awesome, but you know what would make them even better?"

"I can't imagine." Beth had intended to eat only one, but the moist bar with dark chocolate chips and caramel drizzled on top tasted so amazing, she'd indulged in several.

"Roasted marshmallows sandwiched between two of them." He grabbed another from the plastic container, took a bite, and nodded. "Yep. Note to self. Next time bring marshmallows."

Next time? Was she included in that?

Ty downed the dessert and eased back in his chair. "You mentioned bears. Are they a problem around here?"

"Nothing to worry about." Beth shrugged nonchalantly. "And I carry bear spray in here." She held up the canvas bag sitting next to her.

He appeared amused. "Okay, but they shouldn't bother us unless we scare or provoke them—or leave food out to tempt them. Right? Not that I've encountered a lot of bears, but that's been my experience."

"True, but we Girl Scouts are always prepared for the unpredictable."

"I can respect that." He finished his coffee with one last gulp and stretched out his legs.

Would it be too nosy to ask some questions? Ty seemed unguarded here, and Agatha wanted Beth to know him better. "What's your story, Tyler Sharp?"

"My *story*?" His forehead furrowed. "What do you want to know?"

"I understand wanting to help people, and you can do that as a social worker. But what draws you to prisons? Why did you choose that path?"

"Multiple reasons. For one, I . . ." Ty paused, seeming to think through what he wanted to say next.

He let out a huge sigh and then gave a feeble smile. "People are people. As I learn more about their individual stories, I often understand better why they made the choices that led them to prison."

She flinched at his words. "Lots of people struggle with hard times, but not all break the law. I don't think it's wise to give lawbreakers a pass because they were dealing with some challenges." Beth's own family had been deeply affected by someone who had taken selfish risks and put others in danger. If Tyler had experienced trauma like she had, would he still be tolerant and understanding of criminal behavior?

"That's not what I'm saying." He opened the lid to the brownies and held the container out to Beth.

She waved it away. "No, thanks. I've reached my limit."

Tyler grabbed a chunk for himself and snapped the cover

onto the container. "All should be punished for their crimes. But I believe in second chances, and sometimes assistance is necessary."

"I believe in giving people that too, if it's justified."

"I get that." His eyes held hers. "But who gets to decide if another person is deserving? And what's the criteria?" Tyler asked with a quiet, gentle tone.

How open should she be with him? He'd shown up in church with Agatha, but had he gone to appease his aunt? Or did he have a heart for God and a relationship with him? "It's tricky, even though it shouldn't be," she began. "Jesus wants us to forgive seven times seventy, right? And forgive others as he has forgiven us."

Beth couldn't stop now. "But it's not okay for people who have done wrong to manipulate the system for their benefit. Another question? How do we find balance in doing what is considered the right thing, like offering forgiveness, while also protecting and caring for ourselves?"

"It's not easy." Ty popped the last of his brownie into his mouth and finished off the morsel. He leaned forward and propped his forearms on his thighs. "I walk through those prison doors every day with my eyes wide open. I'm not willing to let anyone take advantage of me. But I also pray that I regard each person as a child of God—a human being whom he loves dearly and wants to see reconciled. That's how I approach each inmate placed in my care."

Beth, now completely transfixed by the campfire and Ty's words, nodded to affirm she'd heard him. Could she ever feel the same kind of empathy for the person who had taken the lives of her loved ones? She told Harmony she'd forgiven the woman but had she really? At times, anger and resentment still burned in her gut. Shouldn't she experience something different inside? Shouldn't she feel *lighter*?

"In my position, it's not my job—nor is it appropriate for me—to be a spiritual advisor, but I can still treat inmates with respect and with God's love." Ty straightened and laid his forearms on the chair armrests. "While I don't approve of or like many of the things my clients have done, I still want the best for them."

She saw Tyler in a new light. He must be a caring man if he could view his tough job with that perspective. Indeed, the fact he'd chosen his profession demonstrated a compassionate side, didn't it?

"When individuals are released and return home, it's not easy to acclimate. So it's part of my job to determine mental health, social, or personal needs. Social workers give individual counseling, provide treatment assessments for appropriate programs, assess at-risk prisoners, and facilitate group programs. We're supposed to enhance and support rehabilitation. And hopefully, we end up with some success stories."

"That helps me understand more about what you do and why." Beth sipped her coffee, still processing everything he'd shared.

"Good. I'm glad." The corners of Ty's lips turned up, and he released a quiet sigh, as though relieved he'd gotten through to her. "It's a ripple effect. It's hard to see families torn apart—children separated from their fathers or mothers. Of course, sometimes it's necessary for kids' safety, but other times, it's heartbreaking."

"I can imagine. Children aren't responsible for their parents' mistakes, yet they suffer the consequences." Beth's eyes stung and watered, but not from the campfire's smoke. It was endearing that Ty cared so much about those kids, but what about the heartbreak brought to those whose lives had been unraveled by criminals' actions? What about them? What about her own family's suffering and loss?

≈

Ty worried he'd run his mouth too long. Beth went silent, so something he'd said had triggered her. Despite her turning away, he'd caught her using her coat sleeve to wipe a streak of moisture from her face. He didn't think smoke had irritated her eyes—the breeze was carrying the gray haze in the opposite direction. Was she touched by how kids were affected when their parents were incarcerated?

Time to change the subject. "Is Beth a nickname for Elizabeth?"

Beth snapped to attention, as though her thoughts had taken her elsewhere, and she gripped her coffee mug between both hands.

"No, I was named after Beth, a character from *Little Women.*"

"Haven't read the book, but a former girlfriend convinced me to watch the movie because she loved it."

Beth snickered. "What did you think?"

"Don't hate me. I don't care to see it again. But if I remember correctly, Beth was the sister who died in the story."

"You're right. She was willing to sacrifice for the good of others, and her death had a strong effect on her sisters. They realized they wanted to live with more consideration and care for everyone." Beth caught his gaze and held it. "Even as a tween, the story made me feel a responsibility to live up to the name."

He'd only spent a small amount of time with her, but he didn't doubt that one bit. "And your sister, Harmony? Does she live up to her name as well?"

Beth belted out a laugh that made him grin. "Oh, no. As soon as my sister escaped the womb, my mother heard her screaming so loud, it sounded like Harmony was scolding everyone in the room. My parents thought giving her the name Harmony might avoid some trouble. Didn't work at all. She is *not* the peacemaker in the family."

"Good to know." Harmony sounded like someone you wouldn't want to irritate.

"My sister was quite a challenge, but as she matured, she became more levelheaded as opposed to being a full-blown spitfire. And as far as being musically inclined, she can't carry a tune. But she's smart, funny, and loyal to her core."

"I'm not much of a singer either, but my best friend is a natural." Ty stretched out his arms then returned them to his sides. "Brandon's also an amazing songwriter, although he can't seem to accept how good he is."

"My sister-in-law has a beautiful voice. Kaylee used to sing cute little tunes when she didn't realize anyone was listening, but she's shy, so never in public. We'd hear her humming in the kitchen in their home or singing in the greenhouses at work. The music stopped after Liam died, but now, she pours her heart into baking."

"Agatha mentioned your dad and brother died because of a car accident." But his aunt hadn't told him much more. In fact, she'd avoided sharing additional information, not that he needed to know details. "I'm sorry your family has experienced so much loss."

"Thank you," she said, her quiet tone sounding sincere. "It's been two years, but some days it feels like it happened yesterday."

Mention of Liam and her dad had brought a rasp to her voice. Ty would try to lighten things up. "When I was a kid, I wanted a sister or brother. We moved so much it would have been nice to have a sibling." Someone to share the good times and the challenges. "You've always lived here?"

"Except while I was away at college."

Was he asking too many questions? He didn't mean to interrogate her like a reporter looking for a story. Ty was sincerely interested. "Have you ever considered moving anywhere else? Had any desire to explore other parts of the country?"

"At one time, but my family has needed me here. Losing my dad and brother . . . well, let's just say, it changed a lot of things. For all of us. But we're finding our way—together."

Ty hadn't wanted to come off as being insensitive to her experiences or responsibilities, and her gentle smile reassured him that she was okay. "I understand wanting to be there for them. It takes time to get your bearings after your ship is blown off course. I was just curious because your situation is different from my experience."

"How? You don't get along with your parents?"

"My folks are good people." Ty wouldn't get into explaining his challenging relationship with his dad. "My father is a chaplain in the air force, and we moved around a lot until we got transferred to a base in Colorado. I was finishing junior high, and Dad managed to keep us there until I finished high school."

Beth's eyes filled with compassion. "That must have been

hard, having to start over and make new friends."

"It wasn't so bad because I learned how to fit in in most places. And where I didn't . . . I knew we'd soon be transferred to another place where I could start over. High school could have been a struggle, but a friend there became more like a brother. We're still close." Even though Ty had made huge mistakes and come close to losing that friendship. If it had been anyone else . . . But Brandon had shown Tyler grace many times over.

"Aunt Agatha mentioned you're a horticultural therapist." He bent over the side of his chair, grasped another chunk of wood, and placed it in the fire where flames tasted then consumed the bark, crackling in delight.

"I don't use that title yet, but I am aspiring to one day."

Ty raised his hand, the palm facing her. "I have no idea what that involves, but I'm interested in learning."

"You are?" Her tone held some disbelief, but then she chuckled softly. "Okay."

It felt good to hear her laugh and see her relax again.

Beth sipped her drink. "Obviously, because of what my family has done for a living, I've been exposed to all kinds of growing things. But I attended Oregon State University in Corvallis. The school has a good horticultural science program."

"It makes sense that you'd want to work with plants, considering your family's business, but don't you get plenty of experience there? What draws you to another occupation?"

"Oh . . ." Beth stretched her legs and leaned forward. "Your Secret Garden has been consuming my time since my dad and brother died. But if I get certified as a therapist, there's potential to help people in numerous situations."

"Like?"

"Well, to start . . ." Beth held up an open hand. "Mental health, physical rehabilitation, special education, long-term care, hospice . . ." She pointed to a different finger at each reference. "People with various disabilities can gain skills and coping methods through gardening."

"I get it. Restorative powers." Impressive how something so simple as digging in the dirt could be so beneficial.

"Right. It's exciting to think about what can be accomplished. Memory can be improved through learning a gardening process. Coordination can be strengthened by planting. And people with emotional and mental disabilities find ways to relate to the earth and their surroundings."

"I like the part about relating." Ty preferred the outdoors to city life because of the peace he found in creation.

"Nature—the feel, the smells, the touch, the vast beauty— it all connects me to God. It's where I often feel his presence in a strong way. I want other people to experience that too. If I could make a difference by using my passion for growing things to help improve people's lives, I'd feel like I'd served my purpose." Her eyes sparkled in the firelight, and her voice filled with excitement and hope.

Ty was captured by her enthusiasm. "Where would you like to put your focus?" Her inspiring vocation felt more like an offered gift instead of a career.

"I'm not sure yet. The potential is endless—rehabilitation clinics, schools, hospitals, nursing homes, psychology offices . . ." She sighed. "But there's one glitch."

"And that is?"

"I need to complete an internship."

"So what's stopping you? If there are so many options of places to work, there must be opportunities all over the country where you'd be welcomed."

"It's not that easy."

"Is anything worthwhile easy?"

Beth fidgeted and set her mug on the ground. "You don't understand."

"Help me then," he said calmly. Ty wanted to understand, and he regretted putting her on the defensive.

She settled back in her chair and took a deep breath. "I'm twenty-nine and should have been certified years ago. But while I was in college, my mom found out she had stage three breast cancer, and the diagnosis shattered my family. So I left school to help care for her."

"I'm sorry your mom went through that."

"Thank you. It was scary—and difficult. But she fought hard, and she's doing well now." Beth raised her focus to the darkening sky. "Praise God," she said under her breath. "I eventually went back and finished my college courses, but I still needed to complete an internship. The school helped me line one up at a children's hospital."

Tyler heard the emotion in her voice, so he gave her a moment. "What happened?"

"My dad and brother's accident. A drunk driver swerved across the line and hit them head-on. Neither made it to the hospital alive." Even now, her voice warbled as she shared more of her story.

Beth rubbed her eyes, then dropped her hands into her lap. "We were all devastated. Kaylee went into a severe depression for a while, but she got help."

The campfire illuminated Beth's face with a soft glow. She turned to him, and with a glimpse into her eyes, he witnessed the pain she still carried.

"I don't know if we'll ever be completely healed. Our hearts were broken, and we miss Dad and Liam every day." She inhaled a ragged deep breath. "So maybe you can see why it's been difficult for me to leave—even for an internship. I couldn't abandon my family."

How could he help her? Comfort her? If only a few words or prayers could wipe out the pain in minutes. "I can't imagine what that was like—to lose both at the same time. You have incredible strength." How could he not admire a woman who was so resilient and unselfish? He was rewarded with her soft smile.

"Thank you. Only by the grace of God."

Maybe there *was* a way to help her. He might have an answer to achieving one important goal. "Beth . . . what if you didn't have to move to complete your internship requirements?"

"Well, that would be amazing. Once I get certified, I can start my own business and work in a variety of settings here in the area. But we're not in a large city, and there aren't opportunities for an internship close enough that I wouldn't have to move for some months. There are reasons why I can't do that. At least, not yet."

"When you listed off places where your kind of therapy is used, you didn't include penitentiaries. But that's another possibility, right?"

"Yes . . ." she answered, sounding suspicious.

Excitement brewed within Ty. "I might have a solution."

"To what?"

"I recently met Lisa Randall at a team meeting. She's the program manager for the horticulture projects at the prison, and it was mentioned that we partner with the Sustainability in Prisons Project."

Beth's eyes narrowed, the area between her brows creased. "I've heard of SPP and its success, but I didn't realize it was being used at the women's correctional facility in our area."

How could she not be aware of this option when she was so passionate about her career and when the penitentiary was so close to home? "I haven't had a chance to talk with Lisa one-on-one yet, so I'm not sure how it works." *Mental note— set up a time to meet with Ms. Randall soon.*

Her body stiffened. "That's great news—that the facility's gardens are being used to teach inmates some skills and responsibility." Hesitation came through in her tone, as though she didn't believe her own words.

"Even better news if there's a possibility of getting an internship there. Right? I'd be happy to connect you with Lisa." Maybe he'd said too much. He'd only just met the woman, and he didn't want Beth to face more disappointment. But Ty would be willing to advocate for her.

"I appreciate your thoughtfulness, but I can't work there." Her firm and direct tone relayed there was no chance of her pursuing his suggestion.

Ty wasn't ready to give up—not just yet. Not when it was clear how important it was to Beth to complete that last step for certification. He knew how it felt to have goals in sight but still beyond reach. For some reason, the thought of Beth experiencing that hopelessness disturbed him.

"I get that it might not be your ideal, but if it helps you get to the finish line, why not explore the possibility? The prison isn't that far away. You can make the drive in twenty minutes. It could be the answer to getting what you've been waiting for."

Beth grabbed her empty mug and stood. "It's late. I should go."

"I apologize." Ty hopped to his feet. He'd pushed too hard with his own agenda. "I was only trying to help."

"I believe you."

"But I had no right to act like I know what's best for you."

"True." A cool breeze swept between them, and Beth wrapped her arms around her upper body. "FYI, not even my dad could tell me what to do without me bristling."

"Okay. Got it. Independent woman," Ty said with an accepting tone, and he smiled, attempting to bring some warmth back into the conversation. Maybe entice her to return his gesture. She didn't accept the invitation. Instead, the corners of her lips remained turned down, and her body language screamed *don't come any closer*.

"Look, I know you mean well," she said, her tone becoming less defensive. "But you just met me." Her shoulders slumped. "You don't know the whole story, and I'm not convinced telling you would be in your best interest or mine."

The whole story? What information could Beth want kept from him?

Seven

W hat was she doing here?

Alone in a small room with cement block walls. At least the surrounding color was a pleasant sage hue instead of depressing gray. And the cushioned chair wasn't uncomfortable, but the stale air made her appreciate the light, welcoming fragrance of Your Secret Garden proclaiming life within. She'd return there as soon as this meeting was over.

Beth had arrived at the penitentiary early to make sure she was processed before her appointment. She'd shown the guard her pass, and then she was screened much like a passenger going through security at an airport. Outer clothing like jackets and shoes were removed, as well as any jewelry that could set off a metal detector. Her purse, notebook, car keys, and cell phone were placed on a conveyor belt and X-rayed.

Her watch read twelve fifty. Only ten more minutes before she'd introduce herself to Lisa Randall, the horticulture program manager. Beth's palms sweat. Was she making a mistake?

A week had passed since the night Tyler had suggested she request an internship at the prison. She'd given him several flimsy explanations as to why that was impossible, but they didn't include the strongest motivation to stay away—her connection to an inmate there.

Out of respect for her wishes, Agatha had agreed to leave it up to Beth as to when she'd share that information. She'd explained to Agatha that it might be best for Ty to get settled first before discovering any personal ties to potential clients in the prison. But now that didn't make sense, even to her.

Why was she still being so guarded? Ty would find out regardless of what she did or said. Meriside was a small town, members at their church were aware of her family's tragedy, and people talked.

And now that she might be working at the prison herself? It felt kind of foolish to think she might have been protecting him from any boundary issues.

After going home from sitting around the fire with Ty and then experiencing a sleepless night, she'd confessed to Mom, Harmony, and Kaylee what he'd suggested. With their encouragement and blessing, she'd followed through and allowed him to connect her with Ms. Randall.

She might be on the verge of finishing the requirements of her certification! But at what price?

Oh, yeah . . . her family. Beth had overshared that night with Tyler. She shouldn't have been so free with information about Mom, the girls, and herself. But he'd made her feel so comfortable, and in the moment, it had felt good to talk.

Although drawn to him, it was best to keep things professional. If he became involved with Abbey Ward's case, any relationship with Beth could be considered a conflict of interest. Another reason—he was planning on moving to Colorado as soon as possible. She had plenty to juggle without trying to fit in anything more, and despite being a strong woman, she couldn't handle another heartbreak.

Beth would keep some distance between them going

forward, whether she got an internship here or not. Working with him on the house now seemed like a terrible idea. If he still wanted to hire an expert to help with landscaping, she'd find someone else to assist him from Your Secret Garden. No sense in turning paying customers away.

What a conundrum. Beth needed an internship, but she'd prefer working *anywhere* else but the prison where Abbey resided. However, there was no other position available close enough to home where she could still help her family. Not that she had a job locked down at this facility. Ms. Randall could still refuse her application.

Earlier that morning, Agatha had invited Beth for coffee, muffins, and prayer. She'd asked God to give Beth wisdom and peace of mind. Agatha had closed with "thy will be done," and Beth realized she wanted that even more than she wanted to control the situation she was about to encounter. Maybe she *was* growing in that area and learning to let Jesus take the wheel.

A woman, possibly in her fifties, and wearing glasses, opened the door to the room. Dressed in a navy suit, she wore her strawberry blond hair short with bangs swept to the side. Her bright smile and sparkling blue eyes lit up her freckled face—a welcome change from the cold surroundings.

"Beth Miller?"

"Yes."

"Nice to meet you. I'm Lisa Randall."

Beth stood and accepted the woman's handshake. "Nice to meet you too. Thank you for giving me some time."

"My pleasure." Ms. Randall gestured toward the hallway. "We can talk in my office."

She led the way to a small, pale-yellow room with a desk.

A bookcase, two filing cabinets, three chairs, and several plants that were desperate for water also filled the room.

Beth fought the urge to pick off the dead, brown leaves and relieve their thirst. *Too soon, Beth, too soon.* A few reproductions of impressionistic paintings on the walls. She recognized Monet's *The Water Lilies.* The sun beamed through a lone window, and the light added some cheer to the space.

"Please sit and make yourself comfortable." Ms. Randall pulled one chair closer in front of the desk. "Would you like some water?" She pulled several bottles from a small fridge set on a table next to the wall behind her desk.

Beth cleared her throat. "No, thank you. I'm fine." She settled into the chair, similar to the one she'd just vacated, and folded her hands in her lap. Another prayer wouldn't hurt. *Lord, please stick close. Guard my words, help me listen and discern, and let your will be done, regardless of what I desire or think is best.*

Ms. Randall opened her water, took a sip, then sat on the opposite side of the desk. "I'm going to be blunt with you, Beth. A year ago, I agreed to bring an intern into our program, and it didn't go well. I'd rather not go into details as to why, but it left a sour taste in my mouth, and I've been hesitant to try again."

There it was—already—the red flag that signaled this might not be an option for her. But the sick feeling in her stomach at Ms. Randall's disclosure? Did that mean Beth wanted the position more than she'd realized?

"I'm sorry to hear that," Beth said respectfully. "But that makes me appreciate this opportunity to speak with you even more and determined to prove that I'd do everything I could to not disappoint you."

"Some years ago, I worked as a horticultural therapist myself. Then for a variety of reasons, I decided to take a different career path and accepted the job as manager for the horticulture programs here. I can tell you without hesitation that prison life is unlike any other situation you'll come across."

Ms. Randall moved a file from a stack next to her, placed it in front of her, and opened the cover. "Are you sure you're up to working with offenders? Some are striving to turn their lives around while others may try to use the program to their advantage. It's cliché, but we need to separate the wheat from the chaff."

"I understand." She did, and she believed she could manage potential judgment concerning any inmates. But what if she was assigned to Abbey? Beth's heart pounded at the thought. "Ms. Randall, no matter my position—an intern or a bona fide therapist—I may encounter challenging situations and clients. Older people can get feisty, younger children sometimes act out, and teenagers might rebel."

"Good point, and please feel free to call me Lisa." A quick smile, then she removed a sheet of paper from the open folder. "Your application and records." Lisa glanced at it and laid it down. "You come highly recommended."

How was Beth supposed to respond to that. *Thank you?*

"Let me tell you a little bit about what we do here."

"I'd like to hear everything, or at least, whatever you feel free to share."

"We're partnering with several Washington State Department of Corrections programs. Corrections Hope Gardens help supplement food banks, elementary schools, and childcare centers."

"That's fantastic."

"It is, and involvement gives inmates opportunities to give back to our local communities." Lisa took a drink of water, then twisted the cap back on the bottle. "The Sustainability in Prisons Project not only gets inmates out of their cells and outside, it also focuses on education, including college courses. We currently have fourteen students enrolled, and they earn credits toward certification in horticulture. Those students are being mentored by two master gardeners who are offering their time. Those volunteers are also members of the Horticulture Advisory Board."

Beth nodded. "Would you mind if I took notes?"

"Not at all. There's a lot of information to process. I'll pull out some handouts and formal documentation for you to take when we're finished chatting, but I think it would be helpful for you to jot down your thoughts."

"Thank you." Beth dug into her purse for the notebook she always carried with her and a pen. "What else do prisoners experience besides working in the vegetable gardens?"

"They plant and care for hanging baskets, and they use perennial and annual pollinator-friendly flowers through-out our facility. Last year, the horticulture group planted over four thousand flowering plants on our grounds."

"I never thought that making a penitentiary pretty would ever be a priority. I assumed whatever was grown would be . . ."

Lisa gave a slow nod as she said, "Practical and edible."

"Yes." Beth wrote several lines in her book.

"Thought has gone into everything we do. Besides providing food for those in need outside these walls, our inmates seeded, grew, harvested, and delivered over eight thousand pounds of vegetables for the prison kitchen. Our floral department provides decorations for special government and fundraising events."

Beth stopped writing and looked up. "And in return, the women are learning skills that help them feel better about themselves."

"Humans are connected to nature. If you could see the impact working in our gardens and studying the environment has on women and men who spend most of their days inside concrete cages, you'd never look at horticulture and prisons in the same way again."

Beth no longer needed to see it in person to change her perspective. Just listening to what Lisa shared had accomplished that.

"Our programs don't mandate that incarcerated people participate. They're available as an option."

"And if they don't comply with the rules or engage as expected?"

"We're not obligated to keep them." The corners of Lisa's mouth turned down. "If they step out of line, we'll give them another chance if we believe they deserve it. Third chances don't exist, but it's rare that a situation ever gets to that point. Our inmates love what we provide, and for those who don't at first, most come to appreciate it later."

Lisa eyed Beth for a moment. "I've been doing a lot of talking. Tell me how *you* think horticultural therapy can help our women."

Beth moistened her dry lips and cleared her throat. She should have accepted that bottle of water. At least her heart rate had slowed compared to earlier. "I believe that regardless of whether a person is in a hospital, a nursing home, or behind bars, there are many benefits. The kind of help I offer can improve memory, cognitive abilities, language skills, and socialization. People can learn to work independently, problem solve, and follow directions."

"Our inmates can benefit from all of those."

"Are the women allowed to have houseplants in their cells? It's been shown that hospital patients who keep them in their rooms display less fatigue, pain, and anxiety."

Lisa's eyes lit up. "We've been considering that option."

The two talked about what the programs involved and Beth's potential role until Lisa glanced at her watch. "I have another meeting in fifteen minutes, but there are a few more things we need to cover. To complete your internship, you need to put in 480 hours within a minimum of three months and a maximum of two years."

"Yes, I'm aware."

"Although you don't need to be a student to intern, I'll contact the college you attended. But as your supervisor here, any information, difficulties, or questions relating to clients, staff, or performance needs would be brought to me."

"I'd feel completely comfortable discussing any of those issues with you."

"Good." She pushed her glasses higher on her nose. "Let me read this to make sure I don't forget anything." Lisa picked up another sheet of paper from within the folder, and after taking a glance, returned the information to its former place. "Oh, yes. As with any professional institution, you'd need to comply with the current privacy rule of the Health Insurance Portability and Accountability Act provisions."

"HIPAA. No problem."

"And we can't forget the AHTA Code of Ethics. Horticultural therapists must refrain from practicing when their personal problems or conflicts may cause harm."

"Of course." Beth's heartbeat went from a steady, relaxed rhythm to a full-on gallop. What she had to reveal could end their discussion, and she could leave without any hope of an internship here, but honesty now might protect her from potential controversy. "Could you tell me if an inmate by the name of Abbey Ward is involved with your program?"

Lisa stood and opened the second drawer of a filing cabinet. "Why do you ask?" She thumbed through until she reached the contents farther in the back, then she pulled out a green folder and riffled through the pages inside.

"Two years ago, she committed a felony. She drove under the influence and killed two men in a head-on collision."

"That's true. A father and son, if I remember correctly." Lisa scanned more documentation. "Names were David and Liam Miller." Her head snapped up, and her gaze revealed that she'd made a connection. "Any relation?"

Beth nodded sadly. "My dad and brother."

"Oh, dear. That could be a problem." Lisa sighed and laid the folder on her desk. "You wouldn't be the only person working with our students, as we prefer to call them. Because there's potential for a conflict of interest, I could possibly arrange to keep some distance between you, but I can't promise complete freedom from encountering Abbey." Her forehead creased. "Could you focus on your responsibilities and keep personal feelings aside?"

Could she? "I'm not sure."

Lisa settled into her chair and laid folded hands on the folder. "The situation might test you. But you won't like everyone you provide services for, regardless of where you're hired. People come from all walks of life."

Beth's palms were sweating, but she had to be honest,

regardless of the consequences. "I'm aware, but this is different. Abbey Ward's mistake changed my family's world."

"True. And I haven't experienced the kind of pain you've all carried." Lisa leaned forward. "It's not the same, not even close, but you might encounter difficult clients in a nursing home as well. Some are sweet—but those who benefit from our type of therapy the most might be mean and nasty at times. Patience and kindness must be drawn upon in any situation. I've worked in rehabilitation facilities where pots, dirt, and plants have been thrown at me because someone got frustrated. Our role as a therapist can be extremely rewarding, but it can also feel challenging and frustrating."

Was Lisa defending Abbey or trying to convince Beth to still consider the job?

"I can only imagine what you feel toward Abbey." Lisa drummed manicured nails on her desk. "Unfortunately, I can't share any information about her background since you're not on staff here, but I can tell you that she's come a long way and isn't the same person who walked through our prison doors almost two years ago."

"I'm glad to hear that." It still didn't change things. Mom and Kaylee were still going to bed at night without their husbands next to them.

"We've already discussed ethics." Lisa paused, seeming to take a minute to think. What was she mulling over? "I might be able to provide some distance until I can get a handle on whether you two can work in the same environment. I'll need to get a feel for Abbey because she'll remain my priority in this situation. She's made great progress, and it wouldn't be fair to remove her from the program."

"I understand." She got it. Beth was only there asking for

a job that would last about three months. Abbey would remain here long after Beth had moved on.

Lisa glanced at her watch again, then stood. "The meeting I mentioned starts in a few minutes. A guard will walk you out to the entrance."

"Of course." Beth dropped her notebook in her purse, joined Lisa at the door, and shook her hand. "Thank you for your time. Oh, and I think you should know—Tyler Sharp had no knowledge of my connection to Ms. Ward when he asked you to consider me for an internship. He's still unaware."

"That's good to know." Lisa thought for a moment. "Today is Thursday. I'll get back to you on Tuesday to discuss this further." She shook Beth's hand. "In the meantime, we *both* have a lot to think about."

Eight

T y rapped a pen on his desk and shot a glance at the wall clock. Beth should be meeting with Lisa now. Curiosity over the outcome kept distracting him from his work. He *could* casually walk by Lisa's office in hopes of running into Beth before they left, but it wasn't his place to drill either woman. He'd find out one way or another if Beth was accepted as an intern at the prison.

Why was he so personally invested? It wasn't like he and Beth had become close friends. He thought they'd hit it off the night she showed up at the house he'd purchased, but something had changed since then. Ty would describe her response to him as being more distant than cold. She didn't seem to have time for anything more than a wave or a hello, and invitations to share dinner with him and Agatha had been turned down. His aunt had noticed too but encouraged him to give Beth some space.

His cell rang, signaling his buddy wanted to video chat from Colorado. He picked up the call. "Hey, there."

"This still a good time to talk?" Brandon grinned back at him. His dark hair was a bit longer and wilder-looking than Ty's, and his short beard wasn't as neatly trimmed, but because of those traits and their similar eye color, they were often taken for brothers instead of friends.

"Yep. I can take my lunch break now, so no problem." Ty picked up his cup and saluted the screen before he downed a gulp of tepid but strong coffee.

"Man, I hope you have more than liquid caffeine on hand." Brandon wiped his mouth with a paper towel.

Ty narrowed his eyes. "That better not be Ralph's Barbecue you're chowing down on."

His friend thrust toward the screen a large bun stuffed with meat and dripping dark red sauce. "There's a pile of fries sitting here too."

"You're killing me, bro. I can almost taste it from here." Ty missed the hickory-smoked pork from Ralph's. "And it looks like you picked up the supersized order—enough for two people."

"Hey, my work is physically demanding. I need the calories." Brandon chuckled. "I don't have a desk job, like some people I know."

Ty laughed. "You got me there."

"So fill me in." Brandon took a swig from a water bottle. "I only have ten minutes. Dad's delegated me to install trim in this house we're building in the Woodlands." He grabbed a few fries and shoved them between his lips.

"Upscale neighborhood. Good for you."

"Thanks," Brandon said out of the corner of his mouth. He finished chewing and swallowed. "I'm hoping to contract a few special projects for the owners. They seem interested."

"Show off your woodworking skills."

"I don't often come across opportunities that challenge me, and if they like the results, I might earn some referrals for other jobs."

"Brandon, your craftsmanship is above any I've seen." Ty envied the way his friend could envision something beautiful and then create it out of plain pieces of wood. "Once the public realizes how good you are, you won't be able to keep up with the demand."

"Thanks. I wish my dad understood my need to be creative. But for him and my brother, leaving clients happy and making a decent living have always been the goals. That's all they need to feel satisfied, and to them, spending numerous hours on one rocker or cabinet that potentially will draw a small buyer pool and profit doesn't make sense."

"They'll come around. Just give it some time." Isn't that what Agatha had encouraged Ty to do concerning Beth?

"Yeah—maybe." Brandon propped his phone on something in front of him. Then he took a huge bite of his sandwich, and holding it with both hands, chewed thoughtfully. "Can't wait until you get that job at the prison here and we can do our own thing and develop our kids' program. Man, I need to feel like I got more purpose than pounding nails all day."

"You know, I won't be the only person applying when there's an opening."

"Sure, but God's in this. He must be. We're both feeling led to help troubled youth." Brandon picked up a french fry and dipped it in ketchup. "You aren't having second thoughts, are you?"

"No, not at all. I just—" Even talking to his buddy hadn't completely distracted Ty from wondering how Beth's meeting with Lisa would end.

"Out with it. This is me, remember?" Brandon chomped on his fry. "You can talk about anything. Safe place."

Ty couldn't have asked more of his friend. Brandon had been loyal to him and stood by him when others had decided to write him off and remove him from their lives. A lot of guys wanted the kind of friendship they shared but didn't know how or where to find it. Partly because of ego and partly because many held their cards close to the vest. How did women open themselves up so easily and share their *stuff*?

"I think Beth is meeting with Lisa about the possible internship."

"You *think*?" Brandon's eyes narrowed. "But you don't know for sure?"

"I might have overstepped and pushed too hard for her to apply. We've barely spoken since. For all I know, she might have changed her mind and canceled the interview."

"You were just trying to be helpful."

"Maybe I should have told her about my stretch in prison. Knowing that I turned my life around because people believed in me and gave me a second chance might help her understand the value in what she has to offer here."

"Anything stopping you from spilling now?" Brandon wiped ketchup from the side of his hand and tossed the towel aside. "Any chance your aunt will tell Beth about your past?"

"Agatha left it up to me to share what I want and with whom." Ty shrugged. "Maybe it's best that I don't disclose the part about being incarcerated. I don't know what Beth would think."

He rubbed his eyebrow. "Would it make any difference? In how she approaches working with inmates? Or what she feels toward me? Sometimes I think I should tell her. On the other hand, nothing is going to happen between us anyway. So it probably doesn't matter."

"What's that saying? Something about protesting too much? The way you're rambling, it's clear to me she's become important to you."

"Look, if she gets an internship, we'll have to relate professionally. Regardless, my plans involve moving back to Colorado as soon as I can make a way, so a casual friendship is the most I can offer or accept." Even if he was attracted to Beth and tempted to see if there could be more between them.

"Okay. But what about the house? Didn't she agree to help with the interior and some landscape design? How are you going to handle that?"

"Not sure. We haven't talked about it since she found out I'd bought the place, so that's another thing to resolve. She may decide to back out. It's not like we signed a contract, so I can't hold her to anything. And I wouldn't want to anyway."

"Sounds like you have some things to sort out."

"Probably shouldn't procrastinate too long."

"Right." Brandon smiled. "I might have some news that will cheer you up."

"I could use some." Ty downed the rest of his coffee, now cold, and dropped the empty cup into the trash can sitting next to his desk.

"There's a good chance one of our projects will get delayed. If that happens, I told Dad I'm taking a four-week break. After no vacations for two years, I think I'm due."

"Good for you, B. Are you planning to focus on one of your own woodworking projects? Or fly to some tropical paradise?"

Brandon chuckled. "I'm heading your way, Ty. I figure you could use some real expertise on that house of yours."

"Really?" Ty's spirits lifted tenfold. "You'd do that for me?"

"As long as you let me do more than drywall and show me the best hiking trails in the area."

"You got it. And my aunt might be open to you staying in

the extra room at her place."

"If there's running water and electricity at the house, I can bunk there. It will be like I'm glamping." Brandon winked. "And I'd like to meet Beth . . . since she's so *unimportant* to you."

"Oh, you would?"

"Get squared with her soon, Ty."

Nine

H ad it been less than twenty-four hours since she'd spoken with Lisa? Beth, her mind on the potential internship, had only dozed all night.

Could she handle running into Abbey Ward when she didn't even have the courage to tell her family that the job might require her to associate with the convict? They'd assumed Beth wouldn't be placed in that position and would have the option of being completely separated from the woman. And she hadn't corrected their assumptions.

Sure, Lisa had said it might be possible to keep them apart, but she couldn't promise anything. She also wanted time to think about having Beth on-site, even though the need was immediate. And although she hadn't been enrolled at the college for the past two years, Lisa wanted to check in with Beth's former advisor. This wasn't a typical situation.

Numerous texts from her mom and sister had flooded her cell the day before, and she'd responded that she still hadn't made up her mind about the internship, nor had there been a firm offer, so she was taking the rest of the day off to run errands, assuring them she'd explain more in person.

Beth arrived at Your Secret Garden twenty-five minutes before opening. Next to Saturday, Fridays were one of their busiest days, and with it being the third week of April, customers seemed eager to get plants in the ground. Since rain was forecast for Sunday through Wednesday, people would take advantage of the dry weather now and focus on yard work.

Mom and Harmony stood at the counter, raising their eyebrows in unison as soon as Beth strolled through the door. "Wow, I think your ears are bending toward me. Not eager to hear all the details, huh?"

"Well, can you blame us?" Her mom scowled. "Who makes a mother wait in suspense to hear about her daughter's job interview?"

"Not quite the same thing as an internship, but I understand." Beth slipped off her light sage jacket but hung on to it. She'd need it as soon as she stepped outside again. "I didn't mean to shut you out, but I wanted a little time to process and pray."

Harmony leaned across the counter. "Will you accept the position if it's offered?"

"The job would be interesting and challenging. And after I got certified as a horticultural therapist, I could start my own business. As my own boss, I could still help out here as needed, so it could be a win-win." This would also be a paid internship, so Beth would receive a small check every two weeks, and that money would come in handy. If finances didn't improve for Your Secret Garden, she might need to take a pay cut.

Mom smiled, but her eyes relayed concern. "Oh, honey, you've put everyone else ahead of your personal ambitions for so long, I hope you seriously compare the positives with the negatives."

Harmony grabbed a dainty-looking cinnamon roll covered with white frosting from a large square tin sitting on the counter. She pulled off a piece of the delicious-looking pastry and popped the morsel in her mouth.

Beth peeked inside the container, and her mouth watered. "Kaylee baking again?"

"That's not all." Harmony pointed to a platter behind her. "Wait until you taste her pecan pie cookies. They're incredible—thin, chewy, caramelized bites of rich goodness."

Beth laughed, grateful for a moment of levity. "You've been eating cookies for breakfast?"

"Hey, Kaylee must have spent all night in the kitchen. I wasn't going to wait to enjoy her hard labor."

"About her work here . . ." Mom said, sounding concerned. She and Harmony exchanged a worried glance.

Beth braced herself. She'd sensed that Kaylee was still struggling to keep on task with her responsibilities. "What's going on?"

"Don't be too hard on her," Mom said. "She's trying."

"She didn't forget to water the starts, did she?" Last week, Beth had asked Kaylee to manage the larger greenhouse after one of their experienced employees broke his leg and another asked for vacation time so she could attend her grandmother's funeral in another state.

"No, she turned on the watering system yesterday morning but forgot to turn it off before she went home. No one realized it until this morning. I'm afraid we may have lost most of the plants." Mom's frown relayed more than her words. "Hopefully, some can be saved."

Her eyes stung as Beth tried to control her disappointment. They didn't grow everything on-site. Much of what they offered in trees, shrubs, perennials, and annuals were shipped from other growers. But it had been Liam's pet project to cultivate the vegetable starts, and he'd also begun experimenting with more varieties of flowers in a second greenhouse.

How could Kaylee let him down? She'd been receiving Liam's paycheck since his death without contributing anything to the business. They had given her space to grieve without putting pressure on her to jump in immediately, but they'd reached a critical point of needing her help. Now that Your Secret Garden was struggling financially, could they continue providing Kaylee an income if they had to hire someone to fill Liam's role?

Beth found her sister-in-law alone in the smaller greenhouse, sitting on a bench, bent over with her head in her hands. "Kaylee?" she said, more sternly than intended.

Kaylee lifted her head, and her long, brown mane fell in a curly mass around her shoulders and down to her waist. A watery glaze covered her honey-brown eyes, and tears trailed down her face. "I'm so sorry, Beth. I drowned the starts and made a mess of everything."

"No, you haven't." Beth swallowed her anger and the initial response burning on the tip of her tongue. Her sister-in-law was brokenhearted. Twisting the knife wouldn't stop the emotional bleeding. "I'll check the roots. We might be able to save some plants."

"I should be standing in for Liam. He'd be so hurt . . ." A quiet sob escaped her lips. "I'm so ashamed." Kaylee dried her face with her palms, and she sat up straight, releasing a burst of air from her lungs. "*Ahh!* I wanted to love this place just as much as Liam did, but I don't. I wanted to be a natural at this job, but I'm not."

It was Beth's turn to feel ashamed. She'd broken her promise to her brother to take care of Kaylee. So consumed in trying to control everything because she believed it her responsibility, Beth had never asked her sister-in-law what *she* wanted—what *she* needed.

Beth sat next to Kaylee. "To be honest, we all hoped you'd take Liam's place and enjoy working here. We've needed your help."

"I know," Kaylee whispered.

Lord, help me find the right words. I don't want to cause more hurt. Beth filled her lungs with air and released a slow breath. "But . . . this business was Liam's passion. It doesn't need to be yours." She gripped the edge of the bench on both sides of her. "Talk to me. What are you feeling? Be brutally honest."

"I—I don't know if I can," Kaylee said, sounding shocked by Beth's request. "You and I have never been . . ."

"Close."

"Not like you and Harmony. But I understand. You don't know me that well. No one in your family does. Only Liam saw the real me."

"And that's my—*our*—fault." Beth sighed. For the first time, she understood so much more. "I'm sorry if we made you feel like an outsider. It was never intentional."

"Thank you." Kaylee twisted the wedding band still at home on her finger. "I've wondered, now that I'm no longer Liam's wife, if I'm still a part of the family."

"Of course you are!" An employee stepped inside the greenhouse, but Beth motioned for him to leave, and he took the strong hint.

Kaylee's eyes flooded, and she shook her head. "I don't know why I'm still so emotional. I want to be strong like you."

"Hey, don't be fooled," Beth said in a gentle tone. "We're

all still working through our grief." She laid her hand on Kaylee's shoulder.

"I miss Liam so much." She let out a heavy sigh. "He wanted to start a family right away, but I wanted to wait. I regret that. If I hadn't been so selfish, he could have experienced being a father, and I could still have a part of him."

Guilt weighed Beth down as though she'd swallowed a wrecking ball. How could she have gotten so consumed with herself when Kaylee, the love of Liam's life, was suffering?

A memory surfaced of a conversation Beth had shared with Liam the week before the accident. Even in all the chaos following that horrible night, she'd somehow tucked it away until the right time to remember what he'd confided.

"Kaylee . . . Liam once mentioned that you wanted to open a tearoom or a small coffee shop—a place where you could use your business degree and passion for baking."

Her face hinted a smile, but her eyes held so much sadness. "We wanted to find a location before we put a business plan together. I worked as a hostess at a tearoom while in college, and I started thinking about what it would take to run my own place. I even made a vision board."

Wasn't that what Beth was trying to accomplish too? Create something of her own? "I don't want you to give up on those aspirations."

Kaylee's eyebrows knitted. "But my responsibility here . . ."

"Is not where your heart is drawn." Beth rubbed her sister-in-law's shoulder to comfort her. "We'll figure it out."

Liam had always been there for Beth, supporting her in everything she wanted to pursue. During her senior year in high school, she was invited to go with Jody's family skiing for the weekend. But Beth had committed to working those two days at Your Secret Garden for an employee on vacation.

Without her asking, her brother gave up going to a concert he'd saved and bought tickets for months in advance. He was sixteen, and it would have been his first real concert, but he said there would be others. He'd covered her shifts at the garden center so she could go have fun with her friend. What other teenager would be willing to make that sacrifice? But Liam was like that, always the big brother even though he was two years younger. The only thing he'd ever asked of her was to take care of his wife.

She needed to fix this for Kaylee. But how?

Ten

"What a day!" Beth watched Carmen, an employee, stroll toward the red Ford pickup where her husband sat waiting. After they left, only the family's vehicles remained in the lot. "I know it's good business to stay open until seven, but these twelve-hour workdays are killers."

"I'm glad we schedule our crews in shifts." Harmony locked the front door to the floral department and gift shop. "It's one thing for us to put in more hours but not fair to expect the same from everyone else. People need a life."

"So . . . you're insinuating that *we* don't?" Beth teased as she perched her hand on her hip.

Harmony held up the chrome ring holding keys for various doors and gates to the property. "It's all in perspective, Sis. Right now, I'm starving, and all I can focus on is my growling stomach."

"I'm glad Kaylee is coming to family dinner tonight," Mom said as she removed a bouquet of white, yellow, and peach tulips from the case filled with floral arrangements. "These will brighten our table."

She wrapped the blooms in paper and tied the bunch with a ribbon. "I filled the slow cooker with chicken wild rice soup this morning, and there's a fresh loaf of hearty grain bread from the bakery waiting for us at home. The fridge is stocked with veggies for a large salad. You girls can put one together while I finish making the soup."

Beth zipped up her jacket. "There's something we need to talk about before dinner."

"Can't it wait?" Harmony rubbed her stomach. "Remember? *Starving.*" She drew out the last word and feigned collapsing. Often thinking only of herself, and always the comedian.

"No, it can't, Carol Burnett wannabe." Beth leaned against the counter. They were all tired, but it felt important to make them aware of her earlier conversation. "It's about Kaylee."

Mom's shoulders fell. "She didn't change her mind again about dinner, did she?"

"No, she's still coming, but we talked about what happened in the greenhouse." At seeing her mom's scowl, Beth raised her hand in protest. "Don't worry, I didn't scold her. We merely had an honest chat. Probably the first one we've shared since Liam introduced her."

"About what?" Harmony's ears had apparently perked up.

"Kaylee is trying hard here, but it's not working. We self-ishly assumed she'd help fill the gaps left by Dad and Liam and pour herself into this business like we have, but she's miserable."

Mom laid the flowers on the counter and rubbed her forehead. "I suspected her heart wasn't in the job, but I didn't realize she was that unhappy."

"Why didn't she say something?" Harmony, who normally attempted to keep everything positive and light, sounded worried.

Beth shrugged her left shoulder. "Has Kaylee ever been open about anything?"

"No, not about anything important," Harmony said,

scrunching her face. "When she didn't invite any family to the wedding, Liam didn't explain. He just said to give her some space. She'd share more when the time was right."

"They were married for two years before he died. And in the five years we've known her, she's been so private, we've barely learned anything about her." At least, not until today, when Kaylee had shared her grief with Beth.

"What did the two of you talk about?" Mom asked.

"Do you remember Liam mentioning that his wife wanted to open a tearoom or small café?" At the questioning expressions shot her way, Beth sighed. "Well, I do, but we all were so consumed with our responsibilities here, we forgot the two of them were making plans for her to have something of her own."

Harmony gave a quick shrug. "Liam was always fantasizing about doing this or that. Our brother processed his ideas by talking about them. Until he took actual steps to make something happen, I learned to not take him seriously."

"He was a visionary—and a dreamer. But he was more intelligent than you and I combined. I think Kaylee is very much like him." Beth was finally beginning to understand her sister-in-law better. "I think we owe it to Liam and the love of his life to help make what she's imagined a reality."

"Honey, I feel bad that we've neglected Kaylee's needs, and we'll try to do better, but you continue to place too many burdens on yourself." Her mother's voice was heavy with concern. "You've got to accept that you can't fix everyone's problems."

"I'm aware, Mom, but Kaylee is family." Beth squeezed her eyes shut. "And I need to bring up something else." Her eyes opened. "I only know this because I've been going over the books with our accountant. Our current reality is that we're barely keeping this business operating in the black. A year ago, Mom pulled money from her savings and retirement funds to pay the bills here and make payroll."

Harmony's jaw dropped. "Mom! You shouldn't keep that kind of information from us."

"I'm sorry. I didn't want to worry anyone else, and I only needed to resort to that for one month." Mom massaged her right upper arm with her left hand. "You dad and brother had the business smarts and common sense when it came to running this place. It's been a huge undertaking for all of us to step into their shoes. Somehow, we've managed, and I'm proud of that. But with working as hard as we do to keep going here, I don't see how we could possibly help Kaylee start her own business."

"I understand, Mom." Of course Beth wouldn't suggest they gift or even loan a large sum to Kaylee when finances were tight already.

"It's not only the lack of extra funds available to help her," Harmony said. "I'll admit she's a wiz in the kitchen. The blueberry scones she made the other day were amazing, and she has great taste in decorating. But even though she majored in business, she has no experience running one."

Beth couldn't disagree on that point. "I know she hasn't put her education to use, but maybe that's because we haven't given her a chance. She and Liam were ready to put a plan together and apply for a business loan. After the accident, we were all trying to survive and deal with our own grief, so Kaylee's project got shelved. Years later, she's floundering, not even knowing if she has a place in this family anymore. That's not okay."

"If there was some way to come up with the money." Mom

paused and stared into space for a moment. "The woman responsible for your dad's and brother's accident only carried the mandatory minimum insurance—a payment of twenty-five thousand dollars to me and another for the same amount to Kaylee as Liam's widow."

"I hope you tucked that away for yourself." Beth wanted her mother to relax and enjoy some adventures with friends.

"I don't have much left. Your dad and I had tried to put away what we could over the years for retirement, and the life insurance paid funeral expenses, but after his death, I got behind on a few bills. Then last fall, the house needed a new furnace."

"I'd like to help Kaylee too, but where are the funds going to come from? If she leaves, we'll have to hire someone to take her place here." Harmony unscrewed the top from a bottle of cranberry juice and took a drink. "I want to expand the gift shop, and Mom, you and I were talking about taking on more wedding and special occasion requests. How are we supposed to do it all?"

"It comes down to priorities," Beth said. "Even if she applies for a bank loan, it doesn't mean she'll get approved. Since she's renting a condo, that means we might be asked to put up this place as collateral. As Liam's heir, she's part owner, so we have to take that into consideration."

"Or . . ." Harmony said, "the bank might be willing to use the new business as collateral, and she'd risk losing everything if all didn't go well."

"True, but even at that, the bank might only loan her a percentage of the funds needed to buy an existing building and renovate it." Beth felt someone walk into the room behind her, and by the embarrassed expressions on her mother's and sister's faces, she didn't need to turn around to know who had joined them.

"Kaylee, we thought you'd left to go home and change." Mom stepped close to her daughter-in-law and gave her a brief side hug. "I'm sorry if you heard anything that made you feel uncomfortable."

"I—I didn't come in with the intention of eavesdropping. I apologize for not letting you know I was here sooner. That wasn't right of me." Kaylee shot a glance at each of them. "More than feeling weird about what I overheard, it made me realize that you do care. I'm not alone."

"Kaylee—"

"Harmony, you were right." Kaylee gave her a weak smile. "I haven't used my education here. While Liam was alive, the family didn't need me. And after he died, I just felt so lost. But I can't continue using his death as an excuse to stop living."

"Honey, we love you, and we most certainly want and need you." Mom wrapped her arm around Kaylee's shoulder but this time kept the embrace.

"When the time is right, I'll find another way to open a teahouse. But in the meantime, I still have some of the insurance money I received. I'm more than willing to contribute it all to Your Secret Garden if it would help."

"That means a lot to us, Kaylee, but there's no need. The business is doing fine right now." Mom gave her a quick squeeze, then released her grasp.

"Okay," Kaylee said as she tucked long strands of curls behind her ears.

"Is there anything more you need to say before we head over to Mom's?" Beth asked.

"I know I haven't shared much about my own family—my

parents." Kaylee chuckled quietly. "Well, not at all."

Beth, Mom, and Harmony returned the smile in agreement.

"Liam knew how embarrassed I was about my past, so he never pressured me to talk about my parents with you. You know that my mom and dad are both gone now, but you were never told that they were both addicts and not the nicest people. The truth is . . . I had a *horrible* childhood." She dropped her chin to her chest.

"I worked hard to rise above my circumstances, and one of the reasons I loved Liam so much . . ." Kaylee's voice hitched, and her head lifted. "He never looked down on me but always raised me up as high as he could." She blinked, and a tear escaped down her face.

Group hug.

How could they not?

They broke apart and gathered their things. Beth hadn't expected that when she brought up Kaylee's desire to have her own business it would also open the door to the four women drawing closer. There had to be a way for Beth to help Your Secret Garden *and* Kaylee. Maybe if she received her certification and earned a good living as a horticultural therapist, it would ease the financial situation for them all.

"What's on your mind, Beth?" Mom set the security alarm, and they headed out the door. "I sense serious brain activity."

"Something else to talk about at dinner." Beth swung her bag over her shoulder. "There's more you need to know about the internship."

Beth savored the toasted multigrain bread slathered with

butter. She normally watched the carbs, but really . . . it wasn't healthy, realistic, or fun to deny oneself continually. Besides, she'd also indulged in a large salad filled with veggies. And although her mom's chicken wild rice soup was one of Beth's favorite meals, she'd turned down a second helping.

Her mother served decaf coffee and set a plate in the center of the table filled with the white chocolate macadamia nut cookies Kaylee had stashed aside for them. Apparently, the crew at Your Secret Garden had downed all the pecan pie cookies she'd brought to work earlier that day.

"Now that we've had a moment to relax, I'd like to hear more about this potential internship and what kind of input you'd like from us." Mom slipped into her place at the table and picked up her cup of steaming coffee. Then she raised her eyebrows and peered at Beth, signaling that she couldn't put off telling them any longer.

Beth wiped her hands on her napkin. Time to bring her family into her reality. "During my interview at the penitentiary, I learned that Abbey Ward is enrolled in the horticultural program."

"Oh, dear . . ." Mom said, sounding alarmed.

At the same time, Kaylee choked on the bite of cookie she'd just taken, and she coughed into her napkin until the spell stopped. She took a drink of water. Mom reached over and held her hand for a moment.

"You wouldn't have to interact with her, would you?" The disgusted tone in Harmony's voice relayed *her* feelings about Beth's involvement at the prison.

"I was up-front with Lisa about my—*our*—history with Abbey and that I'd prefer to keep my distance. That wasn't something she could commit to. And she confessed that Abbey would be her primary concern since an inmate's welfare and success takes priority over my involvement in the program."

Harmony's face flushed. "You mean this Lisa person is actually giving more consideration to that woman's feelings and needs than yours?"

"It's her job. It's the right thing to do." Beth nibbled on her lower lip. "It would only be for three months, and I might not have to work with Abbey at all. It's a large facility, and I wouldn't be the only person on staff working in the horticulture department. Also, the internship isn't a sure thing. Lisa could still decline because of the conflict of interest. The program has influenced Abbey's attitude and goals. Lisa doesn't want to pull her out, and I wouldn't want her to."

"Can't you do your horticultural therapy without certification? Why keep putting yourself on hold for a piece of paper?" Harmony grabbed several cookies from the plate and chomped on one while holding the second in her left hand. "Why would you even consider getting involved in anything connected to Abbey Ward?"

"You're out of line, sweetheart." Mom's tone was soft but firm.

Harmony broke her remaining cookie in two. "Sorry, but it's upsetting."

"I understand. I'm not exactly enthused about the circumstances either, but it's possible for me to get in all the needed hours within three months and still work part-time at Your Secret Garden. I'll even put in overtime in the evenings, if necessary." Beth moved her coffee cup away from her.

"It's a paid internship, so I'd bring in a little extra money, and then once I get certified, I could become a registered therapist. That would make me more legit and open doors to so many more opportunities. I could contract my services to hospitals, nursing homes, and rehabilitation centers in the area, and those are only a few potential places. The added income could help our family business."

Beth picked up her spoon and rotated it in her grasp. "I think it's become more than just finishing my internship."

"How?" Kaylee asked in a quiet, raspy tone.

"I've done some research, and my conversation with Lisa confirmed what I read. We know that exposure to nature improves mental health and well-being. These programs have been linked to lower aggression in prisons, and horticulture classes have been associated with vocational and social skill-building."

What she'd discovered had sparked excitement in Beth. Lives were being changed. "Women released from state penitentiaries aren't guaranteed safe and secure housing. So when they're released, they have nowhere to go except to a shelter. But if they leave with knowledge and skills, they have a better chance of finding employment. One former inmate found a job on an organic farm that offers a transitional residential and employment program."

"It sounds like there's potential for you to make a real difference in how the women cope day-to-day, as well as what happens when they leave that place," Mom said in gentle, thoughtful tone. "Are you willing to be uncomfortable around one inmate for a few months to experience that and also move on with the future you've prayed for?"

"I'll admit I'm intrigued, but I also have to consider more than my feelings and needs." Beth sighed. "What about you? And Harmony and Kaylee?"

She glanced at the two younger women, then focused

again on her mother. "It's a large facility, and other staff and volunteers are involved, so I don't think there's much chance that I'll work with Abbey. But how will you deal with the situation if I am put in that position? She isn't just any prisoner. Because she chose to drink and drive, Dad and Liam died."

"You're right," her mom said quietly. "And she's also paying a price for her mistake." She lowered her eyes for a moment, then raised her gaze and met Beth's. "We all fall short, honey. And even though we may believe her sin is greater than anything we've done, God still loves her. Abbey Ward is still his child and someone who needs forgiveness. Have you forgiven her?"

"To be honest, I don't know." There were times when Beth thought she had reached that point, but there were still days . . . "Sometimes, it feels like I've moved on. Then I have moments when I'm still so angry."

Harmony gave her a weak smile. "You're not alone in that. I feel the same way."

If Beth truly forgave Abbey from the depths of her heart, would that suggest all was good? That Beth had put the past behind and forgotten all the pain suffered? Would it diminish the tragedy and imply her dad and brother's lives weren't as valued? Or would they have wanted Beth to forgive and move on?

"We may never get over losing your dad and brother, but we'll figure out how to handle our feelings in healthy ways. Grief can come in waves, and emotions can overwhelm us when least expected." Mom placed her crossed hands on her chest. "It will get better. I promise. And you may not want to hear this, but have you considered that the Lord might give you this opportunity as a step toward your healing?"

"How did you get so wise?" Beth asked with sincerity, but her mother laughed at the question.

"Oh, honey, most days I don't feel smart at all." Mom dropped her hands to her sides. "I just ask the Holy Spirit to speak through me."

"It makes me a little uneasy, the thought of you helping the person who took my husband away from me, but if given the chance, I think you should participate in the program." Kaylee's shaky voice moved to sounding firm and calm as she said, "I know Liam wouldn't want you to pass it up just because it's hard."

"You've sacrificed a lot for this family, so I support you accepting a position at the prison, and I'll pray for confirmation in your heart as to whatever decision you come to." Her mother edged closer. "But know this. I'm proud regardless. And I'm at peace."

Her mother's warm smile and compassionate gaze radiated pure love. "I've forgiven Abbey, and my hope has been that you three girls will also come to that place—for your sake as well as hers. It could turn out to be a blessing for you to work side-by-side with that young woman. I believe she's hurting too."

Harmony groaned and glanced at Beth out of the corner of her eye. Then she faced her, nodded, and smiled. "I don't necessarily like it, but if it will get you certified, I'm on board too, Sis."

"Okay then." Now it was up to Lisa to agree to give Beth the opportunity and God to seal his approval on her heart.

What if this was what he intended all along for Beth? What if her heavenly Father's plan was for her to offer knowledge, gifts, and skills to the woman who had killed those she loved and missed deeply?

Eleven

Aware that Ty could interrupt at any time since he had Saturdays off, Beth had hesitated to accept Agatha's invitation for coffee and banana muffins. He might ask about the interview at the prison, and Beth wasn't ready to talk about her association with Abbey. But she'd missed having time with Agatha, so when the text popped into her cell first thing that morning, Beth had responded that she'd love to join her friend.

"Everything is set up where we can have a lovely view of the gardens. Have you noticed the lilacs are starting to bloom?" Agatha made a waving gesture. "Of course you have."

The old oak floors made a strangely comforting creaking sound when walked on, and the beautiful woodwork throughout the house was a reminder of its history. Not many modern homes boasted the same craftsmanship.

Agatha led the way to the sunroom, where she'd moved her easels and paints to the side. A small table sat between soft, comfortable chairs. They hadn't enjoyed one of these special chats since Tyler had arrived.

A vinyl record played on the turntable, and Agatha turned the volume down low. She was old-school when it came to music. The folk group Peter, Paul and Mary were one of her favorites, and Beth recognized the song playing as "Blowin' in the Wind."

"Spring is delightful, but I'm already looking forward to blackberry season again." Agatha filled Beth's antique china cup with coffee from the carafe and offered her creamer before pouring her own. "Can you believe I've used up all the pints you and I picked and froze last September? I baked blackberry muffins, bread, pies, cobbler, and I also made a few smoothies. Very modern of me."

Beth bit into the banana muffin. "Delicious!" No nuts. Good. She preferred them without.

"Thank you." Agatha broke a muffin in half and took a bite. "Not bad." She wiped her hands with a cloth napkin. "Now, fill me in on your interview."

Beth shared all the details and the discussion that followed with her family last night. "I'm a little worried about how I'll act around Abbey—that is, *if* I get the position. I must assume that I won't be able to avoid her entirely."

Agatha held her delicate painted cup in one hand. "Is there a chance you ever get to the point of *wanting* to help Abbey?"

"I—I don't know." Beth had never considered the possibility of reaching that point in her feelings toward the woman.

"I don't want to seem insensitive to what you and your family have gone through . . ." With her free hand, Agatha toyed with the reading glasses attached to the long chain hanging around her neck.

"You're one of the most caring people I know, Agatha. You would never do or say anything hurtful. Please, speak your mind."

"All right." Agatha moistened her lips. "Consider asking God to help you see Abbey as a person in pain—someone he loves as much as he loves you."

Beth let her friend's words soak in. "I understand where you're going with this, but other people on staff have more experience working in that environment, and they're not personally involved with her. They might be better equipped to help her."

"Maybe. Maybe not." Agatha set her cup down and smiled as though she knew something more—something undisclosed. "But what if you're the *best* person—the *only* person— who can give her what she needs?"

"Last night, Mom suggested that the internship might help me work through Dad's and Liam's deaths, and now you're asking me to also view the position as a way for Abbey to find healing." Adrenaline surged through Beth's body, and her stomach churned. The Lord wouldn't ask that of her, would he? Put Abbey's needs ahead of her own? That would add insult to injury, to say nothing of what it would cost her.

"What happened to your dad and brother was terrible— and painful. But it was an accident, Beth. Abbey didn't set out to take them from you, and my guess is she's suffering in her own way."

Her friend's appearance blurred in Beth's vision, and as she squeezed her eyes shut, the water pooling in her eyes flowed down her face. She wiped her cheeks dry with a napkin and then held it in her hands, twisting it tight. Not again! An emotional reaction when least expected. Why couldn't she keep them under control? "I'm sorry. I don't know where that came from."

"It came from the grief you still carry. It's okay to cry—it's good to release those feelings. Time will soften the sharp edges of that sorrow and make it more bearable. I promise you that." Agatha's eyes filled with compassion. "It might help to share the entire story with your family as to what happened that night. Secrets can eat away at you."

Beth swallowed hard. "It's worth it to protect them from more heartache."

"But the cost may hinder your ability to let go, forgive, and move on."

"I thought I'd forgiven Abbey, but now I'm not so sure." Beth dug her thumbnail into her palm.

"In my many years of living, I've learned a few things about forgiveness." Agatha picked up her cup and sipped. "It's not a feeling. It's not pretending you weren't hurt, because the pain doesn't always disappear. And forgiving someone is rarely a onetime event."

"That makes sense." Beth unwound her napkin and wiped her nose. "Because I'm still angry, I may have to keep practicing forgiveness and pray that God brings me to a place where I can truly let go."

"Remember, forgiveness doesn't condone the harm caused. And it can release us from any bitterness that might start to fester inside."

"And poison us and our relationships."

Agatha folded her napkin thoughtfully. "Abbey made a bad decision—a terrifying one. What she did was wrong, but we may never know what was going on in her life and her state of mind at the time. What we can offer her or anyone else who makes a mistake is grace."

"I realize that one mistake, regardless of how serious, doesn't make a person bad." And Beth didn't want to look at Abbey that way.

"Right." Agatha's smile seemed almost sad. "Sometimes life takes those unexpected twists and turns, and there are times when someone you care about falls short of the person you thought or hoped he would be. That doesn't mean redemption can't follow. People can rise from those situations and surprise you."

"Are you talking about someone else now?"

"No—just thinking out loud." Agatha reached for another muffin.

Clearly something milled around in the older woman's head besides Abbey's imprisonment, but it was also obvious she wanted to keep those thoughts to herself.

"You know," Agatha said as she set the muffin on her plate, "we tend to want things to play out the way we envision them, but God often answers prayers in ways we don't expect. Haven't you been praying for an internship?" She raised her eyebrows and grinned.

Beth nodded and smiled. That day in the garden when Ty had shown up, she'd been complaining to God because her career wasn't playing out the way she'd hoped. By Ty's presence and opening the door to a possible solution, was God answering her prayers—her needs—before she even asked and in a surprising way?

Agatha refilled Beth's cup, then set the carafe and the now empty platter that held the muffins on a side table. "I have something to show you, but relax and enjoy your coffee. I'll bring it here." She left the room and soon returned with a large, clear glass bowl filled with assorted shades of sea glass. She placed it on the table between their chairs.

"These are beautiful." Beth was drawn to the soft colors.

"Thank you." Agatha put on her glasses, picked up several pieces, and held them in her palm, fingering them with the other hand. She gave a nod toward the collection. "Go ahead.

You're welcome to look through them."

Beth moved her hand through the pile. She chose two varieties to examine—a pink and a pale blue.

"Each one started out as a bottle, dish, or some other kind of object that was discarded because it was no longer wanted. After being tossed in the sea, the glass began the slow process of renewal and healing as it tumbled through the water and sand. It was transformed, and the rough edges were softened. The broken glass was physically and chemically weathered until the process produced the frosted glass."

Beth rubbed her thumb over the smooth specimens in her hand.

"But the change didn't happen overnight. The evolution took twenty to fifty years." Agatha caught and held Beth's gaze. "It can be the same for people. It takes time and experience to grow. And often, a little assistance is needed along the way."

Lord, a double dose? "I'm getting the feeling that you and Mom are on the same team. You both feel God wants me placed at the prison."

"Like your mother, I'm asking you to be open to the possibility." The corners of Agatha's mouth twitched, and her lips slid into a smile. "I'd like you to take some sea glass to remind you of what we talked about today."

"Thank you, but I couldn't." Beth appreciated the offer, but it felt too generous.

"I insist." Agatha grabbed a handful from the bowl and laid clear, green, gray, and peach fragments side by side on the table. They searched for additional colors while the song "Where Have All the Flowers Gone?" played in the background.

The back door slammed, and Tyler stepped into view in

the doorway to the sunroom. His dark hair dripped water down the side of his face, and his sweatshirt and pants looked soaked. "Sorry, Agatha. I didn't realize you had company. I thought you might have some rags or towels I could use to dry the floor after I take off these shoes." He pointed to his tennies.

Had he been sprayed by a sprinkler? Beth glanced outside. *Huh. Rain.* She'd been so engaged in conversation with Agatha, she hadn't even noticed the shower quenching the gardens of any thirst.

"Not company. Beth is *family.* There's a difference."

"Sure." Ty smiled, then wiped his damp face with his sleeved arm.

Agatha stood and opened a cabinet containing tattered towels. She handed him several. "These should do the job."

"You both having a nice morning?" Ty asked, directing the question to Beth while swinging the towels at his side. A stall tactic?

"Yes. Coffee, muffins, and great conversation." Why was he hanging around, as though he felt an urge to see what they were up to? He'd only been kind to Beth, and she didn't want to be self-centered, but it had been too long since she'd had quality time with Agatha.

A cheerful tune sang from Agatha's cell phone, and she picked it up from where she'd set it on a shelf. "Excuse me. I've been expecting a call from this friend whose husband has been in hospice care." She vacated the room, leaving Beth alone with Ty.

"You're not working at the house today? I thought you were anxious to get things rolling." Beth didn't mean to sound so judgmental.

Ty gave her a sly grin as he slipped out of his shoes. "You

eager to get rid of me?" he asked as he dried the hall floor outside the sunroom's entrance.

She didn't mean to be that obvious. "Maybe," she said loud enough for him to hear as he moved out of sight. Wasn't honesty the best policy?

He responded with a loud belly laugh and stepped back into the room. "Okay, I didn't realize I was such a nuisance. I'll be on my way."

"No! Wait!" What was she doing? Beth took a deep breath. "I apologize. I could say that my only reason for being rude was that I was enjoying this time alone with your aunt, but that's not the entire truth."

He leaned against the doorframe and cocked his head. "And the rest?"

"I'm a bit ashamed of how ungrateful I've acted toward you. You went out of your way to connect me with Lisa Randall, and I've been less than gracious. It's probably felt like I've been avoiding you."

"Did I push too hard for you to talk to her?"

"No, you've done nothing wrong. You couldn't possibly understand my hesitation to work there. I haven't shared all my reasons. But it helped to process the situation with Agatha this morning." Beth paused, relaxed her shoulders, and shared a genuine smile. "I'm grateful for your encouragement too, so thank you."

"You're welcome." Ty lowered the towels to this side. "And you're right."

"About what?"

"I should be focused on making progress at the house, but I've done all I can for now. I've been putting plans together and have asked my friend, Brandon, for his input. I mentioned him the night we had the little campfire up at the property. He's been in the construction business with his dad and brother since he was a kid, so he knows his stuff."

"I can imagine his knowledge has come in handy."

"I have some skills, but his . . ." Ty whistled and raised his hand above his head. "I've submitted the necessary plans to get permits for electrical, plumbing, and some structural changes. It could take weeks to get everything approved, so for now, progress is stalled in those areas."

Beth raised her eyebrows. "You could still get bids on countertops, painting, and tile work."

"True! But remember, someone agreed to give me some insight into design, and she's been a little distracted."

Her face warmed. "I'm sorry . . . I—"

"Nothing to be sorry about," he said, shaking his head. "There's no rush on that right now. It's more important that you focus on getting that internship."

Agatha returned with her cell in hand. "I apologize, Beth, for cutting our time short, but my friend's husband is failing fast, and she's beside herself. It's a three-hour drive over there, so I'm going to throw a few things together and spend the night."

Tyler pushed off from the doorframe and stood straight. "Don't worry about staying longer if needed. I'll cover things here."

"Thanks, Ty." Lines creased her forehead. Agatha was clearly concerned for her friend.

Beth stood and gave her a hug. "Drive safely."

Agatha headed to her room to pack, and Beth gathered the dishes they'd used. She'd take them to the kitchen and wash them before leaving herself.

"I can carry that," Ty said as he threw the damp towels he held over his arm and removed the carafe from Beth's hands. "Any plans for the rest of the day?"

She glanced at her watch—a few minutes after ten. She wasn't expected at her first stop until eleven. "I do. I'm delivering a little love."

"Okay, I'm curious. What does that mean?"

"I'm visiting some people in the community today. While I won't technically be doing therapy . . ."

"I see." He winked at her, as though they shared a secret. "Mind if I tag along?"

Twelve

T yler stood behind Beth while she rang the doorbell to the blue one-story house. The sun's rays warmed his back, and he filled his lungs with fresh spring air. The last week of April remained on the cool side, but the rain shower had ended after his morning run, and the sky held only a few fluffy white clouds.

His thoughts flickered to the inmates and their inability to step outside at will and how he'd struggled with his loss of freedom during his own stint behind bars. *Thank you, Lord, for bringing me through those days.*

A woman with shoulder-length light brown hair and a bright smile opened the door. "Good morning! Please, come on in." Their host stepped aside so they could enter the comfortable-looking home. "Dad is out back on the patio, having his second cup of coffee, so we have a little time to ourselves."

"Nikki, this is the friend I mentioned, Tyler Sharp." Beth gestured toward him. "Ty, meet Nicole Carson."

"Please, call me Nikki." She reached out her hand, and he accepted the shake.

"Ty is Agatha's great-nephew, and he's living with her temporarily until he gets his own place ready." Beth glanced at him and smiled. "He's a social worker interested in how horticultural therapy works, so he's helping me out today."

"Wonderful! Dad will enjoy having another man around the house." Nikki pushed back her hair. "And I'll welcome an hour to myself."

"How has he been doing this week?" Beth asked.

"Some days are better than others. Danny—my husband—stays with him on Wednesday nights so I can attend a support group for caregivers. That's been a blessing, and your visits . . . I can't tell you how much they help." Nikki blew out a stream of air, smiled, and turned her attention to Ty. "When Beth called, she mentioned that she told you my dad has Alzheimer's."

"Yes, she did," Ty said. He knew that George Anderson was eighty-two, a widower, and after he was diagnosed, his daughter had left her teaching position at the elementary school to care for him in her home.

"Dad has memory loss, difficulty completing familiar tasks, and he can get confused about where he is." Nikki sighed. "He's a sweet man, but the disease has taken a toll. We're always prepared for sudden personality changes."

"What kind of changes?" Ty was aware of Alzheimer's and some of the symptoms, but he had never spent time with anyone who had the disease.

Nikki paused, seeming to consider what she would say next. "There are moments when he becomes suspicious, depressed, fearful—anxious. Most of the time, he's okay at home, but even here he can get upset with us or with friends." She gave Ty a reassuring smile. "Don't worry. Dad enjoys having Beth here. He feels safe with her, and his favorite place is in the garden, so have a good time."

"I'm looking forward to it, and I brought what we need for planting today." Beth moved toward the front door. "Ty can help me carry everything around the back to the patio. We'll meet you there."

"Great! Extra potting soil is sitting next to one of the planters, and Dad's gloves and spade are there too. See you out back," Nikki said as she closed the door behind them.

Ty followed Beth to the car and helped unload several boxes filled with plants. More containers were left behind, but he'd retrieve them after they delivered what they could carry now. She flung a canvas bag over her shoulder that held two pairs of garden gloves and several tools. They hauled their supplies around to the side of the house where a wooden gate had been left open to the backyard. Beth closed the entrance behind them.

"The entire backyard is fenced in, and Nikki locks the gate when I'm not around so she can feel comfortable leaving her dad out here by himself. He tends to wander off and forget his way home, but she can't keep an eye on him twenty-four seven."

They rounded the corner of the house and walked into a large, groomed yard with several maple trees planted near the fence, possibly for shade and privacy, several small flower gardens, and three raised beds filled with soil that Ty guessed were used for vegetables.

Nikki leaned over an elderly man sitting in a folding chair. His thinning gray hair did little to cover his head, glasses sat halfway down his nose, and a cane was propped on the small black iron table next to him.

She waved Ty and Beth over. "Dad, Beth is here, and she brought a friend."

"Hi, George!" Beth set her bag and box of plants next to a long, wooden planter that ran along the outside of the large patio. "This is my friend, Ty."

The older man looked at Tyler and gave a quiet grunt.

"How are you doing today, Mr. Anderson?" Without thinking, Ty had almost shouted. *Cool it. George isn't deaf.*

"Fine, fine," the older man said without much enthusiasm.

"I could use some help getting these in the dirt." Beth pointed to the box with colorful, flowering plants. "Are you up for it?"

George pushed his glasses up and gave her a tentative smile. "Watcha got?"

"Violets, yellow and purple pansies, and primroses in every shade I could find. We'll start planting vegetables next week."

"Betty, you always did love those primroses." George slid to the edge of his chair and got up with the help of his cane. "I need to get closer if I'm gonna get my hands in there. Can't do much good from way over here."

"We'll move your chair, Dad." Nikki got him settled.

"Look at that." George settled in next to the planter. "Betty, you found primroses in every color of the rainbow."

Beth put her hand on Nikki's arm for a moment. "We're good. You take a break."

"Thanks. I have a quick errand to run, but I'll be nearby if you need anything. You have my cell number."

"Go. Relax. Grab a latte. We'll be fine." Beth gave a reassuring smile and pulled another chair next to George. "Oh, Ty . . ."

"On it! I'll finish unloading the car and close the trunk."

"Thanks."

Nikki grabbed her purse from an outside table and walked with Ty to the front of the house where her car was parked.

"Your dad called Beth by another name—Betty."

"My mom. When his memory slips, he forgets that she

116 | DAWN KINZER

passed away twelve years ago. Beth looks a lot like she did at that age."

"Beth doesn't correct him."

"No. She's a gem. Beth understands that he'll be more relaxed if we go with the flow. It doesn't work to fight with him or try to make him accept reality." Nikki opened her car door. "His doctor said there's no harm in letting him live in the past during those moments, and he's happier."

Nikki tossed her purse into the passenger seat and leaned against the car. "My mom and dad didn't have a lot of similar interests, but they enjoyed gardening together. It became their common ground. Beth spending time with him, planting and tending to the gardens like my mom did, has been a bright spot in his dim and confusing world. He's a different person after her visits. Dad is more alert—more alive—and happier."

After Nikki left, Ty returned to the backyard and settled in, interacting when appropriate, but also trying not to get in Beth's way. She and George bantered back and forth, teasing. With love, they planted each growing thing, and the process seemed to also give new life to the older man.

Ty and Beth's next stop was at the nursing home and rehabilitation center where they visited an elderly woman, Mrs. Middleton, who was staying there while she recovered from a broken hip. Her husband wasn't equipped to handle her care at home by himself.

The frail-looking, elderly woman with gray eyes spouted anger at having to stay there. Ty was taken aback by her foul language, but Beth listened without interrupting, and when Mrs. Middleton ran out of steam, Beth spoke to her with a gentle tone and calmed her down.

Somehow she understood that the bedridden woman was

more worried about how her husband, Henry, was fairing without her help at home than her own slow recovery. He visited her every day, and the neighbors brought him meals, but she was concerned that he struggled with loneliness in the evenings. They had developed a nightly ritual of playing cards, checkers, or backgammon. Henry didn't enjoy reading or watching TV, so without someone to keep him company, he sat in his recliner all evening, staring at the walls.

Beth opened the bag she'd brought into the room, and when Mrs. Middleton realized the deep purple violet plant was a gift, she brightened and cracked a smile.

"How did you know I have a fondness for violets?" Mrs. Middleton held the pot in her thin, bony hands as though she held a treasure chest filled with precious jewels.

Beth winked. "I have my sources."

They chatted for a few minutes and then said their good-byes.

Ty hesitated before stepping into the hallway. "I often take a quick run through your neighborhood after dinner." He raised his shoulders slightly and cocked his head. "I could stop by and play a few games with Henry some nights, if you think he wouldn't mind taking on a new challenger."

Mrs. Middleton gasped. Her eyes filled with gratitude. "That would be wonderful, young man."

Outside in the hall, Beth whispered, "It often doesn't take much. Sometimes a mere kind gesture makes a difference. Thank you."

Ty was beginning to understand why Beth was so passionate about bringing nature and people together. Powerful healing took place.

Ten minutes later, they stopped to see an autistic nine-year-old boy. Beth had called his mother earlier to ask permission for Tyler to hang out with them, knowing Colton didn't always handle change well.

As soon as they walked into the backyard, Colton ran to her. "I've been waiting for you!" The boy's light brown hair was a mass of curls, and his height almost reached her shoulders.

"That's awesome, because I'm excited to get to work!" Beth touched Tyler's arm. "This is my friend, Ty. He wanted to meet you."

Colton squinted his hazel eyes at Tyler, then looked away.

"How do you greet someone new?" Beth asked, directing the question to the boy.

A hand shot out, and Ty accepted the shake. "Nice to meet you, Colton."

"Yeah." He pulled his hand away. "You can sit over there with my mom."

Wow. Direct. Tyler had gotten his marching orders, and he'd comply.

"Don't take it personally." The boy's mom, with bright blue eyes and a blond ponytail, smiled and gestured toward several yard chairs sitting under a dark green canopy. "I'm Whitney."

"Ty," he said as he slipped into one of the seats. "Thanks for letting me come."

"Beth is a godsend, and any friend of hers is welcome here. But Colton is a little possessive of his time with her, so it's best we stay out of the way."

"I understand." Ty didn't blame Colton for wanting Beth to himself. "I'm just starting to learn how what she does can be helpful for people. You've seen benefits?"

"Oh, my . . . yes. My son is high-functioning and attends school, but he struggles with things like social interaction, controlling his emotions—unexpected changes. One moment he can be content, and then a minute later, something can set him off."

"That must be tough."

"His bad days can be stressful and draining, but Colton is more than autistic. He's also smart and creative." Whitney glanced in her son's direction. "Gardening is a calm, quiet activity, and what he does with Beth helps him learn to follow instructions and work with others. And his teachers agree that her projects are helpful for his sensory and motor skills."

Whitney's cell phone rang, and she glanced at the caller ID. "Excuse me. My mother. I need to take this."

Ty nodded.

She answered the call. "Hi, Mom. One moment." Whitney left her chair and headed indoors. She must have wanted privacy. Ty understood.

He directed his focus on Beth and Colton. They stopped pouring dirt into a large pot to have what looked like a serious conversation. Colton nodded, and she hiked over to Ty.

"We'd like you to join us," she said, gesturing toward the boy.

"You sure that's a good idea?" Ty peeked around Beth. Colton was staring at them. "His mom said he's kind of possessive. I don't want to cause any problems between you two."

"You won't." She glanced back at her planting partner. "As long as you stick to the rules."

"Which are?" What was he getting himself into?

"Sit within hearing distance, but not right next to us. Colton usually asks a lot of questions and the same one more than once. I'll answer and redirect him. As much as possible, I'd like him to explain what we're doing and why."

"You want use this exercise as another teaching tool."

"Smart man." Beth's lips curved into a sweet smile. "You game?"

"I'd be a coward not to be."

"Pretty much," she said in a teasing manner.

Ty carried his chair to a spot three to four feet away from Colton and sat down.

The boy had shifted his focus back to one of the four large pots. He stood and reached for the potting soil. When he gave the open bag a big heave to lift it, he tripped on his spade, lost his balance, and fell on a tomato plant sitting next to him.

Colton rolled over on the grass to his knees and picked up the plant, now broken halfway down the stem, and threw it. He screamed and hit the ground with his fist. "I ruined it!"

Beth knelt next to him. "It's okay. It was an accident," she said in a soothing tone. "Everything will be fine. We can fix it." She continued to comfort him until he calmed down. "Let's try again. Do you remember why we'll put our pots on platforms with wheels?" Beth asked as she scooped dirt.

Colton sniffed, wiped his eyes, and nodded. "So we can move the tomatoes around the yard to sunshine."

"That's right." She held up the damaged plant and removed the broken top piece. "This guy still has roots, so it will grow big and healthy. It might even have bigger tomatoes than the others."

"Really?" Colton sounded excited at the possibility.

They filled all the containers, and Beth complimented him on how careful he'd been to place the plants deep into the dirt, all the way up to the top few leaves so the roots could develop all along their stems.

Overcome with emotion at seeing the sense of

accomplishment on Colton's face, Ty rubbed his eyes free of moisture. When had he become such a softy?

Beth and Colton had buried green bean seeds in small containers two weeks before, and as they checked on the seedlings' progress, they talked through the process of germination and growth, including roots, stems, and leaves. Beth praised Colton for taking such good care of the seedlings, giving them the right amount of water and sunlight to grow healthy. Without being pushy, she gave him the opportunity to share as much as he wanted about the project with Ty.

On the way home, the day's memories filled Ty's brain. Every moment he spent with Beth, he grew more drawn to her.

He glanced at her beautiful face filled with contentment. "Thanks for sharing today. It must feel rewarding to see the difference you make."

From the driver's seat, she looked over at him, and her warm brown eyes shared her joy. "I love what I do, and I hope you got a better understanding of how gardening can touch people's lives."

"I did." Ty pulled down the visor to block the sun's blinding light. "And today's activities were done as gifts from the heart? You didn't get paid?"

"Right. I wasn't hired to spend time with anyone today." She turned the corner and drove down their street toward Agatha's. "I think of those visits as opportunities to use my gifts and minister to people's needs, like God has called us to."

"You're an amazing woman, Beth Miller."

"Thank you," she said with a sincere, appreciative tone.

How often did she receive compliments? He guessed not as much as she deserved. "What I witnessed today reminded me of the verse Pastor read last Sunday. 'Let us not become weary in doing good, for at the proper time we will reap a harvest if we do not give up.'"

"Galatians 6:9. You memorized it?" Beth sounded surprised.

He nodded. "With the kind of work I do, it felt like a good idea."

"For both of us." She grinned as she parked the car. "You must be hungry. I did warn you that we might not have time for a lunch break."

Ty laughed. "You did, and I didn't even think about food." He rubbed his stomach. "But I'll admit, I could eat now. You?"

"I'm famished." Her fingers tapped on her steering wheel. "Didn't Agatha mention leftover lasagna?"

"You read my mind." Ty opened the car door, then closed it. "You know, after watching you in action today, I know you'd be a huge asset to the horticultural program at the prison. They'd be lucky to get you."

"Thanks, but there's a good chance I won't be offered an internship."

"Why? I can't imagine Lisa not wanting you there."

"There's something I haven't told you." Beth shifted her body in the seat and faced him. "Are you familiar with an inmate by the name of Abbey Ward?"

"We've met, but with over seven hundred inmates in the facility and working there for a short amount of time, I still have a lot to learn about the women. Abbey seems to be trying hard with rehab, and she's also participating in gardening projects. Both seem to be helping her make positive changes."

Beth cringed, then she took a deep breath and her expression relaxed. "Lisa might not offer me the internship because there's a conflict of interest when it comes to me potentially working with Abbey."

"Okay . . . What conflict?"

"Abbey was sentenced to a prison term because she drove while intoxicated and ran her car into my dad's vehicle, killing him and my brother."

His jaw dropped. "Wow." The missing piece. Now Ty understood why Beth had initially shot down pursuing an internship at the facility.

"Yeah . . . wow."

Thirteen

O n Tuesday, Beth's cell rang, but later in the day than originally planned. Lisa Randall had sent a text that morning, changing the time of her expected call.

Beth was settled in at home, wanting privacy during their conversation as Lisa held the immediate future in her hands. She'd taken the day off from Your Secret Garden, but she'd work through the weekend. Mom didn't like being open on Sundays, but times and business practices had changed. Now they were open from noon to five so employees could still attend church services.

Her heart pounded at a speed that could have matched a hummingbird's wings while in flight. Would she have the needed internship, or would it be denied?

"Hi, Lisa," Beth said, pacing the floor in her apartment while still trying to sound cheerful and calm.

"Hello! I'm glad you saw my message. Again, I apologize for the delay." Lisa's upbeat tone was a good sign. *Right?* "So, after giving it some more thought, how are you feeling about interning with us? Do you think it's the right step for you, considering the complications?"

Why did she open with that? Was Lisa hoping that Beth had lost interest because of Abbey? The reality was that Beth needed the job. With the paid internship, she could take a pay cut at Your Secret Garden. To alleviate even a small amount of financial pressure at the business and take an important step in making her own dreams come true, Beth would put her personal feelings about Abbey aside.

Beth's throat tightened. "I've been anxious to talk to you about the position." She dropped onto her aging sofa and gripped the thin, white blanket tossed there. "I've thought about nothing else since we met, and I want the position."

Keep going. "I realize that my situation may feel unique, but I'm still a professional. In this type of career—this *call-ing*—not every person I come across will be fun, easy, and open to what I offer. I might not always agree with a person's political or religious beliefs. Regardless, I will always strive to focus on the best therapy for that person."

Silence.

Oh, no. Beth sighed inwardly. Maybe she'd plowed ahead and said too much when Lisa had merely called to let her down easy.

"I'm glad to hear it," Lisa said after a moment that felt like ten. "I'll always be honest with you, Beth. I struggled with my decision, so I talked to several members on our team here, and I looked over your college transcripts, character refer-ences, and referrals from college professors. I also contacted the college and spoke to someone about setting up an internship through them. Anyway, the school is onboard. As of thirty minutes ago, our program has been approved, and you can complete your requirements here for certification."

A quiet sigh of relief escaped Beth's lips. "That's great news."

"And honestly, we really need your help right now. A key person on staff involved with the program had a family emergency over the weekend, and she's taking a leave of absence. I also found out yesterday that several regular volunteers won't be available to help anymore. Not due to anything that happened at the prison but challenges in their personal lives right now."

"I'm happy to do whatever I can to help fill their roles."

"However . . ."

Here it comes. There was still something in Lisa's voice that hinted the internship wasn't a done deal.

"If at any time a staff member or I see that personal feelings are hindering your effectiveness, you'll be asked to leave the program."

"I understand." She would do anything necessary to avoid that happening.

"Termination is rare in internships, so I don't want to go there for the sake of your professional reputation. I think a better solution would be for you to officially make the decision yourself to walk away for personal reasons."

"Such as conflict of interest." Beth heard the message loud and clear. Lisa was trying to look out for both her and Abbey.

"Right." Lisa gave a quiet cough. "Are you ready for this?"

Beth stared at her reflection in a decorative wall mirror. "I am, and I'd like to start as soon as possible."

"Good. I'll put the paperwork through."

"Thanks, Lisa. I appreciate the opportunity."

"Thank *you*. Be at the front desk at nine o'clock on Monday morning, May first. An officer will take your photo and give you an ID card. Then come to my office, and we'll jump into the month by going over project schedules and assignments."

"I'll be there. Bye." Filled with a mix of excitement and dread, Beth hung up and threw her body prone on the sofa.

She'd already walked away from one internship because of her family going through crisis. Could Abbey be the reason for a second failure?

❧

How long had Beth been staring at the ceiling, deep in thought about her new commitment at the prison? She glanced at her cell—six thirty-five. Needing time to process alone, she'd silenced her phone and missed seven texts. Three from Mom and four from Harmony.

Naturally, they were curious about any conversation with Lisa and if Beth was happy with the outcome. She'd probably get chewed out for making them wait, but she hadn't done it on purpose to worry them or make them feel left out.

Beth would call Mom first. There was a good chance Harmony would be nearby, so maybe she could share the news with them at the same time. Kaylee would be next, followed by a chat with Agatha and Ty.

The doorbell chimed. Probably her mom or sister. Beth braced for a slew of questions and opened the door. "Ty!"

"Surprise." He shifted the box and several large binders in his arms. "Were you expecting someone else?"

"No, not exactly. I just thought—never mind." Beth smiled. "Come in."

"These are the tile and floor samples you asked for, but you probably have other things on your mind tonight." Ty set the stash on her coffee table. "Lisa dropped by my office before I left work. It sounds like we have a reason to celebrate."

"We do." Beth sat on the sofa, opened one of the binders but closed it without paying attention to the information it held.

"You don't sound excited." He dropped into a nearby chair as though he was used to spending time in her small apartment and felt at home there.

Even distracted by her thoughts, she still noticed how handsome he looked dressed in jeans and a black T-shirt with sleeves that hugged his biceps. How things had changed since the first day they'd met beneath Agatha's cherry tree. In that moment, she'd never expected to someday welcome his friendship or feel comforted by his presence. But her feelings toward him had gradually shifted.

His clear, bluish-green eyes filled with concern. "Are you worried you made a wrong decision?"

"I *want* the internship, but—"

"Then what's the problem?"

"Maybe this sounds strange, but I'm starting to doubt myself. Am I the right person for the job?" She held his gaze. "What makes me think I can make a difference for those women? I know nothing about what they've been through or what they experience every day. How am I supposed to relate to them?"

"The same way you connect to anyone else." Ty rubbed the back of his neck. "You don't have Alzheimer's or a broken hip, and you're not autistic, but I saw you impact people with those challenges."

Beth smiled. "You're right. I can do this."

"They may live behind bars, but I think you'll see that inmates are like most people. They want love, respect, and a good life for themselves and their families. Some are tough and difficult to reach, but others have big hearts and want to turn their lives around. They've learned from their mistakes."

"You seem to have a lot of understanding and empathy for them."

Ty tilted his head back as though searching the heavens for an answer. He shifted and leaned forward in the chair and put his head down. His hands were clasped together in front of him. Was he praying? His head came up, and he looked straight into her eyes.

"Do you trust me, Beth?"

"I'm starting to," she said in a teasing manner, attempting to lighten the mood. Where was this leading, and why, given all the discomfort in his expression, did she feel the urge to hug him?

"I wasn't sure how or when to confide in you about something personal, but Brandon has been pushing—*encouraging*—me to not put it off."

"Brandon, your carpenter friend."

"Yeah."

"Ty, you're making me nervous. What is going on?"

"I served time. Two years in the Colorado State Penitentiary."

"What?" Beth asked the question with a quiet breath as her stomach dropped to the floor. "Why? And how can you be a social worker in corrections when you have a record?" She'd almost lost an internship at the prison because of her history with a prisoner. Why wouldn't his past disqualify him from being hired there?

Ty slid back in his chair. "I was nineteen and hanging out with some guys who stole a car. I didn't know what they were doing until it was too late, but we were caught cruising later the same night. We'd also been drinking. It was a nonviolent crime. No one got physically hurt, and I didn't have any priors, so I got a lesser sentence than what could have been thrown at me."

"Wait. Drunk driving?" The news rattled deep into a place Beth didn't often let herself visit. No use trying to hide the grimace she wore. Except the rest of this didn't add up. "But how?" Questions flooded Beth's thoughts, and she mentally tried to detangle the mess inside her head. "Your life now?"

"Those of us who have gone through the system have a better understanding of that life and what it takes to start over." Ty rubbed his hands together. "Although I wish I'd never done a stint in prison, my experiences help me do my job. It would be different if I'd been convicted of a violent crime, but I wasn't. I did my time, got out, and have been on the straight and narrow since."

Was Ty justifying his criminal actions? Beth had begun to trust him, but should she? "You were raised in a Christian home and your dad is a chaplain." Beth was trying to wrap her head around Ty's mixed past. "Your parents must have been devastated."

"So how and why did I mess up?" He gave her an understanding smile. "It's not easy being a preacher's kid. Add the military to that mix. It puts pressure on a guy."

"To perform? Follow rules?"

Ty nodded. "Hindsight helped me realize that I might have wanted my dad's attention. He was so focused on serving other people and helping keep their families intact, I felt a little left out of his life. My dad was furious when I got in trouble. He forgave me, but my actions created somewhat of a chasm between us. Mom still doesn't want to talk about what happened. She'd rather pretend it didn't."

It was easy for Beth to forget that not all children grew up with understanding, supportive parents like hers. "And your relationship with them now?"

"We keep in touch, but we don't talk about anything too deep or personal. I hope that will change someday." He stared at the floor, hunched over, then sat upright as though he'd decided to continue the story. "When I was a boy, I wondered if military rules and the expectations to be strong and brave kept my dad from showing affection. Then I watched other men on base hug their kids, and I believed there must be something wrong with me."

"Did your dad ever tell you that he loved you?"

"No." Ty scratched his head. "Other actions showed he cared about me, but he never said it. And because of that, I've never expressed in words how I feel about my parents either. But I'm praying for that to change, and hopefully, it will one day."

Hugs came easily for Beth's family, and "I love you" was spoken daily. She would miss those gestures deeply if they were no longer a part of her life.

"When I was incarcerated, Brandon was the one person who really came through. He never gave up on me."

"You've mentioned that you're close."

"Like brothers." Tyler's smile hinted mischief. "Military brats have the option to attend public school, and that's what I wanted. Brandon and I became buddies in junior high. We remained best friends because my dad took steps so the family could stay longer than the normal four years at one base. Dad wanted me to have more stability and not have to change schools during my teen years. I give him credit for looking out for me and making that decision. It made a difference."

Beth swallowed her questions and listened, giving him space to spill.

"Brandon and I were roommates in college, but I started hanging out with some guys who were doing stupid things. I didn't realize just how stupid and dangerous. Brandon tried to warn me, but I didn't listen. I'd tasted freedom after years of living under my dad's strict dos and don'ts. I was tired of being the chaplain's son and having someone always looking over my shoulder, and I rebelled."

"And that's when the car theft happened."

"Yeah . . . that woke me up." Ty shook his head, as if in disbelief he'd been a part of that crime. "I wasn't driving, but that doesn't excuse me being in the car and drinking that night. I could have easily ended up behind the wheel."

His voice was filled with remorse. "Brandon never turned his back on me, even after I'd refused to listen to his begging me to stay away from those guys. He wrote, visited, and prayed for me while I was in confinement, and then helped me get back on track when I got out."

"Loyalty like that can't be bought."

Ty let out a long sigh. "I'll never take it for granted again. I owe him more than I can ever repay, but I'll try."

"Hmm . . ."

"We have a plan—a dream—to help and mentor at-risk kids. And with my prison connections, we're looking at ways to connect what we do with teens on the path to serious trouble or who are coming out of juvie. Kids who have incarcerated parents also need support."

"I'm sure you're aware a county juvenile detention center is located outside of town." Why had Beth never considered offering her therapy services there? *Slow down. See how working in a prison feels before you jump into a similar situation.*

Ty chuckled. "I am. The women's penitentiary is a twenty-minute drive, but still . . . how did Meriside end up getting two facilities in the area for criminals?"

Beth raised both hands and shrugged.

"Brandon is still committed to his family construction business, but I promised him that as soon as I can get hired at the prison in the area where he lives, we'll start developing our program for teens. Hopefully, we can make a difference in some lives before they end up with a rap sheet."

"Thanks for finally telling me about your own time in prison—and about your relationship with your parents. It's probably not easy to share that history. I understand why you might not want to blast that info to the entire town." *Be truthful.* Truthful while keeping her emotions in check. She clenched her hands together. "But Ty, I confided about what happened to my dad and brother. I explained why I was struggling with potentially having to work with Abbey Ward."

Beth caught his gaze and didn't let go. "I'll confess that I'm a bit frustrated and angry that you didn't share your story then. Her eyes softened. "Maybe disappointed is a better word for how I feel. I wish you could have trusted me."

"I don't blame you." He inhaled a deep breath. "I wanted to but knowing how you felt about her and what she'd done, I didn't know how you'd react."

"I get that."

"People often struggle with having faith in former convicts. They don't want to be associated with even a reformed criminal who has moved on." He knelt in front of her and took her hands in his. "I know our actions—*my actions*—the night we stole that car could have devastated another family like yours. Please believe me. I have never driven drunk, nor will I ever do anything intentionally that could cause another person harm."

His incarceration and the story behind it had her reeling, but Ty was a good man. Right? His passion and heart for people—for kids—who needed help in turning their lives around was admirable. His loyalty to his friend . . . Beth could relate to that devotion.

She couldn't deny wanting to get closer to him, despite now knowing more about his past. Beth admired and respected him for becoming the man he was today, but the reality sunk in once again that he didn't plan to make Meriside his home. A good reminder to keep her heart in check.

But those eyes filled with truth, his sincere plea . . . How could she deny his request to have faith in him?

"Ty, trust me to trust you."

Fourteen

B eth had tried to eat breakfast that morning, but nerves eradicated any appetite, and even a few bites of toast were difficult to manage. She touched her bag holding contents that had made it through security. The granola bar tucked inside might come in handy later.

Lord, I believe and trust that you've provided this opportunity. You opened the door, and I'm walking through it, but I need some help taking the next step.

"Good morning, Beth! Come in and make yourself comfortable." Lisa waved from behind her desk. "Excellent. I see you've been given your ID card. It must always be worn and visible. Volunteers, interns, sponsors, contractors, and vendors are given red cards. Blue, yellow, pink, orange, or green relate to other roles within the system. You'll learn the differences."

"I want to absorb everything I can while here." The chair with the padded seat gave relief to her shaking knees. *Get a grip. You wanted this job.* She took a deep breath and relaxed her tense shoulders.

"You seem a little apprehensive, and that's okay. It's understandable. But I think you'll soon find that your job here is much like what you'd do outside these walls." Lisa's calm and welcoming demeanor felt comforting.

Beth nodded. "Where do I start?"

"Before I show you the grounds and introduce you to a few people, I'd like to go over some things. When you came in for your interview, we talked about boundaries and potential for conflict of interest. I think we're clear there. Right?"

"Yes. If at any time I feel that I can't handle working with Abbey, I'll remove myself from the program." Beth would do everything in her power to avoid that. With God's help and support from family and friends, she'd somehow manage.

"Within these walls or out there in the world, your role as a horticultural therapist is to always put your client's best interest above personal feelings. As therapists, we must respect diversity and not discriminate against clients because of age, color, culture, disability, ethnic group, gender, race, or religion. That also includes sexual orientation, marital or socioeconomic status."

"Understood." *They're all God's children.*

"Sexual relationships are prohibited. Romantic relationships can impede the judgment of the horticultural therapist and harm the client."

"No worries there." That would be an easy rule to follow, inside the prison and out.

"I didn't think so. But it's something to remember in terms of ethics when you're certified and dealing with clients in the future." Lisa reached for a coffee mug sitting on her desk. "It's also important that we take steps to protect clients both physically and psychologically during therapy activities."

"Of course."

"That's heavy stuff to absorb and remember, but on a happier note . . ." Lisa took a drink and set the mug down. "We have participants ranging in age from eighteen to sixty-five. As I mentioned during your interview, the Washington State

Department of Corrections has implemented a plan called Corrections Hope Gardens, and garden expansion projects are underway at penitentiaries across the state. The purpose is to give more incarcerated individuals an opportunity to garden while also increasing the amount of produce we can donate to local food banks and community kitchens."

"I'm excited about those connections." Beth couldn't wait to get her hands dirty, both literally and figuratively in terms of starting the work.

"I also mentioned that we partner with the Sustainability in Prisons Project. The benefits for the inmates and surrounding communities involve more than gardening. Our facility partners with mostly nonprofits, and our prisoners contribute by making crafts and furnishings from reclaimed materials, refurbishing bicycles, wheelchairs, and computers. Another example is the pet program. Inmates care for cats and train dogs for new owners."

There was so much more going on here than Beth had imagined. "Alternative ways to learn a trade, feel productive, and have purpose."

Lisa nodded. "Research has shown reduced recidivism rates among participants in gardening programs, lower rates of depression, and improved mental health. We've also seen cost savings because of better nutrition and exercise for inmates."

She stood and moved toward a wood cabinet about four feet tall set against a wall. "Would you like coffee?"

"Yes, thank you." Now more at ease, Beth could use something in her stomach.

"Creamer?" She pulled a bottle from her small fridge. "I have vanilla or caramel flavoring."

"Caramel, please. Thank you."

Lisa handed Beth a blue ceramic mug filled with steaming coffee and then refilled her own mug from a large stainless-steel thermos. "A combined staff kitchen and dining area is located down the hall and around the corner. You're free to use the refrigerator, microwave, and other appliances there. Just remember to clean whatever you use."

"Of course." Beth would keep that in mind, as well as bathroom locations. She'd noticed both men's and women's restrooms on her way to Lisa's office.

"Back to our role here." Lisa returned to her chair behind the desk. "The gardening we do enables us to contribute to community food banks, nonprofits, elementary schools, and childcare centers. The partnerships with the state programs are priceless."

During their first meeting, Lisa had mentioned growing food used in the prison kitchens and donating extra to those in need. But now adrenaline rushed through Beth's veins as awareness took root within her heart. She was becoming part of something bigger than influencing one person at a time or finishing a requirement on her career path. What they accomplished here carried an impact that extended beyond these walls.

"Along with vegetable gardens, we've included flower gardens, boxes, and baskets throughout the grounds to attract bees and butterflies."

"For pollination."

"That's one important reason. Their beauty is also therapeutic, and hopefully, we'll add several water features in the future. We also have plans for a diversity garden where cultural groups will be allowed to grow food and flowers for their special events." Lisa's enthusiastic smile relayed her excitement.

"Currently, houseplants are only used on the hospital floor, but you asked during our initial meeting if inmates could have small plants in their cells. Only one prison in Washington has allowed it, but we're confident that option will soon be approved for women in our program as well."

Beth could imagine how having healthy, growing vegetation in a depressing cell could uplift spirits. How could she help get that established?

"Ready for a tour?"

"Yes, please."

Lisa stood and grabbed a white sweater draped across the back of her chair. "The sun is out, but these early days in May can still be a bit cool."

Temps were predicted to reach around a high of sixty-five, so Beth had worn a lightweight coat, and she threw that on and grabbed her large bag containing notebooks, wallet, car keys, and that granola bar she wished she could devour right now.

"You can leave that here if you prefer. I always lock the door behind me."

"Okay. Thanks." It would be nice not to lug it around. Beth pulled out a small journal and a pen to make notes, then tucked the bag into an empty space in a tall cabinet.

Lisa led her through a maze of hallways until they reached an exit to the outside. She unlocked the door, swung it open, and they were bathed in light.

Beth raised her face to the sun and embraced the warmth, getting a sense of what it must feel like to leave a dark cell and breathe fresh air—how it must release something within. She glanced around the yard filled with small and large gardens where women currently tended plants pushing up through the dirt.

"This is C yard where bell peppers, broccoli, cabbage, carrots, cucumbers, green beans, and lettuce are grown. The far section over there is devoted to herbs," Lisa said. "We have more acreage allocated to vegetables farther down on prison property where onions, potatoes, tomatoes, squash, and zucchini are planted. I can't recall the full list without my spreadsheet."

"You must have a great system in place to get everything in the ground." Beth scanned the area, noticing the well-kept gardens void of weeds and the vegetables neatly planted in rows. Yet, it was a facility like you would envision in any penitentiary, with large metal gates, chain-link fences, and razor wire sectioning off different yards.

"We do—we *need* to. Our program runs year-round. We've been studying botany, plant reproduction, and indoor plant care since January. In February we focus on selecting seeds for planting in the spring. The women get excited to flip through seed catalogs and imagine what they might grow."

Lisa started walking down the path between several gardens, and Beth kept to her side. "We've used compost created here at the facility to build up the soil."

Inmates took notice of her presence but acted more curious than threatening. Beth clutched her journal and gripped her pen tightly. But as Lisa greeted various prisoners and chatted with several, Beth felt more at ease. These women wouldn't be given this privilege if they were dangerous.

Still . . . Beth kept an eye out for a familiar young woman. She was bound to run into Abbey at some point but hopefully not today—ideally, those encounters would be rare.

"Once the seeds arrive, the inmates—or students—choose five types of annuals or perennials to start themselves in the greenhouse. Some students like that activity, but others enjoy making potting soil. A select few take on the important task of watering the newly planted seeds, and all are encouraged to observe the daily changes of seedlings."

"Where is the greenhouse?" Beth asked.

"We have three—two small and one quite spacious." Lisa pointed to her left. "The houses are on the other side of that building where they have southeast exposure to the sun."

Beth was pleased to hear it. South would have been even better, but a southeast facing structure was doable. It would get the morning sun, which would heat up the greenhouse after it cooled down overnight. And it was more important that the main plots had southern exposure.

"This time of year, we take walks and observe the changes in the garden, the budding of trees, and the various bulb plants popping through the earth." Lisa opened a gate, and they strolled into another area filled with flower gardens. "The tulips have passed their peak, but they were gorgeous and a welcome sight after winter."

"The columbine is pretty." Beth had noticed regal red and yellow flowers as soon as they stepped into the area. "And the iris are close to blooming."

"These gardens will explode with color soon." Lisa sat on a bench and motioned for Beth to join her. "It can be challenging to motivate the women into action during the shift from winter to spring. Some are anxious to get busy, but others are perfectly happy to sit and talk. Our responsibility is to find the 'in' with individuals and balance their needs with those of the gardens."

"That makes sense." Beth leaned back. "My goal with any client is to *not* make it about me, my needs, or completing a task. I believe relationships are more important. Ultimately, therapy will be more helpful if we've connected with the person we're trying to help."

"Well said." Lisa crossed one leg over the other and laid an arm along the back of the bench. "You know, critics of the program point out that participants are carefully chosen. Those with a history of serious or violent crimes aren't eligible. Therefore, these women are less likely to re-offend to begin with. But they don't see what we see."

"What *do* you see?"

Lisa tilted her head. "Well, for instance, what I've observed in D yard. The garden there is located far from the visiting public. It's only physically accessible to program facilitators and participants, but inmates often stop by the yard, comment, and interact with us through the fence. The garden space is a visual focal point, and even though there isn't access to inside, the splendor resonates through the fences."

Beth let that soak in.

"With our vibrant gardens, we create beauty in a harsh environment. Our program is centered around the belief that by growing a garden and learning about the natural world, a woman incarcerated here can still grow her inner self."

Beth gave thought to what Lisa shared. "How you describe it feels like you were reading from a promotional brochure."

Lisa raised her eyebrows, then narrowed them. "Hmm . . ."

"I think it's simpler than that. I believe that being a good therapist is not about growing the best-looking plants. It's about using nature to help a client cope with trying issues, whatever they may be—physical, mental, or emotional."

A bright red ladybug traveled across Lisa's thigh. She picked up the small insect and held it gently in her palm. "Hello, there!" She turned her hand over as the bug crawled to the other side, and then she placed the critter on the ground. "First one I've seen this year. She and her friends keep the aphid population down."

"I didn't mean to sound arrogant by what I said." Beth didn't want to overstep today or *any* day in the future. Hopefully, her enthusiasm for the work hadn't led her down that road.

"You didn't, and you're right." Lisa grinned, then chuckled softly. "After speaking at several functions with government officials recently, I'm afraid I've slipped into the roles of both educator and public relations."

"That must be difficult—to be in that position."

"It comes with the job, and it's worth it. And really, our program has received wonderful support because of what we've accomplished for the inmates and the surrounding communities."

"My eyes have been opened to so much already, but I know I still have a lot to learn." Beth took in the surrounding area. "It's clear that the gardens provide avenues for the inmates to let out their emotions, stress, or anger. Gardening provides a form of exercise, but at the same time, digging in the dirt can be calming. The fresh air must be invigorating for the women."

"All of that is possible for anyone, but it's perhaps even more true for someone who has been incarcerated for years with little to no contact with family or the outside world. By showing a commitment to living things, the women take responsibility and learn how to function in a team."

Beth was beginning to understand better the opportunity given her, and she felt the earlier flicker of excitement grow within. This was a taste of what she'd always wanted to do. Make a difference.

"You and I know from experience that gardening can help a person deal with success, failures, and problem-solving. Not every plant grows into a healthy specimen. Sometimes we need to figure out what went wrong and how to fix it. Was the soil, the amount of water, or the location the issue?"

A woman dressed in jeans and a blue sweatshirt opened the gate to the flower garden area and led two inmates dressed in khakis inside. They approached Lisa and Beth.

Something felt familiar about one of the prisoners—the woman's gait. She walked with a slight limp, permanent due to an injury from the accident. Convicted of vehicular homicide, sent to prison, and unable to attain extensive surgery and physical therapy, Abbey would be forced to live with a reminder of the damage she'd caused.

Beth's stomach curdled, and her heart raced. *Not today, Lord. Not today.* Perhaps he wanted her to get the initial meeting out of the way. She wouldn't have to fret about it any longer. *Remember to breathe.*

"Lisa, I'm sorry to interrupt," the woman in blue said. "I just need a minute of your time, if that's okay."

"Beth?" Lisa glanced at her with questions in her eyes. She must have realized how awkward this situation was for Beth and was offering her a way out.

"Take whatever time you need." Her focus landed on Abbey Ward standing in front of her. Beth meant to only glance, but her gaze caught and held the inmate's as recognition filled the young woman's large blue eyes. That acknowledgment morphed to what Beth recognized as fear, but Abbey stood still, rigid. The magenta color in her hair had faded out, and the natural light brown hair had grown past her shoulders.

"I'd like to make some introductions first." Lisa stood and Beth joined her. "Sheila, this is our new intern, Beth Miller. You'll be working together in the upcoming months. Sheila is one of our master gardeners who volunteers regularly with the program. She has a wealth of knowledge about soil preparation, planting, pruning, you name it."

Beth shook Sheila's hand and noticed that she also wore a red identification card. With short graying hair and ice-blue eyes, she reminded Beth of a former high school English teacher she adored. The warm smile and twinkle in Sheila's eyes confirmed for Beth that they'd get along fine.

"And meet two of our stars, Melissa and Abbey," Sheila said as she gestured toward each one, sharing their names.

"Hi," Beth croaked out.

Melissa held out her hand, and Beth accepted it. But then, though it seemed expected that she and Abbey would shake hands, they froze, staring at each other.

She wanted to be strong. They were almost through these awkward, horrible introductions, but Beth couldn't stay there. Her heart raced ahead, and if her breathing had caught up, she would have hyperventilated. Her mouth went dry. She wasn't ready for this—acting like Abbey was just another person Beth was called on to help.

"Excuse me, everyone." Beth turned to Lisa. "While you help Sheila, I'll take a walk around the yard to get a feel for what plants are getting ready to bloom and what might be poking up from the ground."

Lisa nodded, giving Beth permission to take a moment for

herself.

She turned, and keeping her back to the small gathering, Beth strolled toward the far side of the yard, trying to catch her breath, and feeling more alone than she had in a very long time.

Fifteen

P rison days started early and ended early. A typical workday for Ty began around 7:45 a.m. and ended at 4:30 p.m. But this wasn't a typical day. Beth had officially begun her internship, and that fact had kept him distracted.

That morning, he'd followed the normal routine. He'd been searched, his belongings were scanned, and then he walked to the cellblock where the program was housed. Ty completed paperwork, like writing treatment plans or printing and signing notes until about eight thirty. Once the count cleared, the inmates were released from their cells.

Around nine, after the staff meeting, the clinical day started. Ty usually met with individual prisoners or groups until eleven when they went to lunch. He took a break then too. Sometimes he ate alone in his office and took time to think or make personal calls. Other times, like today, he ate with the staff. It was usually a mix of chitchat and checking in on inmates, an informal opportunity to do some case consultations or problem-solving.

He'd been intentional in having lunch with the group today, hoping to catch up with Beth and see how her morning had gone. But she, Lisa, and a volunteer were engaged in what looked like a serious conversation, and Ty didn't want to interrupt. So he kept his distance, and when he caught Beth's eye, merely waved and said a prayer for her.

Back in his office, Ty glanced at the wall clock. One more group session and three individual meetings to fit in before 3:00 p.m. After that time, inmates would be locked back in their cells, and he'd lose access to them. Paperwork until around four thirty, and then he'd head home.

Some people might think him crazy, but he enjoyed the challenge of working with "mandated" clients. They often had no genuine interest in participating in groups or any other programs, but they attended or finished other requirements necessary for release or reduced sentences.

Ty had been honest with Beth about his past. She was surprised at first, and he'd expected that reaction. But she'd also been disappointed, even a little angry that he hadn't told her sooner. Still, she hadn't walked out on him. Ty hoped that revealing his criminal record would help her view the inmates here—one in particular—with new insight.

At four twenty, while he was clearing off his desk, someone rapped on his door, and he called out, "Come in!"

Lisa poked her head through the opening. "You got a few minutes to talk?"

"Sure." Ty shuffled papers into a stack, then stood and moved comfortable chairs to the side of the room where they could sit without the desk between them as a barrier. She slid into her spot, and he closed the door for privacy. "What's on your mind?"

Lisa adjusted her glasses. "I hesitate to bring this to you, but we're all on the same team, right?"

"Right." Ty sat on the edge of his chair. By her intro, something had gone wrong earlier. Was Beth okay?

"We want what's best for the women here. We want them

to be successful in taking steps to get their lives back on track." She paused and looked down, appearing to struggle with what to say next.

Warning sirens went off inside Ty's head. He wasn't going to like what came next, but he had to ask. "What's going on, Lisa? How can I help?"

Her shoulders relaxed, her head tilted, and a tentative smile appeared. "I don't want to overstep, but you're Beth's friend. You came to me and asked that I consider offering her an internship."

"Guilty. I did." Ty leaned forward. "Today didn't go as well as hoped?"

"It wasn't horrible." Lisa laughed softly. "It actually started out quite well. Beth and I talked about her role as a horticultural therapist, and we're on the same page. I gave her a tour of the gardens, and she seemed comfortable enough around the women working there."

It sounded like the successful beginning he'd prayed Beth would experience. He didn't want her leaving the prison feeling discouraged or wanting to quit the first day. "What changed?"

"It wasn't anyone's fault." Lisa shook her head. "Or maybe it was mine. You and I are aware of her unfortunate connection to Abbey. But in keeping Beth's personal life private, out of respect for her and Abbey, I didn't share their history with any of my staff or volunteers. I still believe that was the right thing to do, and Beth agrees."

"I think that's best, unless there is a need-to-know situation."

"Anyway, while we were outside this morning, one of our volunteers was working with two of our students, and she had some questions. So she brought the women over to where

Beth and I were sitting, and . . ."

Ty didn't need any more explanation. "Beth and Abbey came face-to-face." His gut clenched. He could only imagine the emotions that coursed through Beth.

"Yes, and without any warning." Lisa folded her hands in her lap. "They recognized each other, but both kept quiet. Beth excused herself and wandered off until I was free to join her."

"That must have felt uncomfortable for everyone."

"Very. Beth and I decided to share why she'd responded that way with my volunteer during lunch. I knew Sheila would understand and would be sensitive to the situation going forward."

The three must have been discussing Beth's reaction when he'd spotted them together earlier. "That's good."

"Ty, I sincerely want Beth to succeed. I like her, and I believe she has a lot to offer. But I can't go out of my way to protect her feelings. In our line of work, clients come first, and we often must put our personal emotions aside. That's something she needs to learn and embrace."

"I understand."

Lisa pulled one earlobe. "There's something else." She dropped her hand in her lap and sighed. "And I'm not sure how to approach this. Abbey spoke to me. After Beth left for the day."

"Okayyy . . . what did she want?"

"She wants you to mediate between them."

"What?" Was Lisa joking? "You're the program director. Isn't that your job?"

"It is—and I will be discussing their responsibilities to the program and how important it is that they're at least civil to each other when it's necessary they interact." Lisa's tone and crossed arms showed she was dead serious. "But you also have a role here as a social worker. Abbey has no idea that you and Beth are friends, and I think it's in everyone's best interest that be kept private."

"We want two success stories here, not failures." That would be an amazing feat, but it also put Ty in an awkward predicament. He'd already talked to Beth about trying to see the inmates as not only criminals but women who had families, hopes, and dreams. But trying to get past Abbey's mistakes? That was personal for Beth. How was he going to convince her he wasn't taking sides?

Ty parked his truck in Agatha's driveway and leaned back in the seat to think. How could he possibly approach what happened today at the prison without Beth feeling forced to meet with Abbey? He'd try to choose his words carefully, and hopefully, he wouldn't be misunderstood.

Maybe if Beth could somehow see how much Ty had grown to respect and admire her, she'd feel supported in her work. Despite her reasons not to take the internship, she still chose to do it, and that showed courage. Beth was also compassionate, and that attracted him to her. They both wanted to make a difference and help people better their lives.

Should he wait and talk to her in the morning? Ask to meet in his office? It might be best to keep their professional and private lives separate. But he wouldn't sleep tonight if he didn't find out how Beth was feeling, and he wanted to assure her that he and Lisa had her back.

Suck it up. Be a man, and just talk to her. Ty knocked on the door to Beth's studio apartment.

"Hey, buddy, I'm over here!"

Ty turned around. Beth sat under the cherry tree—on the very bench where they'd first met six weeks ago. It was a few minutes after eight, so the sun hadn't fully set, and there was enough light to see the gardens—*and her.* With a light blanket draped over her shoulders, she looked cozy even though a cool, salty breeze blew through the yard.

"Hey there, yourself!" Ty sauntered over and dropped next to her. "I didn't see you here."

"Apparently not. You walked right past me." She smiled, and her warm gaze penetrated his heart. "You seemed pretty determined to reach my door. Something urgent? Anything to do with the reno?"

"Ah, no, not the house." Ty scratched his neck. "Although I just came from the property. Went there straight from work and spent several hours reviewing plans. I was notified today that the electrical and plumbing got approved. Now I can get those guys scheduled, and we can finally move ahead."

"That's great news!" she said, her face brightening for a moment.

"Yeah. I picked up light fixtures and faucets, but when you have a few minutes, I'd like to make final decisions on tile and countertops for the kitchen and bathrooms."

"Sure, any time," she said, now sounding distracted.

"And your big day?" He raised his eyebrows. "How did it go?"

Beth pulled the blanket tight around her body, as though protecting herself. She released a large sigh. "It was wonderful—at first. I started to realize the potential and how much good the horticultural program could do for the women. How much they learn and how therapeutic gardening can become for them. Instead of being nervous or anxious about my role there, I felt excitement over what was already being done and what was possible."

"And then . . ."

"And then I ran into Abbey." Beth rubbed her gorgeous brown eyes. "Not literally, of course. But there she was—standing right in front of me. We recognized each other, and neither of us knew what to say—how to act."

"So what *did* you do?" Beth looked so beautiful—so vulnerable—he wished he could protect her from any more hurt or disappointment.

She bent her head down, as if ashamed. "I abandoned the conversation, turned my back on her, and walked away. When I left the prison, I went to Your Secret Garden, saw Mom and Harmony, and broke down and cried."

"I'm sorry that part of the day was so hard. I'm glad you were able to talk to your mom and sister." *Lord, help me.* What was he supposed to say? The truth. Always the truth. "Lisa stopped by my office late this afternoon."

Beth's head jerked up, and she faced him. "She did?"

The fear in her eyes tore him up inside. "She wants the internship to work for you, more than you realize." Ty rubbed his hands together, but not because they were cold. He needed to focus on the reason he was there, not on his own emotions and how he wanted to take her in his arms and hold her, tell her everything was going to be all right.

"It sounds like seeing Abbey today was unexpected, and how it affected you—and Abbey—worried Lisa. It shook everyone up."

Beth's eyes narrowed. "So, you knew we'd met, and that's why you knocked on my door," she said in an accusatory tone. "I thought you were checking on me because you merely cared about my day. Why lead me on with questions when you already knew the answers?"

"I wanted to hear your side of the story. I wasn't trying to keep anything from you." She wasn't going to like what he had to say next. "Abbey doesn't know that you and I are friends, and Lisa and I agreed to keep it that way. But Abbey has requested that in my role as a social worker that I mediate a meeting between the two of you. It's something I do on a regular basis with prisoners and family members—or others affected by an inmate's actions."

"You've got to be kidding."

"I'm not. But it's up to you and whether or not you're willing to try." He'd thought about it since Lisa brought it up. "It could be helpful."

She glared at him. "Are you unbiased?"

"No, but as a professional, I need to put my personal feelings aside. We've talked about how important that is in our roles." Ty's insides were tearing up. Even though he'd do anything to not hurt her, he also couldn't do anything unethical. He had to consider Abbey's best interests too.

"Ty, I can't. I won't." Her eyes shimmered with tears. "I'm not having a sit-down meeting with her to sing 'Kumbaya.'"

"The other day you said that I should trust you to trust me." He wanted to slide closer and comfort her, but he gripped the top of the bench instead and stopped himself. Boundaries. "That's what I'm asking you to do now, Beth. Trust me."

Sixteen

T wo days later, Beth stood outside Tyler's office. Her heart raced, her breathing had grown shallow, and she shivered from cold sweat.

Every instinct told her to run, but she didn't break promises, and Beth had made a commitment to meet with Abbey. Ty had asked her to pray about the outcome, and he urged her to have an open mind.

The night he'd brought up mediation, Beth initially thought she'd rather quit her internship than consider it. Her heart and mind had wrestled with the idea that making peace with the inmate meant Beth no longer grieved for her dad and brother. It took a sleepless night and hours of prayer to realize that she wasn't doing this for Abbey. Beth was doing it for herself. She wanted to fulfill her calling, and it was the right thing to do for everyone involved.

Beth inhaled slowly, then released her breath at the same pace to calm her nerves. One more time . . . in . . . out. She knocked.

Ty opened the door wide, and facing her, shared a welcoming smile and a small wink, signaling he was there for her. He gave a nod for her to join him inside, and she slipped by him. The door closed behind but was not shut entirely—safety precautions. She was left inside with him and the person who had devastated her family.

No turning back now. Beth sank into the empty chair sitting some feet from Abbey, ran her damp palms down her thighs, and then folded her hands in her lap. How long could she avoid looking at the other woman?

The room felt too small. Would any space feel large enough?

Ty dropped into his chair and rolled it up close behind his desk. Did he want the barrier for protection? Beth didn't anticipate a cat fight. She wasn't a violent person. Was Abbey?

"You both know why you're here, so I don't think we need to cover that ground," Ty said in a calm tone. "It's important that each of you are successful in the horticulture program, and for that to happen, we need to find a way for you to work together."

He paused. "No one is asking you to become besties. Lisa and I are only asking that you be civil, focus on cooperating with the needs of the program and each other, and don't sabotage your success."

Ty grabbed a pen from his desk and held it between his hands. "It might be helpful to say whatever is on your heart and mind and get it out of your system. And that goes for both of you."

Beth understood the importance of Ty remaining impartial, but it still prickled that he also supported Abbey and her needs.

"Nothing held back—if you can do it in a respectful manner," he continued, as though urging them to speak.

"Seriously?" Beth asked, whipping a glance at him. "We can say anything without it being held against us?" As a probational intern, the risk scared her.

"Yes, without being malicious." He rapped the pen on the desk several times. "From my understanding, the two of you have never talked, so you've never had the opportunity to share your gut or hear what the other has to say."

Carte blanche was something she hadn't anticipated. Ty leading them in a mutual agreement of cooperation, sure, but saying anything she needed or wanted to, just to get it off her chest? How did you avoid lashing out when you'd suffered so much loss and the guilty party was only a few feet away?

"I gave an impact statement in court," Beth said, fidgeting in her chair. "And Abbey apologized to my family at that time."

"But wasn't that primarily done for the court? The judge?" Tyler raised his eyebrows. "Time has passed. Is there a chance there's more to say?"

"Yes, there is," Abbey whispered so quietly, Beth could barely hear her speak.

She turned to face the prisoner, and the watery gaze took Beth by surprise. *She* was crying?

Abbey blinked several times and cleared her throat, but she didn't turn away from Beth's stare. "In court, I confessed to doing wrong, and I apologized. And I meant what I said, but the words didn't carry the weight of what I feel now."

She wiped her eyes and sniffed. "I've been sober for two years, and my head is clearer than it was even a year ago. Since the accident, I've had time—*so much time*—to think about the pain I caused. I'm sorry—so sorry!" Abbey's voice shook, and her lips quivered.

Beth heard the sincerity ringing in her adversary's voice, and it broke her. All the hidden truths and pent-up emotions busted through the lock. "I—I don't know if I can do this."

"What's going on inside, Beth? Talk to us." His genuine concern and gentle voice gave her courage. Maybe he wasn't solely on Abbey's side in this. Maybe he was on her side too. She held his kind gaze for several moments, connecting. Gearing up.

"Abbey, I can't see you without being thrown right back there again." Beth's voice caught in her throat.

"What do you mean, Beth?" Ty asked. "The courtroom?"

"No." Beth swallowed. "I was at the accident scene, soon after the crash." She rubbed her eyes. "I've never told anyone, except for my friend, Agatha." She glimpsed Ty's head jerk slightly at the reference to his aunt, but she focused on Abbey.

"I can't be in the same room with you without seeing the flames, smelling the smoke, and feeling the horror. The memory—the pain—it all comes rushing back." Beth sucked in a ragged and shallow breath.

"I don't remember seeing you there," Abbey whispered.

"You were drunk out of your mind and restrained by two police officers. You walked away with some cuts and bruises, but my dad and brother *didn't survive.*"

"Beth, how did you end up there?" Again, Ty's voice carried incredible gentleness, urging her to tell the entire story. Providing a safe space.

She didn't blame him for wanting to know, but she could only share the partial truth. "I'd come back to Meriside for a few days before starting an internship at a hospital in Seattle. We'd had a busy day at Your Secret Garden, and our floral delivery guy needed help, so I took a large order to the farthest location. I was on my way back when Liam called my cell. He was gasping for air, but I understood enough." *Just get through this.* "He'd tried to reach his wife, Kaylee, but she didn't pick up, and he was so disoriented, he didn't think to leave a message for her."

Beth took a moment to rein in her emotions. She didn't want to lose it and break down in front of Ty and Abbey. "He was able to give me a rough idea of where they were. I called 911, but they'd already been alerted. By the time I reached my dad, he was gone." She choked down a sob. "Liam breathed his last breath while I held his hand."

Tears streamed down Abbey's flushed face, and Ty offered her the tissue box.

"I told my mom, my sister, and Liam's wife that it was a coincidence that I'd come across the accident while on my way home. I convinced them that Dad and Liam had already been taken away in an ambulance." Beth paused to take a breath, the vision of that horrific day playing out in her mind once again.

Her chest tightened, and her breathing quickened. The door—her escape—was right behind her. Beth wanted to stand and bolt, but instead, she closed her eyes and focused on calming herself. *Breathe in. Breathe out.* She would be okay. It was important to continue her story.

"I didn't tell my family that I'd seen Dad and Liam—their broken and smashed bodies covered in blood." Beth sniffed. "Kaylee's cell phone had died earlier, but Mom had gone over to tell her in person about the accident. I've kept Liam's attempt to call his wife a secret. I didn't know if it would help or hurt her more to know that she'd missed her chance to tell him she loved him one last time."

"You never mentioned any of that in court," Abbey said, wiping her nose.

"No. I didn't need to testify. There was plenty of evidence

of the crime, and I didn't include it in my impact statement because I wasn't ready for my family to know. I felt the need to carry that experience alone."

It took merely a look to know Ty was supporting her silently, and most likely, praying for her. His eyes filled with understanding, and he slid his hand forward on the desk, as though to let her know he was reaching out in the only way he could.

Abbey pulled another tissue from the box and wiped her eyes. She sat up straight and appeared to work at gathering her thoughts. "I can't change what happened then, but what I do now might help make it easier for you to offer what you can to the other women here. I want to continue taking responsibility for my actions, so I'll do what's right. I'll withdraw from the program."

"Abbey, that's an unselfish offer." Ty cleared his throat. The glance he shot at Beth let her know he wasn't abandoning her, but he also had to be fair. "You've contributed so much to the gardening projects, and I think the work has benefited you too. I want you to think this through before making any rash decisions."

Beth heard Agatha's voice in her head. What if Beth was the best person—the only person—to give Abbey what she needed to walk out of here and start a new life?

Really, Lord? This is what you require of me? After all I've sacrificed? Shame washed over her. Whatever he asked, it wouldn't come close to what Christ had done for her. What if learning to love Abbey as God did would free Beth to move on herself? Was that even possible?

"No, Abbey," Beth said firmly. "I want you to stay."

Abbey's eyes widened. "Really?"

She nodded. "Don't leave."

"Why? Why would you give me the chance?"

Tell her. God's voice whispered the message clearly within Beth. *Tell her the story.*

She filled her lungs slowly, then exhaled. "Abbey, when I was a little girl, I used some of my mother's red nail polish without permission, and I spilled several large drops on her dresser. Of course, she was angry. My sister was too young to blame, so I told Mom a neighbor had polished my nails." Beth focused on her hands, as though the incident had happened earlier that day. It felt good to concentrate on something other than the accident.

"Go on," Ty said quietly. "What happened?"

"Well . . . she knew I was telling a fib. My mom was the disciplinarian in our family, but that day she gave me one of those *wait until your father comes home* threats." Beth glimpsed Abbey sitting attentively, waiting for what came next. "That night, my dad sat me on his lap and asked me to explain what happened. I could never lie to him, so I told the truth. Because I confessed, my dad said all was forgiven. There would be no punishment."

"It sounds like your dad was full of wisdom and kindness," Ty said.

"Yeah . . . that and more." The backs of Beth's eyes prickled as she caught his compassionate gaze. "As a child, I wasn't familiar with the term, but now I know. That day, he gave me the gift of *grace.*"

She sighed and faced Abbey without wavering. "I believe there's something bigger than us going on here." Peace blanketed her heart. "I look in your eyes, and I believe you're genuinely sorry. Maybe this is what we both need to heal. Working in the gardens side by side where God can meet us both with grace."

Seventeen

A fter the meeting between Beth and Abbey ended far better than expected, Ty had felt encouraged these past days by the flow created in the gardens. The two women found ways to work around each other while in the same space, limiting their interaction.

Today was a different story. Why couldn't he get through to this one?

Tyler had gone rounds with other stubborn inmates, but this gal with the strawberry blond hair, freckled face, and the girl-next-door look twisted his insides. Maybe he wanted so desperately to fix things for her because he saw a part of himself in her. Ty was trying to help her find ways to succeed during confinement and when she reentered the outside world, but she wasn't making it easy.

He leaned across his office desk. "Emily, you're young. You still—"

"Have time to change and build a great future?" Emily grimaced. "Yeah . . . I've heard the speech before. It's over for me. I don't get a do-over. So don't waste your breath on me."

"A life sentence wasn't handed down at your trial. Someday, you'll walk out the prison doors. I'm hoping you won't make a return visit."

Emily jerked back. "Isn't that what always happens? Once

an offender . . .? I'm hopeless."

"No, you're not." Ty sensed a soft heart underneath, despite her tough attitude. "I don't see a throwaway sitting in front of me. You're a valuable human being who has a lot to offer. The question is, are you willing to give it? Are you willing to put in the work while *in here*, so you can thrive when sent *out there*?"

"Like I said. You're wasting your time. I don't have to join any of your programs, your groups, or your little clubs if I don't want to."

"No, you're not mandated to do any of it. But refusing will only make it harder to get released."

"I don't care." Emily bit her lower lip and fidgeted with her hands. "I don't have anywhere to go anyway."

Ty sensed she was scared, maybe even terrified, and cared a great deal more than what she was willing to admit. He'd do whatever he could to help and inspire her. Without hope, people tended to lose their desire to pursue any goals.

"Don't give up, Emily."

"I already have." She tried to stare him down, probably to make her point, but he won. Emily broke her lock on his eyes and turned away. "Can I go now?"

"Yeah." Ty stood and walked her to the door. "But we're not done talking about this."

She glared at him. "Why do you care so much?"

"Why does it matter?" He grasped the edge of the door with one hand and splayed his other hand across his hip.

"You're still going to try and convince me to get into a program, aren't you?"

"Yep. You can give me an answer as to which one at our next meeting."

Emily rolled her eyes and shook her head as though she were thirteen instead of twenty. Then she headed back to her work assignment in the laundry department.

Ty closed the door and returned to his desk. He rubbed his temples, trying to alleviate the ache. A massage would feel good. The muscles in his neck and shoulders were tight, and pain ran from those locations into his head. It had been a rough week, and it was only Tuesday.

One of his group meetings with prisoners on Monday had not gone well. Several individuals had given him attitude, and two others got into a verbal fight. Feeling beaten up and exhausted after that wreck, he'd retreated to his office, shut the door, and prayed.

During an appointment, an inmate had broken down at hearing her mother had died the night before from a heart attack. That prisoner wanted to cling to him and weep, but it was important to keep boundaries, so he forced some distance. She misunderstood his actions and believed he didn't care she'd been shattered.

This morning, a prisoner had flirted and offered sexual favors in exchange for personal items and privileges. He shut that down fast. At first, she believed he was teasing and found that humorous. When she realized he was serious, she got angry.

And then there was Emily, who had pushed back on every attempt he'd made at getting her to see that not all was lost. She could still have a good life.

What would the next three days bring?

Three raps sounded on his door.

"Come in," he called.

Max Waters stepped inside. "You free to talk?"

"Sure. What's up?" Ty readied himself. By his supervisor's grim expression, Ty guessed bad news was the reason for the unexpected visit.

"Missy Jones."

Ty's heart pounded. *Please, Lord, no.* "Missy is in my recovery group for addicts, and she's been making a lot of progress. We just celebrated her reaching two months of sobriety."

"I'm sorry, Ty." Max dropped into a chair and released a heavy sigh. "This is going to be hard to hear."

Ty crossed his arms on his desk and laid his head down on them. His heavy heart thumped against his chest. She'd been doing so well.

"Are you okay?"

He tilted his head up and witnessed the concern in her eyes. "Not really," he said sadly.

Beth closed the door behind her. "I'm done for the day, and I wondered if you'd like to meet up at the house later to see what the landscaping crew has finished. I think you'll be pleased. They've been doing a great job." She gripped the back of a nearby chair. "I'd like to make some final decisions on paint colors for the bedrooms too, but if you're not up to it, we can do it another time."

"Oh, that's right. The rest of the plants were scheduled to be put in." Ty sat up and rubbed his eyes. When she wasn't at the prison, Beth had been putting in time overseeing the landscaping project at his house. "As for paint, my head isn't in the right space to think about color schemes right now."

"Need to talk?" She slipped into the chair and dropped her backpack next to her on the floor. "About why you're upset? Or is it confidential?"

"Upset?" Ty massaged the back of his aching neck. "I'm not sure what I feel. Maybe disappointed. Guilty. Frustrated. Sad." He sunk back into his chair and nodded. "Yeah, all of the above."

Beth sat quietly with hands folded in her lap, but her attentive gaze let him know she was willing to listen.

"It's been a day." How much should he dump on her? "One challenge after another, and I also just got informed that one of the inmates who was participating in my support group for recovering addicts overdosed earlier today and died." The words left a bitter taste in his mouth.

"Ty, I'm so sorry." Beth's comforting tone made him feel less alone in his grief.

"She'd been sober for several months and was excited about staying clean and starting over, but a few days ago, her husband was shot and killed in a drug deal gone wrong. I knew she was spiraling, so we talked at length about ways to cope."

"So, you did what you could."

"But did I really?" Ty took a deep breath and tilted his head back to stare at the ceiling, but as hard as he searched, he found no answers written there. "Could I have done more? I feel like I failed."

"No matter how hard we try, we can't save any of these women." The sheen in her eyes relayed how deeply she cared. "They have to want to save themselves."

"You're right." Gratitude filled his heart for her empathy and understanding "And thank you. I needed to be reminded of that." In his work, there were rewarding opportunities to make a difference in people's lives, but the job was also stressful and demanding. It wasn't surprising that there was such a high burnout rate for social workers.

"May I ask?" Her brows knitted together. "I don't mean to sound naïve, but how did drugs get into the prison? All people and items are searched prior to entering."

"They still find ways in, and unfortunately, drug overdoses kill a huge number of inmates." It wasn't his first experience with a death in prison, but he'd carried so much hope for Missy. "Narcotics are sometimes delivered through visitors, packages, or letters. Strips of paper soaked with drugs have been tucked into pieces of mail or books, and if they get past the mailroom, inmates eat the strips, or roll them up and smoke them. Incoming prisoners swallow drugs or hide them in body cavities."

"If only they'd put all that creativity into something positive."

"Yeah, if only . . ."

"Something else on your mind?" Compassion filled Beth's eyes, inviting him to share his thoughts and feelings with her. "When I came in, it sounded like you'd been through a lot today, aside from losing an inmate, which was upsetting enough in itself."

"Another prisoner has me spinning. Maybe because she reminds me too much of me." That had to be why he felt so personally invested.

"I'm happy to listen."

"Thanks. Maybe it will help to process her situation out loud." Ty gathered his thoughts. "Emily is twenty, and she's in for theft. Her first offense."

"Okay, what's her story?"

"She was a sophomore at the University of Washington. Emily has three brothers and two sisters. Her parents work hard but they couldn't afford to help with college, and they didn't live close enough for her to live at home and commute. A small scholarship covered the cost of books, but she didn't receive any financial aid."

"So, her parents didn't make enough income to pay for school but too much to get the help needed." Beth grimaced. "I get it. Several college friends dealt with the same thing and worked on campus to help pay for tuition."

"Emily was employed as a waitress. But with working late hours, attending classes, and studying, she was behind in school and struggling financially."

"It's difficult to find balance." Beth crossed one leg over the other and covered her knee with folded hands. "This may sound judgmental, but did she ever consider slowing things down?"

"She was planning to cut back on classes and work more hours at the restaurant, but an acquaintance convinced her that helping him and his friends would be an easy way to pick up money. When Emily understood it involved theft, she tried to back out at the last minute, but one guy threatened her."

Beth's eyes widened, and she leaned forward. "Why?"

"He was afraid her conscience would influence her to report them to the cops. He scared her, so she agreed to help them once and only once. Emily believed that if she was involved with one job, they would trust her not to turn them in."

"Because she was guilty as well and would want to protect herself."

"Right." Ty understood her reasoning, but Emily hadn't factored in one important thing—the possibility that it would take only one incident to land her here. "One of the guys worked at a warehouse for an electronics retailer, so he knew what was stored and where. He'd fixed the monitoring system—or so they thought—so they wouldn't get caught. But another employee realized that something was wrong with the system and rebooted it.

"So after they'd broken in and taken laptops, TVs, and other gadgets, they got caught in the back parking lot and were arrested. Because of the value of the stolen property, she was charged with a first-degree felony."

"A person's life can change so quickly because of one bad decision." Beth turned her focus to the side for a moment, then she returned it to Ty. "What she did was wrong, but I still feel sorry for her."

At hearing Beth's confession, Ty's heart warmed. The beautiful woman sitting in front of him carried so much empathy for people. Her heart was bigger than the Grinch's after learning the meaning of Christmas wasn't about food, presents, or decorations.

"Emily acts tough, but I believe she's a softy underneath." Ty had witnessed the emotion in her eyes when talking about her family. "She disappointed her parents. They can barely look at her, and she can barely look at herself in the mirror. I'm afraid Emily has given up. She believes her future is hopeless."

"How long before she gets out?"

"Her lawyer got her a reduced sentence and a lower fine. But she'll still be incarcerated for seven years, maybe five, if she can get early release on good behavior."

"That's a long time." Beth sighed. "It will be hard to start over once she leaves here."

"I've been trying to redirect her—get her involved in something that can build her self-esteem and restore her hope in the future. But she's been pushing back."

"This job isn't just a paycheck to you or the means to get a more prestigious position, is it? You sincerely care." Was that admiration in her eyes? Or something more?

"Yeah, I do care."

"What if I tried?"

"Tried . . .?"

"Reaching Emily." Beth propped her finger on her lips as though thinking through some possible methods. "I'll talk to Lisa and ask permission to approach her about participating in one of our gardening projects."

"I suggested your program, but she wasn't interested."

"And I appreciate the referral." Beth gave him a mischievous grin. "But as a woman, I may have a different way of conveying the benefits."

"You'd do that?" Relief washed through Ty's body from his head down to his shoulders and all the way down to his big toe.

"Of course. You and me, we're a team."

He liked the sound of that—a lot. "Thanks."

"You're welcome." She stood and grabbed her backpack. "But for now, I should head home and let you finish up for the day. And it sounds like you're not up to working at your house later."

"I'm pretty worn out." As much as he'd like to spend more time with her, she'd already spent a chunk of time listening to him talk about work and its challenges. It wouldn't be fair to take up her evening with shoptalk too. "Would you mind if we skipped it for tonight?"

"I understand," she said in a tone that conveyed she did. "We can do it another time."

"Beth, please wait," he said before she reached his office door. He stood and moved closer to her. "Can I take you out for dinner on Friday? If you don't already have plans?"

"Like a date?" she asked, tilting her head, and sounding surprised.

"I enjoy spending time together, and I want to know more about you."

He looked down, immersing himself in her enticing brown eyes. "Would that be okay?"

"I like you too." Beth placed her hand over his heart. "You're a good man, Tyler Sharp." She patted his chest gently, then stepped back. "It's a date."

Eighteen

"Thank you for bringing me here, Ty. It's lovely." Beth glanced around the quaint restaurant. The Bridge had recently opened in Meriside, and to reach the entrance, guests crossed a small bridge built over a stream. With only handicapped parking in front of the building, the location felt even more picturesque. "I've wanted to come ever since I heard about this place."

The comfortable booth set against a wall of exposed brick gave them some privacy. The last of the sun's rays filtered through the vaulted glass ceiling, and baskets filled with realistic-looking silk foliage hung from wooden beams. Lush plants were set on the floor around the building's interior.

"I'm glad you like it." Ty gave a quick glance at their surroundings and smiled. "I overheard you mention it once to Agatha, and after one of the prison guards described it, I knew I wanted to bring you here."

"Because of all the greenery?" It was sweet of him to choose a location he thought would please her.

"The guard said the place was beautiful, but he also mentioned that after a ridiculously hard day, the atmosphere felt calming." His eyes twinkled. "I couldn't think of anything more appropriate. You're gorgeous, and you have a similar effect on me. You're a great listener, and when I'm with you,

I feel . . . more at peace."

"Hmm . . . like a cocker spaniel that will snuggle up to you," she teased, her face warming at the compliments.

Ty let out a belly laugh. "No, more like the genuine and caring person I'm getting to know."

"I'm glad you see me that way." His comments made her feel seen, appreciated . . . and a little uneasy. She wasn't used to such praise. Beth, redirecting the conversation, pointed to the waterfall painting hanging on the brick wall. "I recognize the signature."

"The restaurant's website mentioned displaying work by local artists."

"Do you think Agatha would be interested in having her art showcased here?"

"I wanted to check the space out first before bringing it up, but I'll definitely mention it to her."

The waitress arrived at their table to take their orders. Beth decided on the smoked salmon Caesar salad with a slice of grilled French bread, and Ty chose the walnut-crusted halibut with rice pilaf and a side of roasted vegetables.

She studied Ty while he chatted with the waitress about contact information if someone was interested in submitting a painting for sale. Beth appreciated how respectfully he treated the woman.

As soon as he'd shown up at her door earlier that evening, she was struck by how handsome he looked in his khaki pants and green polo shirt. Beth had also been relieved that she'd deviated from her jeans and casual shirts and worn her favorite blue dress with the full skirt. A brown belt, dressy sandals, silver earrings, and her dainty silver cross necklace completed her outfit for the evening. The attire felt comfortable and

174 | DAWN KINZER

flattering—a winning combination.

The waitress left, and Ty turned his attention back to Beth. "Would you mind if we made a pact to not talk about work? Just for tonight? It's been a long time since I've asked anyone out, and I'd like to leave our jobs behind and just spend the evening getting to know each other better."

"I'd like that." Beth sipped her lemon water. "Why haven't you dated? There must have been plenty of girls—women—ready and willing."

He gave her a sly grin. "Why would you assume that?"

"Um . . ." *Just be honest.* He'd been free with his compliments toward her. "You're smart. Polite. Kind. Unselfish. You have integrity, and . . . you're quite attractive." There. She'd confessed the truth.

"So you think me handsome." His grin could compete with the Cheshire cat's.

"That's all you got out of my list of attributes?" Could her face get any warmer? Time to divert. "Getting back to why you haven't dated in a while . . ."

He unwrapped the dining utensils from his napkin and dropped the cloth on his lap. "There have been a few potential opportunities—women who said they were willing to accept my past. But I don't think I completely trusted that. And I was so wrapped up in my work and proving that I'm a changed man, I don't think I would have been present the way I think a guy should be if he's serious about a future with a woman."

"But you believe you're ready now?" Why did she want so badly for him to say yes?

"I think so, but . . ."

But?

Ty's brow furrowed, as though he was thinking over his

answer. "This may sound like a cop-out, but I'm relying on God to let me know who, when, and where."

His words felt reassuring. "No, it's not a cop-out." Beth stopped talking while the waitress refilled their water glasses and assured them their food would be ready soon. "Any relationship, regardless of how healthy, can go through rough patches. I think it's important to always have God in the center."

"And you? I can imagine you're asked out a lot." Ty sat back, appearing relaxed, but his gaze locked on hers.

"It depends on what you mean by a lot." Beth gave him a weak smile. "The reality is that I haven't been on an actual date in over a year."

"That's hard to believe."

"It's true. Like you, I've been focused on other things."

"Any serious relationships in your past?"

Since she'd asked personal questions, it was only fair that she answer in return. "At one time, I thought a boyfriend and I were heading in that direction, but I broke his heart . . . or so he said."

"What happened?"

"The accident that killed my dad and brother and having to abandon my initial internship in the city where he'd found a great job. I chose putting my family first over what he wanted. I understood that he wanted his feelings and needs to be my priority. I did. But he wasn't willing to give me even a season to grieve and help get things settled here."

"I don't want to offend," Ty said, sounding tentative, "but the guy sounds selfish, not willing to compromise. I think you're better off without him."

"Maybe we were both selfish. But I think you're right. If

he'd sincerely loved me, he wouldn't have moved on so quickly." And if she'd truly loved him, she would have been more hurt than relieved.

Their dinners arrived, and after Ty said a short prayer of thanks for the company and food, they sat quietly for a moment and tried their first morsels.

Beth bit into the bread's buttery, crunchy goodness. A bit nervous about the evening, she'd noticed her appetite had waned during the day, but now that she felt relaxed, her desire to eat had returned. She glanced up at Ty and caught the delighted expression on his face as he dined on the halibut.

"Good?" she asked, then smiled.

"Incredible." He wiped his mouth with his napkin. "That guy you were seeing obviously didn't realize how much he was losing. Not only more time with you, but also with your relatives. I'm grateful that I've met your mom, Harmony, and Kaylee. You're lucky—*blessed*—to be so close. Not everyone has a family like yours, and you've discovered from my stories that I don't."

"Do you miss not having siblings?" Beth tried to eat her salad quietly, but the croutons were crunchy, and the fresh romaine wasn't doused with dressing, so it had remained crisp.

"Sometimes, but as I've mentioned, Brandon has been like a brother to me."

The moist smoked salmon was just how she liked it. She dabbed her mouth with her napkin and dropped her hands in her lap. "You shared some things about your dad and your relationship with him. Tell me more about your mom."

Ty laid his fork down. "We're not close. She grew up in a wealthy family, and her parents had plans for her. But she fell for my dad, and that changed the path she might have taken."

"Love will do that to a girl," Beth whispered as she peered into his clear sea-green eyes and dove into their depth. *Don't drown!* She forced herself to surface, then cleared her throat. "Go on."

Ty blinked and took a gulp of water. Had he been lost in the moment as well? He shifted and took a large breath. "Ahh . . . well, now as an adult, I understand her situation, or at least I *think* I do. It can't be easy for her to make friends, get to a point of feeling comfortable in that environment, and then have to move on." He took another bite of fish.

"As a chaplain's wife, she feels the pressure to meet certain expectations. She supports my dad and is a great role model for other military wives." Ty stabbed a piece of broccoli with his fork. "I think that gives her purpose, but she doesn't have the freedom or time to pursue her own desires."

"I'm sorry your mom has given up some personal goals." She'd found something in common with Ty's mom. "I understand what it feels like to give something up you want so desperately because the people you love need to be the priority. I feel so fortunate that I'm now able to pursue my own path, so I hope that someday, your mom can too."

"Thanks." His warm smile was like a hug of affirmation. "I appreciate that."

"It hasn't always been easy with my mom either. We struggled with each other for a while. Normal teenage battles. My dad was my refuge."

Ty raised his eyebrows. "The story you told Abbey about the nail polish got me here." He pointed to his heart. "I'd like to hear more."

"Okay." Beth searched internal files and retrieved a

memory. "As the oldest child, and maybe because I was also a girl, it was a rare occasion when I was given permission to drive one of our two cars without a parent in the passenger seat. Contrary to my situation, my brother drove often."

"Different standards."

"And maybe they had a good reason to limit my time behind the wheel. I wasn't a very good driver." Beth held up her pointer finger. "But in my defense, I didn't get much practice."

Ty chuckled. "Hard to get proficient without it."

"Anyway, during my senior year of high school, I asked to drive to a nearby town for a football game and take Jody with me. I was shocked when my parents gave the okay, but Mom warned me to be careful."

"Good for them—and you."

"Yeah, it was great until it wasn't." Beth scrunched her face. "We got lost in a neighborhood and ran through a stop sign. Mind you, the sign was hidden by a large pine tree, but it was still my mistake. Another driver hit the back side of the car. We contacted the police and reported the incident, and then I made that awful call to my parents. The car was still drivable, so we turned around and went straight home and missed the football game."

Ty leaned forward, appearing eager to hear more. "Then what happened?"

"I dropped Jody off at her home. My parents were waiting for me in our driveway. Mom glared at me, then turned around and went inside the house without a word. I knew she was angry about the damage done to the car, the cost of having it fixed, and what the insurance company would say."

It had taken years for Beth to realize there might have been more to her mother's reaction. "But I think she was also freaked out about what *could* have happened. She just didn't know how to express those feelings."

"And your dad?"

Beth's eyes prickled, and she fought tearing up. "He was so cool about it. Dad just gave me a hug and said, 'Welcome to the club. It was bound to happen sooner or later.'"

"Your dad was quite a guy."

"He wasn't perfect, but he was a good man." Beth sniffed, then regained control of her emotions, and smiled. "I miss him, but I'm grateful for all the memories we created together. And if I marry someday, I'd like my kids to have a dad like mine."

Ty reached across the table and grasped her hand. "I'd like to be the same kind of father as yours to my own kids." The room had darkened, and in the candlelight, his eyes reminded her of the sun's rays reflecting on a clear body of water.

Warmth spread up her arm and into Beth's heart. What was Tyler hinting?

Nineteen

Ty stood next to the porch railing and surveyed the exterior of his home and the large yard, still visible in the lowering sun's rays. The place remained a work-in-progress, but without his inheritance from a grandfather he barely remembered, making the huge investment would have been challenging, if not impossible. Social workers didn't earn large incomes. *Thanks, Grandad.*

And thanks to Beth's tenacity, necessary and desired changes were coming along. He admired her ability to see the big picture and also keep track of details.

She sat on the porch with her feet planted on a step below, focused on the horizon, and looking relaxed in worn jeans and a red, long-sleeved T-shirt. Beth peered up at him, and her familiar gentle smile appeared. "Thanks again for last night at The Bridge. The meal was excellent, the atmosphere was certainly lovely, and the conversation . . . well, I enjoyed learning more about you."

He returned her smile. "I hope we'll have more times like that. Good food and great company. It was exactly what I needed after a rough week."

And after walking Beth to her door at the end of the evening, Ty had fought off the urge to cover her soft-looking lips with his. But it felt too soon for even a casual good-night kiss.

Although he felt close to her and cared deeply, there was still so much uncertainty in his future. Would it be fair to her if their relationship grew serious?

"This is pretty awesome too," she said, gesturing toward the view.

"It is . . ." Ty poured decaf coffee into a paper cup and handed it to her. "Careful. It's hot."

"Isn't that how coffee should be served?" She chuckled.

"Well, unless you've requested an iced latte."

"True. Unfortunately, I can't offer you a fancy drink right now. Maybe never in my own home. I'm not the kind of guy who buys expensive espresso machines or loads up on ten flavors of syrups and creamers." He winked. "I'm pretty simple when it comes to food."

"I see. Although . . . the fixings you've laid out for s'mores seem beyond the basics." She gestured toward the tray laden with marshmallows, graham crackers, large chocolate chip cookies, a jar of Agatha's homemade raspberry jam, and an assortment of chocolates. Beth tasted the brew. "Not bad. Strong, just the way I like it."

He poured a cup for himself. "I had to reward you somehow for taking time off on a holiday weekend to come up here and talk about the house, and on a Saturday night at that. And then on top of everything else, you brought dinner." Ty had worked all day at the property, but she'd also spent hours at Your Secret Garden.

Beth had been more than generous with her time helping him with his new home, but to feed him a home-cooked meal . . . Her caring gesture touched him. "I hope I didn't ruin any plans."

"No, I didn't have anything else going on tonight." She

wrapped her arms around her knees. "It's important to make some final decisions on design, but the process should also be fun. I've been looking forward to it all day."

Sure, they needed to talk about tile and paint, but after their enjoyable date the night before, he'd been more interested in just hanging out with her.

"Memorial Day weekend is a time to honor the fallen military, but it also feels like the beginning of summer. A lot of people spend the three days enjoying picnics, camping, hiking, or just relaxing." Beth shooed a fly away with a sweep of her hand.

"But my family has always been tied up on this weekend with business." She gave a small shrug. "Homeowners some-times start or finish yard projects, so the garden center is always in a flurry. Mom also brings in temporary help to assist with floral arrangements because many gravesites are decorated with fresh flowers for Memorial Day."

Ty sat next to her. "With my father in the military, we always attended the ceremonies, honoring those who had passed. I grew up knowing it was a somber holiday but also a day to be grateful for those who were willing to serve." He slapped his knee. "I have some news."

"Oh?" Beth cocked her head. "Good, I hope."

"Definitely." Ty took one gulp of his drink. "I've mentioned Brandon several times."

"The carpenter who has been like a brother to you."

"A man of *many* talents. He'll be here next Friday, and he'll stay for as long as possible—at least a month—to work on this house. It's his dad's busiest time of year, but Brandon hasn't taken any vacations in several years, and he's hoping to prove that the construction company can do just fine without him." Because one day, it would have to.

"That's amazing, Ty. You've gotten so much done here already, but I know it's been difficult while working full-time at the prison."

The fact that she understood trying to find a balance felt strangely comforting. "It's been tiring, but working here has also felt like therapy."

"You know, when I first heard about the potential sale of this property, I couldn't stand the thought of a new owner doing shoddy work and destroying the charm." Her face lit up. "It's wonderful to see the craftsmanship and care that has gone into a house where so many wonderful memories were created for me."

"Thanks." Pride filled his chest at hearing her praises. "I do care—very much." Even more so, knowing what the home meant to her.

"Before we dine on three-cheese tortellini and chicken soup and then eat ourselves into a sugar high with dessert, I'd like to get a tour." She set her cup down. "Let's assess what's been done and what still needs to be addressed."

Beth stood and headed down the steps. "Since we decided on a clean and fresh look with a touch of soft grays, greens, and blues, I brought some samples for you to consider for the kitchen and bathroom countertops, backsplashes, and shower walls. They're in my car." They'd already carried in a slow cooker she'd brought filled with soup and plugged the appliance in to keep their dinner warm.

Ty followed her, and they lifted several boxes filled with tiles and quartz samples. They'd already chosen laminate flooring. It gave the appearance of stained wood but would be water resistant, scratch resistant, and more durable than hardwood.

Before he'd done anything else, Ty had made it a priority to bring the electrical and plumbing up to code. The steps and porch were repaired. A soft green shade of paint now covered the exterior red brick. He'd ripped off the damaged front siding and applied a log siding that looked natural and fit in with the surroundings. A new wood door and new windows were also added.

The extended porch stood three feet in height from the ground, so to bring it up to code and make it safe, he'd added a railing. Although glass would have provided a nice, see-through barrier, it would take work to keep it clean. Who wanted more maintenance to worry about? So instead, he'd opted for cable rails that offered a sleek, modern look and didn't obstruct any views while sitting on the porch.

Inside the house, Beth showed him the samples she'd brought, and they made some final decisions. "The landscaping is done, but I'd like to walk around the yard and explain what's gone in."

"Sure." Ty held the door for her, and they headed back outside before twilight.

She removed the blue sweatshirt she'd tied around her waist and put it on. "It's getting chilly. A fire will be nice tonight."

They strolled around the yard, and Beth showed him areas where she'd planted multiple shrubs and flowers. "I didn't want the yard to look formal, so no rhododendrons or azaleas. Not in this wooded setting.

"Instead, we used a variety of hostas, foxgloves, and closer to the house, we planted climbing rose bushes that will bloom for months. Foxgloves come in a rainbow of colors, including red, pink, yellow, white, and purple. The flowers will draw bees, butterflies, and hummingbirds."

"I hadn't thought about animals dining in my yard." Her knowledge about plants was impressive, and he appreciated the efforts made to add sustainable beauty to the property.

"Deer and rabbits might be your biggest threats, but I wanted to add some color to this gorgeous setting, so I took the risk." Beth pointed to a garden where green, thriving plants grew. "The lupine will grow about one to three feet, depending on the variety. They're easy to grow and deer resistant, and since lupine is a perennial, the plants will blossom year after year."

"Nice. We won't have to replace them." He grinned. "*Hopefully.*"

She smirked. "My crew also planted coneflowers in a variety of colors—purple, pink, yellow, and white. Another perennial. Deer may not bother them, but unfortunately, rabbits like the stems and leaves. And to be safe, we've applied deer repellant around the entire area."

"It might be nice to see them wander through the yard, but I get it. We don't want all the pretty plants to become their garden salad."

"Trust me, they have so much vegetation to choose from in the forest, they won't go hungry." Beth nudged him, playfully. "Are *you* hungry?"

He responded with a gentle shove. "Always."

They returned to the porch where Ty set up a card table and two chairs while Beth ladled soup into bowls. They each carried their portion to the table, and then she returned with a basket filled with cheddar and herb biscuits.

Ty tasted the soup filled with shredded chicken, tortellini, carrots, red pepper, onions, fresh parsley, and spinach. "Wow, this is amazing. It has a slight kick to it." "It comes from the combination of onions, fresh garlic, and a small amount of red pepper flakes. Too spicy?" "No, not at all." He took another bite, savoring the flavor. The biscuits complimented the meal. "Thanks for bringing dinner. I appreciate the offer, especially when you're so busy at the garden center."

"I don't cook much. It feels like too much effort for one person." Beth broke a biscuit in half. "So when I have the opportunity to make a meal for someone, it's fun."

They inhaled the food, and between bites, talked about the renovation. Trying to be discreet, Ty watched Beth as she soaked in the remaining daylight. Where had her mind wandered off to? What was she thinking? By her expression, she felt at peace. He understood. This place did the same for him. It calmed him. Made him feel God's presence.

It felt natural for him to share this moment with her. Like they could remain like this for days, not saying a word, yet completely comfortable with silence. He'd never experienced this before.

Her trance broke, she returned to the present, and smiled at him. If only Ty could tuck that lovely expression away and carry it with him.

Beth attempted to hide a large yawn and leaned back in her chair. "Excuse me. Along with working at the prison, I've been putting in a lot of hours at the garden center. And I'm still popping in to visit George. You remember him? The gentleman with Alzheimer's?"

"There were moments when he thought you were his wife." And she'd been so kind and gentle with the man, never correcting him.

"I try to spend time with the other people you met that day as well—Mrs. Middleton, the lady who broke her hip, and Colton, the little boy who is autistic. There are several others who benefit from digging in the dirt. But the three you met have all asked about you." She grinned. "You made quite an impression on them."

"I've stopped by to see Mr. Middleton a few times and played backgammon. He served during the Vietnam War and has shared some of his experiences. Not all vets want to talk about what they went through."

"You're a good listener." She leaned back and closed her eyes, and her face glowed from the sun's rays as the orb lowered farther in the horizon.

Was this woman an angel? Everything about her convinced Ty that she could be one in disguise. Beautiful was an understatement, but how she continued to sacrifice her time to serve others daily blew him away. Did she ever put herself first?

"Beth," he said, his voice almost carried away with the breeze.

"Yes?"

"I think . . . I think it's time for you to step back from working on this house."

Her eyes opened, and she bolted into sitting straight in the chair. "Why?"

"I've asked too much. You're already carrying a heavy load with trying to balance your time at Your Secret Garden, the prison, and making personal visits to people in the community." He shook his head. "I don't know how you do it and still find time to sleep."

Beth frowned. "How much I can handle is for me to decide," she said, sounding defensive. Her body relaxed, and she sighed. "I'm sure you're only trying to be considerate. I can appreciate the thoughtfulness."

"It's not that I don't want and enjoy your input, but now that the yard work is done and most of the interior design has been figured out, I thought you might be anxious to have the time back that you've been putting in on this project."

"Ty, being here and working on the house has been a nice distraction from my other responsibilities. I've loved every minute." The corners of her lips curved up into a teasing smile.

"And as for landscaping, it's not like I've done all the labor myself. I've basically made decisions and then given instructions to employees as to what to plant and where." Beth grinned. "I'm great at giving directions."

A hearty laugh erupted from his gut. "I believe you." He settled back in his chair. "Okay, then. I'll trust you to know when enough is enough."

"Thank you."

She'd done an incredible job. Stone pavers were laid through the flower gardens to the patio where the stone firepit was now located. A roof built over that area provided shade from the sun, which could get hot in the summer, and protection from the rain. But the placement of the roof didn't obstruct the view of the water and mountains from the porch.

Ty would put a grill out there for cooking, along with a table and comfortable chairs for dining. He could grill steaks or salmon without worrying about the weather. "I've been thinking about putting in a covered deck. Composite materials are more expensive than wood, but the deck wouldn't need sanding, staining, or any other kind of treatment in the future."

"I like that idea, but where would you build it?"

"Over there, to the side of the house where there's access to electricity. A hot tub would be nice, and we could still take in the scenery from that spot."

Did she notice he'd said *we*? How could he even think about enjoying the property without her being a part of it? She belonged here. If life were different—if his goals and loyalty to Brandon weren't taking him in a different direction . . .

Beth nodded. "That would feel good on cold, rainy nights, and we get plenty of those around here."

"So, I hear."

"I have a question." Her tone had grown serious.

"Shoot."

"Why are you putting so much into this house when you might only live here a year or two and then sell?" Her gaze penetrated him. "You're putting your heart into the place when many contractors would be more concerned with making it presentable enough to make a fast sale and profit."

"A lot of reasons." Ty unscrewed the cap to his bottled water and took a swig. He held the bottle in hand and fingered the cap in the other as he thought through his answer. "The property is a good investment, and my dad has always pushed me to do my best." It had been an ongoing challenge to measure up, but he still tried.

"Like you, it's become a good distraction from my work, which can be mentally and emotionally draining." Ty chuckled. "Even for a *guy*."

Beth's eyes shone with mischief, and the corners of her mouth twitched. "So you're admitting that men can get emotional?"

"Nope. That's not what I said." He shook his head and laughed. "What I meant in few words is that the women at the correctional facility and their problems can be challenging, frustrating, and . . ." Ty took another drink. "Actually, yes. I can get caught up in the painful stuff they're dealing with too."

Beth tilted her head and gave him a gentle smile. "You're a kind soul, Tyler Sharp."

"Thanks." The way she looked at him. Could she hear his heart beating? Did she glimpse the affection he felt for her in his gaze? He needed to stop staring. Ty shifted in his chair and returned the cap to the water bottle. "There's another reason for pouring so much of myself into this place."

"Oh?"

"It's hard to explain. But like an author who needs to write or an artist who is driven to paint, I have a desire to create. I believe it's something God planted inside of me. I can only go so long without finding an outlet before I start to feel anxious and irritable."

"Agatha has talked about similar feelings, and that's why as long as she breathes, she'll find a way to make art."

"Right. And I don't have her gifts, but I get a lot of satisfaction in finding a house like this one and making it functional and beautiful again." Ty had helped Brandon's family remodel other homes, but this one felt special. "And of course, selfishly, I want to enjoy the place until I need to sell."

"I wish I could afford to buy it," she said wistfully. "But I know I don't stand a chance of making a worthy bid after all the improvements you've made."

"Beth . . ."

She lifted her palm to hush him. "It's okay. Really. It's given me joy to help bring the place back to glory again. The former owners will be happy and proud of what you've done, and I am too."

"Thank you." *Don't give up hope, Beth.* He kept telling himself that he was making improvements to make a profit later, but he kept envisioning her living there.

How that was going to happen, he didn't have a clue, but he couldn't let those visions go.

Twenty

During Beth's initial meetings with Lisa about four weeks ago, they'd discussed a desire expressed by inmates to have plants in their cells, and Beth had a keen interest in bringing their request to fruition.

Last week, on a rainy afternoon not suitable for outside work, Beth had gathered twenty women together. They'd spent an hour transplanting succulents and African violets into large plastic cups to take back to their rooms, and they'd also potted larger plants, such as ficus and Norfolk Island pine, into roomier containers for display in a common area.

She'd made a commitment to Ty, and she'd encouraged Emily North to participate in one of the horticultural programs with no success. Beth had also invited her to the planting activity, but neither Lisa nor Beth had been successful in convincing the inmate to join in. Determined to reach the young prisoner, and not wanting to let Ty down, Beth wasn't ready to give up on Emily yet.

While the project didn't require many gardening skills, the activity did involve social interaction and cooperation, which, Beth was learning, was no small task in a prison setting.

Now she greeted the women as they sauntered into the classroom with their personal plants and dropped into chairs placed behind four rectangular tables facing her. Beth had called each one by their correct name without prompting. *Progress.*

Abbey walked in and chose a seat in the back of the room. Beth caught her eye, nodded, and mustered a small smile. Since their meeting in Ty's office more than three weeks ago, they'd coexisted in the gardens and the classrooms by keeping some distance and only interacting when necessary. Each taking time to get used to the other one's presence.

Lisa slipped in last and sat next to Abbey. It was expected that the program manager would observe at times, but this occurrence had come with no warning. Beth shot up a quick and silent prayer for guidance. She was earning the inmates' trust, wasn't she? Yet, how could she feel completely optimistic? Several might be playing her, thinking she was totally naïve.

True, Beth hadn't even come close to experiencing and surviving what any of them had faced, but she empathized with wanting more from life. She understood loss, grief, and having goals for herself and her family. Those feelings—those desires—weren't exclusive to one group.

Beth remained standing and scanned the room. She released a pent-up breath and smiled. *Relax. You got this.* "Good. You all brought your plants with you this morning. I'd like to hear about your experiences this past week."

Felicity, slouching in her chair, looked up. Her forehead furrowed. "Like what?"

"Well, how has it made you feel to be responsible for keeping your plant alive?" Was that too deep of a question to ask right from the start?

The inmate scratched the back of her neck, then shrugged. "I guess it made me feel good. My grandma liked violets, and seeing these flowers next to my bed every morning reminded me of her." Felicity sat up straight. "And it got new blooms too. I think my grandma would be proud." She nodded. "Yeah, keeping this thing alive made me feel like I'm not a total screwup."

"I think your grandma would be proud of you too. *I am.*" Beth's heart warmed at seeing Felicity's freckled face flush with pale-pink pleasure before she ducked her head. When was the last time the young woman had received a compliment or any words of affirmation? Beth stepped closer to the group. "Have any of you noticed growth or other changes in your own plants?"

A hand shot up.

"Tania?"

The expectant mother rubbed the swollen belly carrying the child she'd deliver soon. "I don't know what I'm doing wrong." Tania's frustration and disappointment carried through in her tone. She thrust a pot holding a wilting philodendron in the air, then returned it to the table.

Marcy, her dark hair pulled back into two tight braids, guffawed and pounded on the table several times. "Man, how does she think she's ever going to take care of her kids when she can't even keep that thing alive?"

"You shut up, hag!" Tania shot back. Others chimed in, supporting her.

Antagonizing the other women had become a sport for Marcy. She might not make it much longer in this program where leaders stressed the importance of teamwork.

Beth understood Tania fighting back. At least she'd done it with words and not her fists.

It wouldn't be safe for the baby to get into a brawl. Her infant would be cared for by her sister, along with Tania's two other young children, until she was released and got her life together. She was one of the fortunate women whose family still stood by her, willing to help. Her children wouldn't be separated and placed in foster care.

"Marcy." Beth waited for the inmate's attention to focus on her. "It's not okay to be mean. You don't have to like anyone, but if you believe it's impossible to show respect toward the other women in this group, you can return to your cell, and I'll remove you from the roster," she said, calmly and firmly.

Beth smiled and held Marcy's gaze with what she hoped was a piercing one of her own. "It's up to you. You're in control of whether you stay in the program or not."

Heads turned toward the troublemaker. With all eyes on her, Marcy caved. "I'll stay." Her tight lips revealed she agreed begrudgingly.

"Good. I'm glad." Beth walked over and picked up the distressed plant that started the clash. "Tania, you've made a common mistake. I promise the plant isn't doomed. It will be fine. Philodendrons turn yellow when the roots are sitting in too much moisture." Beth removed the unhealthy leaves and tested the dirt with her finger. "Wait a week, then start watering sparingly, and see what happens."

Tania's shoulders straightened. "Thanks."

"You're welcome." Beth glanced around the room. "I'd like to hear more thoughts on this project."

She gave each participant an opportunity to talk. With few exceptions, most were eager to have a turn, and they said the plants brightened their own rooms as well as the common area. For some participants, the group activity had triggered positive memories or brought a sense of community. They used words like homey, peaceful, and calm to describe how they felt, and how the greenery improved their environment. Abbey chimed in with the others.

Their time together came to an end, and Beth excused them back to their cells.

Lisa waited for the last prisoner to leave and then approached the front of the room. "Nice job, Beth."

"Thanks." With an exaggerated gesture, Beth wiped her brow.

"You held your own today with Marcy. I wasn't sure there for a minute if I'd need to step in and remove her."

"I was relieved she settled down." Beth released a large sigh. "Overall, I think allowing the women to have greenery in their cells has been a positive move."

"They expressed that today, but we need to be cautious in our assessments. We don't know how long these feelings will last. Still . . . even in this short amount of time, I can tell the project has had some impact."

"I agree, and I'd like to pursue additional options."

"I'd like to hear your ideas. You know, a common complaint from outsiders is that individuals who are incarcerated don't deserve things they label a luxury. But studies show experiences like these are a necessity." Lisa pulled out a chair from behind a table and sat. "And I don't want our focus to be on merely making prisons prettier. I want to make this place feel more humane while we still provide separation from the community. My *hope* is that we'll promote accountability and health."

Beth moved another chair from behind the table and joined her. "I've been reading the research you gave me to look over. I knew that exposure to nature improves mental health and well-being, and horticulture classes have been associated with vocational and social skill-building. But I found it interesting that even watching nature videos has been linked to lower aggression."

"Fascinating, isn't it?" Lisa crossed one leg over the other and cupped her hands around her knee. "I'd love to get approval to purchase a large-screen TV for a common area where we could run ongoing videos of forest, ocean, and mountain scenes.

"With today's technology," she continued, "we have films available of plants growing and caterpillars morphing into butterflies in accelerated time. The possibilities are numerous. Think of the calming effects on our inmates."

"I love that idea!"

"It won't be easy to convince those in power that not only the inmates but also people on staff will benefit." A hint of a smile graced Lisa's face. "If the prisoners are less agitated, they're less apt to cause trouble."

"Spending time in nature relieves my own stress. There's nothing like the peace that God's creation can bring to the soul."

Lisa nodded. "We can't take the women out of the facility and into the mountains or to the ocean beaches, but maybe we can bring a glimpse of what's still out there waiting for them if they're willing to work hard to get there."

"I'll confess that I accepted this internship a bit reluctantly, even though I needed and appreciated the opportunity." Beth took a deep breath at seeing Lisa's brows rise. "I was worried about what I might face here, especially with Abbey participating in the program. Even without her presence, I was intimidated by the prison setting."

"I sense there's a *but* coming."

"I'm starting to see and know the inmates as women

instead of criminals."

"Ah, well, that's a huge step." Lisa smiled. "I'm glad you've managed to take the leap."

Beth felt relieved—grateful—that she'd grown beyond those first days. She no longer walked through the prison doors with her stomach in knots. Instead, she anticipated her hours in the facility with joy.

She was there to help these women change, yet through them, God was doing a work and changing *her*.

Twenty-One

T yler pulled into the parking lot of Your Secret Garden and turned off the car's engine. The lot wasn't empty, but it wasn't full either.

Brandon, sitting in the passenger seat, faced him. "Wow, you'd think this place would be hopping on a Saturday afternoon."

"They've been dealing with tough competition. A national chain moved into the area this year, and the company ships in truckloads of plants and markets them at a lower cost than what my friends can afford to sell them for." Ty had hoped the warm June weather would entice more customers in to shop—people loyal to Your Secret Garden and the Millers. With as much rain as they'd experienced this past week and gardening delayed, he thought people would be eager to finish their yard projects.

The two friends followed a middle-aged couple through the main doors leading into the garden center, where Beth helped a couple with two young children choose outdoor plants. Ty didn't have a clue as to what they were called or if they would bloom or not.

Beth glanced in their direction and waved. He nodded, hoping she understood they'd wait until she had a free moment. In the meantime, Ty and Brandon explored the area that felt almost empty when the aisles should be filled with customers loading carts with vegetable starts, flowers in an array of colors, bags of soil, and fertilizer.

"Hi!"

Ty felt a tap on his shoulder and turned. Those warm, chocolate-brown eyes melted his heart. He fought to break their hold. "Beth! Thanks for taking a minute."

She nudged his arm. "I always have time for you."

That was true—at least to date—and it felt good to know he could count on her.

"And as you can see, I'm not terribly busy. We were counting on the sale we're running to bring in more people, but it hasn't been as successful as hoped." Beth held out her hand. "You must be Brandon. Ty mentioned you were coming."

Brandon accepted her offer to shake with a grin. "I got in last night."

"So, that must be your truck parked in front of Agatha's. I live in the apartment behind her home."

Ty put his hand on Brandon's shoulder but spoke to Beth. "We don't want to get in the way, but I wanted to introduce him to your family and show him around." He'd been eager for Brandon to meet these new friends he'd become so fond of, and he was also proud of how hard they were fighting to keep their business going after such devastating losses. Their story and how they stuck by each other through challenges motivated him when discouraged.

"I'm glad you came in." She put up her pointer finger. "Give me a moment." Beth scanned the area and headed toward a coworker. They chatted briefly, then she returned. "This a great time for a breather. I think you've seen what we offer here, so let me take you into the floral department and gift shop. My mom and sister would love to see you."

They followed Beth through a smaller area filled with garden accessories and into another attached building that housed the floral shop. Mrs. Miller finished a phone conversation, wrote on a notepad, and tucked her pen in the upper pocket of her apron.

The matron of the family came around the counter. "It's nice to see you again, Tyler," she said in a lighthearted voice.

"Hi, Mrs. Miller," he said, tipping his head slightly.

"Please. It's about time you call me Candace. Everyone around here does."

He nodded again and turned to his left. "This is my best buddy, Brandon Willcox."

"The woodworker from Colorado." Harmony made her boisterous entrance into the room carrying a large basket that held small bags made from see-through material. They were tied with various shades of ribbon and filled with flower petals. "Welcome to Meriside! I'm Beth's younger sister, Harmony."

Kaylee was close behind, her lengthy, light brown curls cascading over her shoulders. Although she offered a warm smile and a small wave, she remained silent.

Brandon's lips curved up as he tilted his head toward her. "Then you must be Kaylee," he said in a gentle tone. "Ty has spoken highly of the entire family. It's nice to finally meet you all."

"Likewise," Beth said. "It's wonderful you've come to help with getting his house finished. I think you'll love the place as much as we do."

Her last comment struck a beautiful chord in Ty's heart. She confessed to loving the home, and she'd said *we*. Boy, he liked hearing her refer to the two of them that way, as though they were partners—or a couple.

"After seeing photos, I'm anxious to check out what's been done on the exterior, as well as the landscaping, which looks phenomenal. But I'm especially interested in seeing the interior renovations," Brandon said, addressing Beth. "Ty has been singing your praises, and the decisions you've already made will make the job easier for me. I can dive in right away and get to work."

"*Easier?*" Harmony chuckled. "You don't know my sister!"

"Beth *is* a perfectionist, but that's because she cares so much," Kaylee said quietly.

Detail-oriented, caring, creative, smart, funny—and beautiful. Ty could go on . . . and he had earlier that day with Brandon.

"Thanks, Kaylee." Beth raised an eyebrow and shot a look of satisfaction toward her sister.

Harmony shrugged, then grinned. "How long are you able to stay?"

"Maybe five weeks. Dad wanted me to take the lead on a job back home, but it's on hold due to complications. One headache after another, so I asked to use some vacation time."

"*Some?*" Harmony drummed her fingers on the counter. "Mom, he works for family, and he gets *five* weeks of vacation," she said in an almost whiny voice. She winked at Brandon. "Just kidding, Mom. I'll take a day when I can get it and be happy."

"That's my girl—always the comic," Mom said in a teasing tone.

Ty slapped his friend's back just hard enough for him to feel it. "What Brandon isn't telling you is that he hasn't taken a real break in over two years, so he's due."

"And you spend your hard-earned vacation helping a friend. Admirable." Beth's eyes brightened. "Ty has been bragging about your woodworking skills, and I'd like to learn more. Coming here must be taking you away from your special projects."

And Tyler couldn't be more grateful for his friend's generosity. But that was Brandon—always there for him when Ty needed anything. And now that his friend had met Beth, he was confident Brandon would pin Ty down on his feelings for her. Brandon always saw right through him.

"I've put requests for custom pieces on hold so I could work on Ty's house and spend time in the Pacific Northwest. It was kind of a no-brainer for me. I've been here for less than a day, and I already love it."

Harmony plopped her basket on the counter. "You couldn't have explored much in less than twenty-four hours."

"No, we'll check out some hiking trails soon, but Ty has been showing me around town. The Sound, the mountains . . . it's all breathtaking. We grabbed lunch at the Seaview Diner at the marina. Best fish and chips I've eaten."

Kaylee perked up. "That's one of my favorite places on the waterfront."

"Okay!" Brandon gave her one of his irresistible grins that pulled women in like a magnet. "Good to know."

"I realize you both have a lot to tackle at the house, but while you're here, you need to visit Hurricane Ridge," Beth chimed in. "The views of the Olympic Mountains are amazing, and we usually see black-tailed deer and marmots. The wildflowers are spectacular in July and August, so you'll need to make another trip back then."

"Oh, that's on our list of adventures." Ty shifted his small backpack. "Along with heading over to Lake Crescent and taking a hike to Marymere Falls. But depending on how much time we need to put in at the house, we may not complete our to-dos this trip." Before Brandon had decided to hang out with him, Ty had considered asking Beth to explore those areas with him, but neither of them seemed to have much free time. He wanted that to change.

Ty elbowed his friend. "What he hasn't mentioned is that we both targeted the saltwater taffy at the ice cream and candy shop downtown."

"There's a reason for bringing his backpack in here," Brandon whispered as though sharing a secret. "He doesn't want to go anywhere without his stash. But I'll go back for ice cream later. That's my vice."

"Flavor?" Harmony asked. "Not black licorice, I hope!"

Brandon grimaced. "Not on your life!" His reaction sent Harmony into a genuine, joyful laugh.

Ty stood back and watched the interaction between his buddy and the women. Unlike his own serious demeanor, Brandon's vibe was charismatic and funny. He engaged that way with everyone. It didn't matter age or gender, he just had a genuine love for people and an interest in them and what they enjoyed. What made them tick. People were drawn to Brandon.

How would Ty feel if his friend showed an interest in Beth? When she laughed at Brandon's jokes, jealousy jabbed Ty. He'd never been envious of his friend before. Brandon was a good-looking, likeable guy. He didn't hurt women intentionally, but he didn't understand the effect he had on them.

Harmony and Brandon continued bantering back and forth, but Ty understood his friend well. Kaylee had caught

Brandon's eye. Ty knew her least of all, but he wasn't confident she was ready for another relationship or that she was even healed from her loss.

Two years had passed since her husband died, but it took time to move on from grief. Ty didn't want his friend to face rejection, nor did he want Brandon to break anyone's heart.

Twenty-Two

N ow that Brandon had arrived, would Beth see even less of Tyler?

Funny how that possibility saddened her. It wasn't as though they were a couple and Brandon was trying to keep them apart. Just the opposite.

Although Agatha had invited him to stay in her home, Brandon had chosen to stay at Ty's unfinished house alone. Plumbing and electricity were available, so he likened it to glamping, and he insisted he was content to use a sleeping bag and cot. On the other hand, Ty opted to remain at Agatha's in a real bed, explaining that he needed to show up for work rested.

Brandon seemed eager to have Beth join them at the house to talk over renovations, and in the few days since he'd visited Your Secret Garden with Ty, Brandon had shown an interest in getting to know the entire Miller family. He'd even surprised them that morning with fresh baked goods soon after they'd opened. Of course, the treats weren't as tasty as the pastries Beth's sister-in-law created, but each flavor was still tempting, and even Kaylee had agreed with a nod and a smile that the donuts with lavender-blueberry frosting were delicious.

Now Kaylee watered the plants while Beth walked the aisles and removed spent geranium and petunia blooms and yellow or dry leaves. It was also important to check for any diseases. It would hurt their profit if they were forced to discard any plants.

How many hours of sleep had she gotten? Three—maybe four. Two cups of strong coffee hadn't helped. Beth blinked her tired eyes. Time to rally and focus. As soon as she'd fallen into bed the night before, her brain switched into high gear, and she couldn't shut it down.

Thoughts and questions swirled in her head. How were they going to save Your Secret Garden from going under? What could they do to help Kaylee find her way out of grief and into purpose? Was Mom doing okay? Was Harmony?

Would Ty be happy with Beth's design decisions for the house? And how long would he be sticking around? Could she trust her growing feelings for him? Did he feel anything for her besides friendship? And if so, would it be wise to entertain any attraction since his plans didn't include staying in their small town?

Beth was managing her responsibilities connected to the internship at the prison, but then what? How would she start her own therapy business?

Sleep had come to her weary mind and body only after she'd downed three glasses of water, visited the bathroom several times, and worn herself out by tossing and turning.

Before heading to the prison, she'd put in a few hours at Your Secret Garden. Then she'd return to finish up the day and close the business that evening. Twelve-hour days were tiring but rewarding, and she'd feel even more exhausted if she didn't love both jobs. Plus, after having to say goodbye to several part-time employees, it was necessary for her to cover as many hours at the nursery and garden center as possible.

A young mother strolled through the aisles with a baby in a denim carrier strapped to the front of her. The woman hummed as she passed Beth. The child she carried slept peacefully. Beth caught her sister-in-law staring at the two. Kaylee watched for a moment, and then she put down the wand attached to a long hose and disappeared.

Beth stashed the bucket she carried filled with plant debris and searched for her. She found Kaylee in the storage shed, staring out the window with shoulders slumped.

"Are you okay?" Beth stood beside her, wanting to put her arm around the sweet and sensitive woman but waiting for a sign her comfort might be welcomed.

"I will be." Kaylee wiped tears from her cheeks. "Most days I do fine but seeing that mom with the baby . . ." She sucked in her breath. "Grief hit me hard all over again—all that I've lost. Liam and I will never have a chance to have our own son or daughter."

"I'm so sorry. It's not fair. Not any of it." All that pain, and yet she'd supported Beth taking the internship and working with the very woman who had destroyed the future Kaylee had envisioned with her husband.

More than ever, Beth understood her sister-in-law's strength and sacrifice. No wonder Liam had loved his wife with complete adoration and abandonment.

Kaylee took a deep breath. "But I'm getting stronger every day, and although the pain is still there, it's becoming more of a dull ache in my heart. I know God cares, and nothing can separate me from his love. I also know that life on earth is temporary for all of us. Liam has just gone on ahead of me." A small smile grew on her lovely face, and she wiped away any remnant of tears. "I'm okay now. We should get back to work."

"You know you still have a family with Mom, Harmony, and me. We'll always be here to love and support you in any way we can."

"I know, and it makes all the difference." She gave Beth a rare embrace, then left the shed.

The members of the Miller family had always been affectionate and quick to offer a hug or a verbal *I love you*, but Kaylee had been more guarded when it came to physical expression, except with Liam. Beth's throat thickened with emotion. She wanted so much for her sister-in-law to find peace and joy again.

Beth entered the prison gardens with a heavy heart.

Abbey stood next to a raised vegetable garden, smiling, and joking around with one of the other prisoners. Beth couldn't get that morning's intimate conversation with Kaylee out of her mind, especially as she heard Abbey laugh from across the garden. Abbey who had taken Liam—Kaylee's husband. Beth's dear brother. Abbey who had wrecked their family with one stupid, selfish, *avoidable* decision. Senseless. Devastating.

Beth had thought she'd been okay. She thought she'd put all this behind her. Tears pooled in her eyes. Clearly she hadn't. And Kaylee's pain only reminded her of that.

Dad won't be here to walk Harmony or me down the aisle. Grandchildren will never hear his corny jokes, work beside him, or feel his strong hand on their shoulders as he shares wisdom or prays for them. And Mom will never again be comforted by his embrace or hand enfolded in hers.

Abbey glanced her way, then she stared for a moment, her eyebrows furrowed.

No, don't come over here. Beth pretended to focus on the pepper plants in front of her, but her vision had blurred, and with her emotions in upheaval, it was worthless to try. The agreement she'd made with Tyler wasn't working. Beth couldn't force herself to be okay around Abbey.

The clank of the gate caught Beth's attention, and she looked in that direction. Lisa led Emily North into the yard and over to the garden where Abbey and several other women worked. Beth couldn't hear the conversation, but she watched Emily accept a trowel from Abbey and start digging out weeds. What had finally persuaded Emily to participate in gardening?

Lisa chatted with the group of women for several more minutes, then she approached Beth. "Well, I never expected that outcome."

"What happened?" Beth sucked in her despair, wiped her nose, and gave a slight nod in Emily's direction. "How did you talk her into trying the program?"

"I didn't. Abbey convinced her."

Beth's jaw dropped. "Abbey? I don't understand." How could she have succeeded where Beth had failed?

"The two women share a cell, so they spend a lot of time together, so there's that. Sometimes peer pressure wins, and sometimes, it's a matter of trust," Lisa said matter-of-factly. "Earlier this afternoon, I received a request from Emily to meet. After our conversation, I agreed to integrate her right away on a trial basis and see how it goes."

So, after Beth had approached Emily several times and been shut down, she'd changed her mind after all. Tyler would be thrilled. He wanted so desperately for her to try anything that might light a spark inside and motivate her. This was great news.

Why didn't Beth feel exhilarated instead of deflated? Because Emily had listened to Abbey and not to Beth? Why did she feel the need to rescue Emily? Was she trying to impress Tyler? Or God?

"Sheila will keep an eye on Emily today. She'll make sure she's given direction and kept busy." Lisa glanced at her watch. "Anything you need before I head back to my office?"

"No. Thanks, Lisa." She forced a smile. "I'll check on the strawberries and see what's ready for picking." Beth picked up a small box and moved to a garden some distance from any prisoners and volunteers, where she could be alone for a minute. She knelt in the dirt, feeling worn out and disinterested in searching for the sweet, red jewels hanging beneath the foliage.

This wasn't like her. She'd always found joy in the feel and smell of the earth. All she wanted to do was lie in the dirt and cry.

Someone moved up behind her, blocking the sun's rays. "Beth, are you okay?"

Earlier, Beth had asked Kaylee the same question. *No, I'm not okay. And I don't know if I ever will be.* Why couldn't Abbey just leave her alone? Beth was exhausted from swallowing her grief.

Abbey knelt next to her. "Can I help?"

She clenched her teeth, then relaxed and took a deep breath. *Lord, I need to be honest with her. I can't pretend something I don't feel.*

"I'm trying. I'm *really* trying, Abbey. But some days it's still hard to see you because it feels like I'm being slapped in the face with loss all over again." Beth sat back on her knees. "I've forgiven you—I have—but I can't forget."

Abbey's eyes glistened, and her lower lip quivered. "I promise. If I could change anything, I would."

"But that's the problem." Beth studied the ground. "You can't."

Twenty-Three

T y tapped another piece of laminate flooring into place with his rubber mallet, then surveyed the area they'd completed. "It's looking good!" What would his father think of the place? Would he be proud of what his son had accomplished?

"Yeah, I like it." Brandon set another bundle of planks close to the action. "The place is coming together."

He'd helped Ty vault and apply pine boards to the ceiling in the family room at the front of the house. The result produced a bright and spacious feeling as soon as one stepped inside. Ty didn't like the outdated red brick fireplace. Instead of destroying the structure, they covered the brick with stone cut in half to limit the thickness and whitewashed it. A large mantel, created from a piece of interesting driftwood, had become an unexpected showpiece.

"I think we'll keep the walls in here white. But Beth wants to add an accent color in the bedrooms. Something that will look nice with the light-colored floors."

Brandon saluted. "Okay by me."

They'd blown out a wall to enlarge the kitchen and were more than pleased with the effect. "Kitchen cabinets will be painted either a pale blue or sage. I'm putting in stainless steel appliances, a white porcelain farmhouse sink, a new garbage disposal, and an instant-hot faucet. Black quartz for the countertops and large island." They'd gone back and forth between white and a dark color but opted for black to contrast with the white walls and the light cabinet and floor colors. "Beth gave me two backsplashes to choose from. That decision will depend on the cabinets."

"Go with blue. Not everyone is a fan of green, and when you decide to sell . . ."

"Gotcha."

"Beth did a great job picking out materials."

"She says they complement each other." Ty grinned. "I obviously needed help."

"So the house needed a woman's touch, but is that all there is to it?"

"Meaning?" Ty sat on the floor, resting his elbows on bent knees.

Brandon tapped his water bottle against his thigh. "I know you all too well, my friend, and I see the way you look at her." He pointed the container toward Ty. "You're into her like nothing I've ever witnessed before. It might be time to act on those feelings."

Relief showered Ty like refreshing rain washing away caked-on mud. He didn't need to worry about his buddy taking an interest in Beth and becoming Ty's competition for her affections. Brandon was encouraging him to pursue her. And his friend wasn't wrong about Ty's feelings for Beth. He was falling hard, but if they got serious about moving forward into something deeper than a friendship, then what? He'd made a commitment to Brandon to return to Colorado.

Would Beth be willing to leave Meriside? She felt responsible for her family's emotional and financial welfare. How could he help her put down that burden? She'd never feel completely free to follow her heart until assured they'd be okay without her ongoing help.

"What about you?" Ty needed to know. Where was Brandon's head? Why would he urge Ty to move ahead with a romantic relationship here? "You and Harmony sure hit it off." Ty actually thought Brandon had been more intrigued by Kaylee, but he didn't want to jump right into that delicate territory with a nosey question.

"Harmony is great. We could become good friends, but if you're asking if I'm interested in dating her, I'm not." Brandon dropped to the floor and sat facing Ty. "I haven't felt a special connection with a woman since college. Remember, I thought Carrie was *the one*, but we didn't want the same things."

Ty nodded. "I *do* remember. She was only interested in her journalism career and traveling, and she didn't want a family." Having kids, whether biological or adopted, was important to Brandon.

"And she couldn't understand why my faith is so important to me. She believes God exists. She just couldn't buy into having a personal relationship."

That was one of many things Ty appreciated about Beth. She understood what it meant to walk by faith daily and to believe that God was not only real, but that he was also interested in her personally.

"Hey, Ty . . ." Brandon cocked his head and stared at the wall.

"Yeah?"

"Have you thought about adding in bookcases and storage on both sides of the fireplace?"

"Yes—and no. I wasn't sure what to do with those areas.

Beth and I tossed around a few ideas the other day, and we looked at some cabinets online, but nothing struck us as being perfect."

"I have an idea, but I'll need more tools than what I brought with me." Brandon stood and walked over to the fireplace. He studied the wall space on either side of the fireplace, then slipped his metal locking tape measure from his carpenter's tool belt and took measurements.

"Are you talking custom pieces?"

"Sure."

"That would be amazing, but that kind of work takes a lot of time." Ty shrugged. "And to be honest, I can't afford what something like that would be worth."

"What if you covered the cost of materials? That might not amount to much if Dad has wood in storage that he'd let me take for free." Brandon placed his hands on his hips and slacked his stance. "But I'm not charging for labor. It would be my pleasure. Think of it as a housewarming gift."

Ty stood and looked his friend in the eyes. "That's too much to ask, B."

"You didn't ask. I'm insisting. It will give me another project to put in my portfolio." He grinned. "I'll post the pics on Instagram and add them to my website—when I have one."

"How and where would you build the units?"

Brandon rubbed his jaw. "I still have two weeks of vacation that I'd planned on using here, but there's nothing left to do on the house that you can't finish without my help, and what you can't do is already contracted out."

"Right."

"So, I'll leave my truck here and fly back home. Make magic in my woodworking shop, rent a truck to haul everything back, and return within a couple of weeks."

"Brandon, are you sure?" Ty rubbed his lower back. "All the time used for traveling and working in your shop could be spent hiking the trails you've wanted to explore."

"Hey, man, I'm excited! Inspired!"

"Okay." Ty gave his friend a quick hug and slap on the back. "You're the best."

"Just promise one thing while I'm gone."

"You got it. Anything."

"Think good and hard about giving you and Beth a chance."

Twenty-Four

Tyler massaged the area between his eyes, not that the action would help much. The pounding in his head had grown progressively worse since he'd arrived at the prison that morning. If it lasted much longer, he'd resort to taking a mild pain reliever.

He could use a win. Was he really helping anyone? Or was he just pushing paper, writing reports, and failing to reach these women? The inmates he'd met with yesterday and today were guarded and defensive. They worked hard to act tough and strong. Their pushback wore on Ty. How could it not feel the same for them? And it was only Tuesday. What would the rest of the week bring?

A female guard knocked on his half-open door. "Mr. Sharp, you got a minute? One of the inmates asked to speak with you. She doesn't have an appointment."

Stacks of files and paperwork filled half his desk. He'd never get through them by the end of the day. If Mary was coming in to complain about the food again . . . Ty rubbed his jaw.

"Who is it?"

"Robin Delaney."

"Ah, sure. Have her come in."

This was out of the ordinary, but he didn't have any

meetings scheduled for another forty minutes. It must be important for Robin to make a request. She'd been assigned to one of his groups, but she never spoke during the sessions.

The nineteen-year-old with two black braids almost reaching her waist shuffled into the room with her eyes focused on the floor.

"Robin, please come in. Take any chair." Ty gave her a moment to settle in. Instead of returning to his place behind the desk, he pulled an empty chair over and stopped a few feet from her. Close enough to hopefully break down some barriers but not so close as to be inappropriate or threatening.

She sat at the edge of the wooden chair with a cushioned seat, gripping the arm rests, one knee bouncing, her attention flitting to every space in the room but his face. It seemed Robin was doing everything she could to avoid looking into his eyes.

"It sounds like you have something important to talk about." Ty relaxed, hoping she would pick up on his vibes. "Take your time. I'm not going anywhere."

"Can I trust you?" Her dark eyes finally sought his, and her gaze held both fear and hope.

"You can," he said in a quiet but confident tone.

She shifted in her seat, but the bouncing knee didn't rest. "What do you know about me?"

"You're nineteen. You were caught selling drugs a year ago in Larksville where you lived, and you have two more years left to go on your sentence." Ty thought for a second, recalling her records. "That was your first arrest. Is that accurate?"

She nodded.

"So, what's going on? How can I help?"

"It's not me who needs help."

Interesting. Then why was she here? "Okay. You'll need to explain."

Robin chewed on her bottom lip.

"Start from the beginning."

"The beginning—sure." Robin took a deep breath, and her body stilled. "My mom died when I was sixteen."

She toyed with one braid. "Me and my brother had to stay with our stepdad. He's got a bad gambling problem. And I mean *bad.* He's a welder at the shipyards, and every time he gets paid—he blows most of his check at the casino. When my mom got sick, she didn't get the medical care she needed because he didn't give a—" Robin stopped before revealing the word she had in mind, but Ty didn't have any problem guessing numerous possibilities that could have filled in the blank.

"Gambling can be an addiction, just like alcohol is to alcoholics."

"He's mean and he drinks some, but he doesn't do drugs." Robin slouched in her chair. "He started sellin' drugs so he'd have more money to gamble."

"A domino effect ending in trouble." Wherever her story was leading, Ty wasn't going to like it.

"He got this *brilliant* idea," she said sarcastically, "that kids my age would trust me more than him, so he forced me into pushing drugs at the local schools." Robin sat up, her back rigid. "I didn't want to do it, but there was *never* any food in the house, and I couldn't stand Marcus crying 'cause he was hungry."

"Marcus is your brother?"

"Yeah, and Luke—our stepdad—said if we wanted to eat, I had to earn it, and the only way was selling dope for him and taking part of the profit for groceries."

Tyler's gut simmered with anger. Luke was a monster.

"I was good at it." A hint of pride came through in her voice. "I also got a job at a fast-food place, but Luke forced me to deal there on my breaks. I couldn't get out of it."

"You weren't old enough to make it on your own." Ty was getting the picture—in full color. "And running away would have left your brother on his own."

"I couldn't leave him behind." Her voice was thick with emotion, and she wiped away the tear sliding down her face. "I was saving money to get a place for me and my brother when I got caught."

"You were eighteen at the time, so you were sentenced as an adult."

"I know I did bad things and deserve to be punished." She sniffed and tugged on her braid. "But I talked to my brother. I use the money I make in the kitchen here to call him once a week on his cell phone, but only when Luke is at work."

Inmates were permitted to call out, but no one was allowed to phone in. Ty read between the lines. If she wasn't making any collect calls to her family, there was a reason. "Are you worried about your brother?"

Robin chewed her lower lip. "He's scared because Luke wants him to start pushing drugs at the middle school. Marcus is only twelve. He's going into the seventh grade. Those kids are too young to know what they're getting into, and my brother doesn't want any part of dealing."

"Have you told anyone else about your stepdad?"

"No." She grimaced. "Maybe if I had I wouldn't be here, and Marcus wouldn't be in trouble. But I was afraid if I reported Luke, my brother and I would be separated and put in foster care."

Tyler sighed. "As a mandated reporter, I can't keep this information private. I'll have to share it with authorities to protect Marcus and keep him safe."

"I know. That's why I'm here." Her chin thrust up, and her eyes gleamed with determination. "You *can't* look the other way. You *have* to do something."

Smart girl. She knew what she was doing. "I'm glad you understand that we need to do what's best for your brother."

"I've heard plenty about horrible places, but I know decent people also foster. A friend at school had a nice home and foster parents who cared. I want you to get Marcus away from Luke. Promise me that you'll find my brother a *good* home. *Please.*"

Three days later, around six thirty in the evening, Tyler and Ms. Palmer from CPS arrived at Luke Hanson's home in Larksville, twenty-three miles from Meriside, and rang the doorbell.

A caseworker would typically bring a police officer if there was concern over safety, but they didn't have cause to request protection, and after Ty asked to accompany her, Ms. Palmer hadn't seen a need for additional assistance.

They stood patiently for a minute, but no one responded. Ty rang again. From the corner of his eye, he watched the front curtain rise from the corner of the window and drop back into place. He looked at his partner, shrugged, and pounded hard several times.

The door swung open, and a lean man possibly in his late

forties with ice-blue eyes, a long nose, high forehead, and a receding hairline stood in front of them. "How can I help you?"

"Luke Hanson?" Ms. Palmer asked.

"Yes."

"I'm Ms. Palmer from Child Protective Services. Mr. Sharp is also a social worker." They'd agreed to not mention Ty worked at the prison. "Your stepson, Marcus, lives with you. Is that correct?"

"He does. Great kid." Luke grinned. "He's not in any trouble, is he?"

Ms. Palmer didn't falter. "There's been a report of child neglect, and we're required to investigate that complaint."

"That's crazy. Who called? That nosey neighbor across the street? She's had it in for me ever since I threatened to call animal control on her dogs." He leaned forward and lowered his voice, acting like he was letting them in on a secret. "Barking all the time. What a nuisance!"

"I'm sorry about the dogs, but as to who called in the report, that's confidential. We can't share that information."

"Ahh!" he growled. "I know who'd lie about me." Luke propped himself against the doorframe and shook his head as though deeply grieved. "My stepdaughter. You know she's in prison, right? Got into trouble, and now she can't leave her brother alone. Bad seed, that girl. Since their mom died, I've tried to do right by them, raise them as my own, but she never liked me."

"I don't know your stepdaughter, but I do need to speak with Marcus." That wasn't a lie. Ms. Palmer had never met Robin.

"I know my rights," he said firmly. "If you don't have a

court order, I don't need to let you in."

"That's true, Mr. Hanson, but it's in your best interest to cooperate now."

"Sure. Come on in. Put your concerns to rest." Luke stepped aside and held the door open for them. The dingy beige carpet was stained, but their sparse furnishings seemed in order and clean.

A young boy with curly black hair and green eyes peeked from behind the door to another room.

"Marcus," Luke said as he waved the boy in. "Come out and talk to these nice people." Luke stood behind his stepson and put his hands on the kid's shoulders. "See? He's all right."

Something was off. Ty expected the man to be angered by their visit, but it was almost as if he was expecting them. Everything was *too* perfect.

"Hi, Marcus. I'm Ms. Palmer." She gave the child a reassuring smile. "We're just here to visit." She craned her neck and focused on an opening to another room. "May we look in the kitchen?"

Luke gave a dismissive shrug. "Go ahead. Don't think you'll find anything interesting."

"Thank you." Ty followed her into the other room. Fresh milk and orange juice sat in the refrigerator, along with a few apples, a loaf of bread, and sandwich meat. A cupboard held three boxes of cereal, along with some pasta, spaghetti sauce, and peanut butter. Frozen dinners were stuffed into the small freezer.

"I've been making a grocery list. Heading to the store after work tomorrow." Luke pointed to a paper held to the refrigerator door with a magnet.

The boy fidgeted and glanced at Ty, who didn't miss the

fear in his eyes. Luke draped his arm around Marcus and drew him close, acting chummy, but the kid tensed up.

Ms. Palmer smiled at the child. "I'd like to speak with Marcus alone." She raised her eyebrows at Luke. "I promise we won't take up much more of your time."

Luke's eyes narrowed, and his smile seemed forced. "Sure."

"Marcus, would you like to show me your room?" She seemed calm and in control. Ms. Palmer must have been in this situation many times before. "It's always interesting to see what kids are into."

The boy slipped out from under Luke's arm and led her down a hallway. Ty heard a door shut. How to keep Luke from intruding? "You a Mariners fan?"

"Not into baseball." Luke gazed down the hallway. "I follow football."

"You think the Seahawks will pull it together this year?"

Luke's focus returned to Ty. "Maybe."

Ty struggled to keep the guy occupied, but Mr. Hanson's mind was clearly focused on the conversation that might be happening in the back bedroom. Ty sighed internally when Ms. Palmer returned with Marcus.

"Thank you, Mr. Hanson, for giving me the opportunity to have a little time with Marcus. You have a wonderful son."

"You done here?" Luke asked.

"Yes, we're finished. I don't have any more questions for either of you," Ms. Palmer said.

"Good."

"Bye, Marcus." Ty held out his hand, and the boy looked at Luke, as though asking for permission to accept it.

Luke scowled at the kid. "Go ahead. Be polite and shake

the man's hand."

Tyler grasped the boy's hand firmly and smiled at him, hoping to send a quiet signal to not give up hope. Ty stepped outside and then turned back toward the door.

From the doorway, Luke glared at him. "Say hello to Robin for me. And tell her to stop making trouble for her brother."

The guy had known they were coming! That explained why he was prepared and willing to let them in. Ty wanted to pound the man, but he was a professional. He'd keep his mouth shut for now, but bullies like that—he bit his tongue. Ty didn't want to make matters worse for Marcus or Robin.

Luke slammed the door.

Ty followed Ms. Palmer to her Toyota and got in. "You find out anything?"

"There's something going on. I can feel it to my core." She slipped on her sunglasses and started the car. "Marcus barely spoke or looked at me." She glanced to her left, steered the car away from the curb, and headed down the road.

"Somehow, Luke knew we were coming." Ty's right hand made a fist, and he punched his left palm. "He let it slip that he knew I have connections to Robin. He was prepared, and he made sure that Marcus kept his mouth shut."

"I agree. Mr. Hanson scared the boy into lying about his welfare in that house."

"So, let's get him out of there. Put him somewhere safe."

"We have to consider the legalities." Ms. Palmer faced Ty, her expression grim. "I can't remove a child on a gut feeling or one person's complaint. I need a court order or proof that Marcus is in imminent danger. Like physical harm, sexual contact, neglect, or firearms left in the open." She stopped at an intersection, looked both ways, then turned right.

"Physical, photographic, and other forensic evidence helps. I didn't see anything in that house that conveyed an unhealthy environment."

Ty heaved a sigh. "What can we do?"

"Our small police department has its challenges, but the officers care about this town and are willing to do whatever they can to serve and protect." Ms. Palmer tapped her fingers on the steering wheel. "I'll ask them to watch for any suspicious activity."

"Good idea." Ty shifted in his seat and considered possible outcomes. "But if Marcus gets caught dealing and refuses to testify against Luke, will the real criminal get off and the poor kid be sent to juvie? That's not best-case scenario, but it would still get Marcus away from his stepdad."

"Other kids are involved. The teens and preteens buying the drugs. We need to also think of them." Ms. Palmer stopped at a red light. "I may need Luke's permission to talk to Marcus in their home, but I have the authority to speak to him alone without his stepfather's approval or presence while Marcus is in school. I'm regretting not starting there." The light turned green, and she moved the car forward. "I'll check in on him and work on building his trust."

"What can I do?"

"See if there's anything more Robin can tell us that will help us gather evidence against Mr. Hanson."

"Robin, how did your stepdad know CPS was going to show up at his door yesterday?" Ty asked with a calm but firm tone. "How did he know I work here?"

"I'm sorry, Mr. Sharp." Robin's eyes misted, and she wrung her hands. "I—I didn't mean to ruin anything."

"What happened?"

"I called my brother yesterday. He was upset because Luke told him before he left for work that morning that Marcus would have to deliver more drugs to a buyer that night."

Ty remained attentive and silent, waiting for Robin to finish her story.

"Marcus didn't want to do it. He was freaking out, even crying. So, to get him calmed down, I explained how you were going to get him out of there, and he started to pull himself together." Robin sniffed.

"And he told Luke?" Ty handed her a box of tissues.

She pulled out a tissue and wiped her nose. "No—well, not by choice." Robin took a deep breath. "He came home before we hung up, and he smacked Marcus for talking to me without permission. Luke was yelling and swearing, and the line went dead. He must have forced Marcus to tell him everything we'd talked about and warned my brother not to talk when CPS showed up."

Anger boiled in Ty's stomach as he imagined Luke harming the boy, but he couldn't let off steam in front of Robin.

"I was going to warn you, Mr. Sharp, but you'd already left the prison for the day, and I didn't know you were planning on showing up at the house yesterday. I didn't!"

"I believe you." The girl deserved some grace. "It wasn't your fault. The timing was merely coincidence."

"So now what? You're going to get Marcus out of there, right?"

If he could, he'd place her brother in a safe and loving home immediately. "It's not that simple."

"But you promised." Her eyes begged him to say what she wanted to hear.

He felt helpless in this situation, and it broke his heart to not give her the reassurance he desperately wanted to provide. "I promised to do all I could to help, and I am."

Tyler picked up a pencil and rapped it several times on the notebook in front of him. Nervous energy. Honesty was critical now. He couldn't sugarcoat the situation. If he withheld the truth, Ty would lose her trust, damaging any potential to guide her in the future.

"When Ms. Palmer from CPS and I visited, the house was clean, some food was stocked in the kitchen, and there was a list of grocery items taped to the fridge. Luke said he was making a trip to the store later. Ms. Palmer spoke to Marcus alone, but he closed up. She couldn't get him to talk about anything that would have helped us."

"Luke probably threatened him."

"That's our guess." Ty raised one shoulder, then let it fall. "We wouldn't have known that Luke expected us to show up, but he couldn't keep his mouth shut. Before we left, he told me to say hello to you."

Robin released several curse words under her breath.

Maybe he shouldn't have relayed that last part. "We can't do anything more until we get proof that Marcus is being neglected or in need of protection."

Her chin quivered. "Then there's no hope. My brother is stuck there forever, isn't he? Marcus is either going to die or end up in prison, just like me."

"Don't give up, Robin. There's always hope."

Twenty-Five

B eth turned on the oscillating fan. The day's high temps had heated her bedroom, and though the sun had now set, the air felt too warm to be buried under a blanket. She crawled into bed and pulled the sheet halfway over her body. Even the thin covering was too much. A quick thrust and it floated to the side.

The digital clock on the nightstand stared, reminding her with blue numbers that time was fleeting. It was a rare day that she managed to retreat to her room before midnight, and this was no exception at 1:17 a.m.

Get some rest. Tomorrow would be a long but enjoyable day. Beth wasn't required to work at the prison and Your Secret, Garden would close earlier than normal. She was looking forward to fun and relaxation. Their competitor advertised staying open until 9:00 p.m. on the Fourth of July, but they'd all leave Your Secret Garden at 1:00, so they and their employees could enjoy the holiday with their families.

With her eyelids now closed, Beth's muscles relaxed as she breathed a prayer. She entered that twilight zone where she was neither awake nor in deep sleep, still aware of sounds.

Her eyes shot open. How could she have forgotten?

Every Fourth of July, she made her dad's favorite cookies— sour cream with white frosting, decorated with red and blue sprinkles. She'd continued the tradition in his memory and had promised her mom and sister that she'd make them again this year.

The ingredients were purchased several days ago, but every spare minute had been consumed by other responsibilities. Kaylee might have been delighted to take over the baking, but pride had stood in the way of asking. Beth was determined to carry out the act herself.

As for now, the cookies wouldn't magically appear. And she couldn't disappoint her mom and sister, even if it meant getting only a few hours of sleep. Beth sat on the edge of her bed, rubbed her eyes, and yawned. *Get up, girl, and get to work.* Once she got moving, her brain would kick into gear, and she'd be fine.

Tyler helped search for a spot at the waterfront park to watch fireworks. He'd enjoyed the day in Agatha's backyard with Beth and her family, but they should have arrived earlier at the park because the place was packed.

He also understood the women not wanting to spend the entire holiday in a crowded area. Instead, they'd shared a quiet afternoon with delicious food, yard games, and engaging conversation that included respectful debates on topics like recipes, politics, and favorite movies.

They grabbed an empty space being vacated by a family with two young children after the parents offered it to Ty and Beth. The couple confessed they'd decided late-night fireworks would be too much for their kids to handle after going all day without naps.

Ty set up lawn chairs for Agatha and Mrs. Miller. Harmony, Kaylee, and Beth spread a large blanket on the ground in front of the other women, then sat and got comfortable. Ty sprawled on a smaller blanket thrown on the ground next to them. The women had set out popcorn, cookies, and soft drinks. The evening temp was somewhere in the seventies—warm, yet pleasant, and the breeze coming off the water helped cool the air that had earlier hit the mid-eighties.

Fireworks shot high into the air, bursting with electric colors, their sparkling effects reflected in the water. People clapped and in unison released their *oohs* and *aahs*. They could stare at the sky, but the glow lighting Beth's beautiful face captured Ty's attention. Her expression mesmerized him, and he couldn't turn away.

She leaned back, her slender legs stretched out in front of her, hands on either side, propping up her torso. Beth closed her eyes and tucked her chin to her chest as though taking a catnap. Not quite her energetic self today. He'd caught her yawning several times and blinking her eyes as though struggling to keep them open.

His hand covered hers, and at his touch, she opened her eyes and smiled. Ty considered himself a strong, solid man. He'd survived a lot in his life, including a stint in prison. How could that one gesture of acceptance weaken him to mush inside?

Face it, you've got it bad for her.

Beth slipped her hand from beneath his, got up on her knees, and didn't move.

"You okay?" Something was off, but how hard should he push her to admit it?

"Yeah." She cleared her throat. "Yeah, I'm fine. I just need some cold water. There are more bottles in the cooler behind Mom."

She didn't *sound* fine, and she looked pale compared to earlier. Even though the water was only a few feet away, he would have gladly gotten it for her, but Beth was already up, so he stayed put.

Four booms filled the dark sky with an array of magical designs. The lingering effects sparkled like diamonds trailing downward.

Ty turned to watch Beth's reaction to that last spectacle, expecting to see pure delight across her face. But her back was turned toward the sky art, becoming a silhouette as the last display fizzled out. Beth's form wavered, as though ready to topple over.

She just needed some water to feel better. *Focus, Beth.*

The night was closing in on her, restricting her vision to a fuzzy tunnel that grew smaller and smaller. Her breathing was too shallow. *More air.* She needed more air. And what was that humming in her ears? Beth's knees buckled. The world went dark.

Heavy eyelids and a foggy brain made her feel as though she was surfacing from a deep sleep. Her eyes refused to open. Muffled voices surrounded her, but her own lips wouldn't respond.

Now she understood words spoken. Her mother begging her to wake up. *Open your eyes, Beth.* Her head cleared, she blinked, and her lungs inhaled fresh air.

"She's coming out of it." Ty, kneeling on the ground, held

her tenderly, as though she were a delicate creature. His comforting embrace felt soothing, like a warm bath on a cold, damp night.

"What happened?" Beth felt a little embarrassed. Had she tripped and fallen? No—that wasn't it.

"Oh, honey, you fainted, and Ty caught you before you hit the ground." Mom knelt next to them and brushed her hand over her daughter's forehead. Then she moved out of the way for a man wearing a dark-colored shirt and pants.

They called a first responder? She'd only fainted. That wasn't serious. "I'm fine. I just needed some water." Beth tried to sit up but was still too weak. Ty helped her but kept his hold on her.

"I'm Adam." The paramedic held a small light in front of her eyes and moved it back and forth. "Do you have any chronic conditions?"

"No."

"Currently taking any medications?"

"No."

"Allergic to any medications?"

"No." Beth lifted a weak, shaking hand to wipe away the trail of cold sweat running down the side of her face.

Adam clicked off the light and tucked it inside his bag. "Fainting can be nothing, or it can be more serious."

While he checked her blood pressure and her heart, Beth glimpsed the concerned faces around her. After a lovely day, she'd ruined it with this little episode.

"Your vitals are looking good, but it's still important to get checked out in the ER. My partner and I will take you in our rig."

She shook her head in protest. "That's not necessary."

Adam smiled. "It *is* necessary, and it's my job, so don't make my life difficult."

"Honey, please . . . you're going." Mom stood with her arms hugging her chest as though comforting herself.

"It's best, dear." Even Agatha seemed convinced that Beth should make the trip.

"All right. I'll go." Beth sighed. "But the rest of you stay here. It doesn't make sense for you to follow us over there. It would be a waste of your time."

"You'll need a ride home," Ty said.

"She may need to stay the night." Adam packed his equipment in his bag.

"The night?" Beth shook her head. "I can't. I have too much to do."

"Let's just take one step at a time, okay?" Harmony, the voice of reason. "I'll drive separately over to the hospital and stay until we know more, and then I'll report to the rest. Okay?"

Did she have a choice?

Several hours later, Beth tugged the hospital bedsheet up to her chest. "Do I really need to spend the night here? I feel fine."

"You collapsed and were out for almost a minute, so it's important we run some tests." The doctor wrote on his iPad with a compatible pencil. "We're short-staffed because of the holiday, but we'll get you through them as quickly as possible."

Beth cringed. "What do you think happened?"

"You could have just been dehydrated, but we need to play it safe. The tests I'm ordering will rule out anything serious." He tucked his iPad under his arm and slid the pencil inside the upper pocket of his white coat. "Fainting can be caused by several things. Standing for a long time, getting overheated, seeing blood, or shock. Fatigue, low blood pressure, or low blood sugar can also trigger fainting. We'll know more tomorrow."

Twenty-Six

T yler rolled his aching shoulders and stretched his arms. Working on the house that evening had been a good distraction. Worried about Beth, he'd been too restless to sleep much last night, but pouring energy into the remodel had tired him. His digital watch showed 11:48—almost midnight. He'd conk out quickly after he got back to Agatha's.

Ty had waited impatiently all day to hear from Beth's mom, praying and hoping for good news. He'd struggled to focus on work, but taking the day off wasn't an option because of important meetings scheduled. Even if the hospital had allowed him to visit Beth, tests had occupied her day.

Finally, Candace called as Ty was leaving the penitentiary and heading to his house. Her mom assured him that Beth was okay and would be released the next morning. However, she was given strict orders by the doctor to slow down and not push herself so hard.

He'd inhaled a deep breath, and with its release, his shoulder muscles had relaxed, and his chest felt lighter. Ty had given a prayer of thanks that Beth's fainting spell wasn't related to any serious condition. Going forward, he'd encourage her to take time off, and he'd also be careful to not add more to her already heavy load.

He glanced around the kitchen and imagined cooking with

Beth, sharing stories about their day, making this place a home—*their* home. A dangerous dream. Ty needed to accept reality. They made a great team, but this season would come to an end when the time came for him to leave this town. Unless he could convince her to go with him.

Call it a night and turn off the lights. Ty stepped outside and pulled a set of keys from his pocket. A chilling shiver ran down his spine. *Why?* Even at that late hour, the air temperature hovered in the low eighties. He stood still and listened, straining to hear any sounds out of the ordinary. A soft, low-pitched *whooo-ooo-ooo-ooo* came from a nearby pine—a great gray owl.

The cloud-filled black sky and thick woods shrouded the area in darkness. Ty could barely see his hands in front of him. It might be time to follow Brandon's advice and install safety lights on both sides of the house that would activate at dusk and a motion-sensitive light on the porch that would be tripped by people, deer, raccoons, coyotes, or other critters in the area.

Lock up and go home. Ty inserted the key. Quick footsteps hit heavy to the side of him on the porch floor, and his left side was shoved with a locomotive force.

Caught off guard, Ty tripped, but he instinctively grabbed the other man and held on. He avoided crashing his head on the floor, but like a bolt of lightning, sharp pain shot through Ty's right shoulder, and he cried out.

The assailant pinned him down. "You're going to regret messing with me!" His hot breath, smelling heavily of alcohol, covered Ty's face, sickening him.

He recognized that voice—Luke Hanson. Robin's stepfather, in a drunken state, had come to threaten Ty and put him in his place.

A hard punch to the left of Ty's stomach forced the remaining air from his lungs, and he gasped. Two blows to his face—he feigned defeat and went limp. Luke released his grip on Ty, pushed off his body, and staggered to a standing position over Ty.

"You're not so tough, are ya?" Luke slurred as his body swayed. The owl called again, pulling his attention away from Ty.

That distraction was just what he needed. Ty sprung up, lunged, and grabbed Luke around the knees, throwing him off balance. He landed on his backside, and Ty threw his body on top of the assailant. They wrestled, and a hard punch to his jaw made Ty's eyes water and mucus run from his nose.

Luke broke away and stood doubled over. Maybe he'd had enough.

"Give it up, Luke." Ty forced his legs to raise his beaten body to a standing position. His chest heaved as he gulped fresh air, but he couldn't waste a second. He pulled his cell phone from the pocket of his shorts.

The man straightened and faced him.

Ty dialed 911, asked for help, and didn't hang up. Instead, sensing Luke was going to reengage, he slid the phone to the side of the porch.

"You stay away from my family!" Luke pulled a switchblade from his pocket and waved the knife in front of him. "Or I'll kill you."

"I can't do that." Ty's heart pumped boiling blood through his veins, and his body prepared to move. He'd learned a few skills while incarcerated. Moves a guy never forgets. "You're putting Marcus in danger. He deserves better."

Luke gripped the knife in his right hand and ran toward him. Ty didn't hesitate. He tackled Luke below the waist, throwing him over. Luke dropped the knife, and Ty kicked it off the porch into the bushes. The drunk and breathless man lay on the porch, coughing. Ty shoved Luke over and sat on him.

"We're done." Ty pulled off his T-shirt, ripped it in half, and tied Luke's hands behind his back as tightly as he could to help restrict the guy's movements.

Time moved slower than a three-toed sloth. Where were the cops? Ty didn't want to retrieve his phone and risk losing control of Luke, who was spewing vile words.

Sweat dripped down Ty's face, and exhaustion threatened to take over his body, but he used his weight and remaining strength to keep Luke restrained.

The sound of sirens carried through the still night air, reaching Ty's ears. Red and blue lights flashed through the trees. Two police cars stopped in front of the house and officers jumped out, the vehicles' lights still flashing.

"Up here!" Ty yelled. "I'm Tyler Sharp. I'm a social worker at the women's prison. This guy, Luke Hanson, attacked me with a knife and threatened my life."

The cops took over and handcuffed the perpetrator.

Ty crawled over to the wall and leaned against it, still catching his breath.

"Hey, you okay?" Ron Metcalf stood over him. Ty had met the officer at church, and they'd talked shop a few times over breakfast at a local diner.

"Yeah, I'm fine." Ty wiped warm, sticky blood from beneath his nose. "Luke must have followed me here after I left the prison and then waited until dark to attack."

He knew better, but Ty had been so worried and focused on Beth's condition, he wasn't paying attention to his surroundings and aware of the possibility that someone was trailing him.

If Luke had come with a clear head and hadn't been drunk and slightly out of his mind, or if Ty's phone had fallen out of his pocket or gotten smashed during the fight, he might not have won this battle.

But God's angels—his mighty warriors—had protected Ty. He truly believed that.

Thank you, Lord.

"After you and I talked the other day, I contacted the department over in Larksville. They've had their eye on this guy for a while." Officer Metcalf rested his hands above his belt. "Now they'll have enough on him to get a warrant to search his house."

"There's his stepson to consider—Marcus." Was the boy home asleep? Did he know Luke was coming here?

"How old is he, again?"

"Twelve, and he needs to be removed from that home for his own safety." Ty stood, but his legs felt weak. "He's a good kid who ended up with an evil stepfather."

"If I remember correctly, someone from CPS is already involved."

"Ms. Palmer. Please contact her."

"Will do." Ron returned a wave from another officer who was getting behind the wheel of the first police car. Luke sat in the back seat, still shouting obscenities. "I'd like you to get checked out at the ER, just to make sure you're okay. Then if you're willing, I can take your statement tonight, or you can get some rest and come in first thing in the morning."

"Tonight. Let's get it all down tonight."

❧

Ty slipped into the chair at the table in Agatha's kitchen and winced. His left side and right shoulder were black and blue from the beating he'd received from Luke. But any bruises were worth it if that was what it took to put that jerk away. The cuts on his face would heal in good time.

"Did you sleep?" Agatha set a large mug filled with steaming coffee in front of him. Her long silver braid was draped over her right shoulder, and it hung down the front of her dark blue robe. Unusual for her not to be dressed this late in the morning. "I don't think I got more than three hours myself."

"I was still pretty riled up after the trip to the police station, but I drifted off for a short time." He brought the mug to his lips, tested the heat, and took a gulp. "I'm sorry I called and woke you up. I should have let you sleep and waited to fill you in this morning."

"Nonsense! After all you went through, I would have been upset if you hadn't told me when you did." She offered him a piece of coffee cake with a crumbly brown sugar and cinnamon topping, and he accepted. "You're an adult and can come and go as you please, but when people live under the same roof, it's natural to worry when someone is out all night without notice."

"Yeah, I get it." He smiled. "And it's nice to know people care."

Agatha placed her hand on her chest. "It makes my heart sick to think what might have happened if you hadn't gotten control of Luke or managed to reach the police. What if he'd had a gun?"

"God was protecting me." Ty had no doubt. "I gave my statement, so I don't need to return to the station. Aside from being stiff and sore, I checked out okay. But the doc encouraged me to take it easy for a few days."

"Good. The last two nights have taken a toll on you and Beth. You both need a break. She was a little freaked out about Luke showing up at your house."

"Beth knows?" When would Agatha have had a chance to speak to her?

His aunt tilted her head and smiled. "It's not like I'm the neighborhood gossip who ran next door to spill some juicy news," she said calmly. "She was released from the hospital earlier this morning, and I was in the garden praying for you when she arrived. Instead of walking past me and pretending I was invisible, she sat down for a moment. It didn't feel right not to tell her."

"I can understand that." Ty downed a large bite of sweetness. He was hungrier than he thought. "She was upset?"

"Concerned. But I assured her that you're okay, Luke is locked up, and you'd fill her in on more details." Agatha broke off a piece of coffee cake with her fork but laid the utensil down without eating a morsel. "I'm worried about Marcus and what will happen to him."

"For now, he's in emergency foster care until other arrangements can be made for longer placement. It's not an ideal situation, but at least for now, he'll be safe." He filled his mouth with cake. If not the breakfast of champions, it served as manna from heaven to a ravenous man.

"Ty, I want to do it."

"Huh?" Ty almost choked on his food.

"I want to foster Marcus."

"Where is this coming from?" Ty set his fork down and wiped his mouth with a paper napkin. "You can't just decide to take in a kid on an emotional whim. It doesn't work that way."

"That's what I was praying about in the garden this morning—that and other things." Agatha stood and refilled their mugs with dark, rich coffee. She added hazelnut-flavored creamer to her own.

"The licensing process in this state can take six to nine months."

"I was approved and licensed over a year ago, but I never followed through. For some reason, it didn't feel like the right time. But now it does, and maybe that's because God had this in his plan all along." She sipped her coffee, then smiled. "I don't need to renew my license for another fifteen months."

"Okay, but consider your . . ." He didn't want to offend this dear woman, but she had to be realistic.

"My *age*." Agatha raised her eyebrows and shot him a teacher's warning look. "I'm seventy-four, but I'm an active senior citizen. I exercise daily, and my mind is still sharp. There's no age limit to being a foster parent, so I could continue into my eighties as long as I remain healthy."

She smiled. "I agree that I might not have the stamina to care for a baby, toddler, or young child. But Marcus is twelve, almost a teen, and quite capable of doing many things for himself."

"True." How could Ty argue against that? Agatha had given it more thought than he'd realized.

"I miss being around teenagers. I miss teaching and mentoring young people."

His mind spun with all the arrangements they'd need to make if they followed through with this. "You've had years of experience with kids his age, so it might work."

"It sounds like he's a nice boy, and I want to give him a home where he doesn't have to worry about where his next meal is going to come from or if he's going to get into trouble and end up in juvie."

"You have love to give, and you have an incredible amount of patience. He would be a lucky kid to have you as a foster parent."

"You know . . ." Agatha's sea-green eyes sparkled as she held her mug in front of her. "Once you move out, I'll have even more room to share. If things go well with Marcus, maybe his sister could stay here as well, until she's on her feet and able to care for him and herself."

Ty chuckled. "Ah, Auntie, let's not get ahead of ourselves."

Twenty-Seven

B lack-eyed Susans, purple coneflowers, blue hydran-
geas, and peach verbena bloomed in Agatha's backyard. Baskets and pots filled with dark pink geraniums and
yellow, blue, purple, and white petunias were placed in various
areas.

A rainbow of color surrounded Beth and her mother as
they relaxed on the familiar bench beneath the cherry tree. Its
blooms were long gone, but the canopy of leaves provided
some shade, and the limbs served as a haven for squirrels and
birds.

Beth was released from the hospital that morning feeling
weary. It had been difficult to sleep the two nights while there,
and then she'd been put through a series of tests, which made
her feel restless and anxious to return home. Fortunately, the
results showed nothing alarming, so she and her family
could relax on that front.

But after chatting with Agatha that morning and hearing
about Tyler's fight with Luke at the house, it was impossible
to rest, even in the comfort of her own home. Agatha had
looked worried, and she'd mentioned Ty's physical state when
he'd returned home earlier. He was exhausted, bruised, and
limping.

Until she had a chance to hear the story from Ty himself,

Beth's nerves wouldn't completely calm. Even now, her gaze kept returning to Agatha's back door, waiting—hoping—he'd step through it and find her.

Her mother had returned to check in on Beth and brought lunch—turkey, avocado, tomato, and lettuce sandwiches made with Kaylee's freshly baked hearty bread.

"Mom, this was so nice of you. My fridge is almost bare. I haven't made time to stock up on groceries." She had no appetite, but not wanting to be rude, Beth forced herself to take another bite of her sandwich. "This bread is amazing."

"I feel bad Kaylee's talents aren't being used to their fullest." Mom held up a plastic container. "She sent dessert too— strawberry, lemon, and mango macarons. And my personal favorite, her chocolate truffle cookies."

"Yum!" Beth took a drink of bottled lemonade. "I feel the same about Kaylee's baking. Sure, we reap the benefits, but I wish we could give her an avenue to showcase what she can do." She bit into a light, airy mango cookie filled with mango buttercream frosting and was transported to heaven.

"Kaylee checked into renting a building and the costs to start up her own business. Liam didn't have much in life insurance. The plan was to increase it as soon as Kaylee got pregnant. Even using money received from the accident claim, she couldn't get a loan big enough to cover the costs. The loan officer said it was too much of a risk. He told her new businesses need to plan for potential losses in the first one to two years, and around 25 percent of them fail in the first year and shut down."

"We'll think of something." Beth would find a solution. Not only because she sincerely cared about her sister-in-law but also because she'd made a promise to Liam.

"Another surprise." Mom reached down next to her for a large bag with handles and pulled out a small pot with pink miniature roses. "From Colton."

"That sweet boy." She'd missed her appointment with the nine-year-old yesterday because of her hospital stay and was worried she'd disappointed him. Autistic children often depended on routine and structure.

"He insisted that he and his mother get flowers for you. Colton wanted to deliver them himself, but his mother told him you needed rest, and I assured him that I'd bring them to you personally."

Beth took the pot of roses from her mother and fingered the delicate blooms. "I'm truly touched."

"People love you, honey." Her mom's grin faded as she tucked the rest of her sandwich into a plastic bag.

"What's wrong, Mom?"

"I—I don't know quite how to say this." She frowned, placed her leftovers in the small cooler she'd brought, and folded her hands in her lap. "I worry about you. You care so much—maybe too much—about your family, friends, and this community. Look at what happened the other night. You've been running yourself ragged. Exhaustion caused you to faint and end up in the hospital."

Beth rubbed her tired eyes. "I know, Mom. I need to slow down for a little while." She'd have to remind herself that she'd lose the ability to help anyone if she truly got sick.

"It's more than pumping the brakes temporarily." Mom folded the floral bag and held it against her chest. "As much as you want to, it's impossible for you to take care of everyone. It's not your responsibility. Can you accept that?"

"I'll try." Beth held her sandwich close to her mouth but

didn't bite. "But maybe I'm not the only one who should receive one of your lectures."

"Hon, I didn't mean to—"

"I was kidding about the lecture. I know you mean well, and you're right." Beth lowered her hand. "After you brought me home this morning, I talked to Agatha. Tyler was ambushed last night by the stepdad of one of the prisoners he's been trying to help."

Her mom's jaw dropped. "What?"

Beth filled her in on everything Agatha had shared. "Mom, he's fine and resting, but Tyler is lucky to be alive. That guy could have knifed him, and the police might not have gotten there in time." Beth's eyes burned from pools gathering. The thought that Ty could have been left lying alone in the dark, bleeding until all life escaped him, made her ache inside.

"But he didn't die. He's alive and well, thank the Lord." Mom pointed to the sky. "Angels were fighting by his side."

The screen door to Agatha's house slammed shut, and Ty made his way down the steps and toward them, his gait slower than normal. At seeing him, the reality of what could have happened hit even harder, and Beth's brimming tears threatened to spill onto her face.

"I'll see Agatha for a moment before I head back to work and let you have time alone with Ty." Mom moved the container filled with cookies closer to Beth and gave her an all-knowing smile. Of course . . . her mother must have figured out that Beth was falling for him.

On her way to see Agatha, Mom stopped and greeted Ty, and they spoke quietly for a moment. She gave him a quick hug, then went on her way.

Beth took that time to wipe her face, take a deep breath,

and pull herself together.

"We need to stop meeting like this," Ty said, narrowing his eyes.

She cocked her head and smiled. "That would mean you never coming around here, because this is a magical spot, and I'm not giving it up for anyone." Was it better to tease and try to take his mind off the fact that Luke could have killed him? Or should she let Ty know his experience scared her? Admit she still wanted to cry with relief that he was okay?

"Stubborn woman, aren't you?"

"I am."

Ty winced as he sat on the bench. "Your mom said you might be willing to share." He grinned and gave a nod toward the container sitting next to Beth.

"Kaylee has done it again." Beth removed the lid and offered him the assortment.

He reached for a chocolate truffle cookie, ate half in one bite, then brushed crumbs from his mouth. What would it be like to kiss and taste those lips? She could wonder for eternity, but that possibility would remain in her imagination.

Their relationship could never move beyond friendship and mutual interest in serving those who needed a little help. Not if his plans to move to another state didn't change. Long distance relationships were difficult to maintain, and she didn't want to get hurt. But what if he decided to stay in Meriside?

"Agatha filled you in." Tyler chomped on the remaining chocolate treat.

"It must have been terrifying to be attacked like that." She laid her arm along the top of the bench and faced him. Agatha mentioned the beating he'd taken. But Beth wanted so much to touch him, and in some small way, comfort him. "I'd like to give you a hug, but I don't want to hurt you."

He chuckled quietly. "I'll heal, and the bruises will eventually fade, but the thrill at seeing Luke Hanson in cuffs won't." His demeanor grew serious. "Actually, I'd welcome a hug."

"Really?" She wanted nothing more right now.

"Yeah. Really." Ty's intense gaze confirmed the invitation. "I could use one." He winked, breaking the hold on her, and his smile held a hint of sadness. "Just don't squeeze tight." He pushed up from the bench slowly and stood.

They'd been so careful to keep professional boundaries, but they weren't at the prison now. They were in Agatha's beautiful garden alone and where the outside world couldn't interfere.

"I'll be careful." Beth rose to meet him. She wrapped her arms around him gently and laid her head on his chest. His heart thumped strong, and hers matched the rhythm.

They remained entwined together, not speaking, for several minutes.

"I've wanted to do this for a long time," he said, breaking their silence.

"You have?" She wasn't alone in her feelings? Warm relief rushed through her.

"I sure have." He squeezed just a little bit tighter.

Beth released her hold but didn't move away. She wanted—needed—to see his eyes.

"Ty, when I heard how Luke attacked you . . ." Uncontainable emotion bubbled to the surface, and Beth almost choked on her words.

"I know. Scary, huh? That's how I felt when you fainted and ended up in the hospital. It freaked me out." Ty stroked her cheek gently, sending shivers of longing through Beth. His eyes searched hers. "But I'm okay, and you're okay. Right? We're standing here, both strong and alive and ready to face whatever comes at us next."

"Right." She inhaled a deep breath.

Ty led her to sit, and they settled back against the bench, but he continued to hold her hand. "Our doctors are like-minded. Yours told you that you need to slow down, and mine advised that I take at least a day to rest. But I told my supervisor that I'd like to spend an hour at the prison this morning. I'd just gotten home when I saw you sitting out here with your mom."

"And to think I assumed you'd stay in bed all day." She shook her head and grinned. "I should have known better!"

They were both stubborn in that way. They didn't allow anything to deter them from what they believed needed to be done.

Ty massaged the back of her hand with his thumb. "I'm exhausted but still too amped up to sleep any more. Robin deserved to hear from me what happened last night and the reassurance that her brother is being taken care of. But my supervisor insisted that I come home after the visit and wait until Monday to return to work."

Beth covered his hand with her free one, sandwiching it between both of hers. "Robin must be so relieved that her stepdad is being charged."

"The attack, along with statements made by Robin and Marcus were enough to get a warrant to check the house. Luke was clever, but they found a large stash of illegal drugs." Ty closed his eyes for a moment, then opened them again.

"The guy was out of his mind last night." He pinched the

area above his nose and between his eyes briefly. "Luke must have followed me after I left the prison. The cops found empty beer bottles on the side of the house, so he must have been drinking the entire time he was waiting for an opportunity to jump me. And they found his car parked down at the bottom of the driveway with additional empty bottles tossed on the floor. He can expect a long prison sentence."

"And Marcus?" Where would his future lead? The poor boy had been through so much with his stepdad.

"He's been placed in emergency care." Ty slipped his hand from Beth's and put his arm around her shoulders. "Turns out, Agatha is licensed as a foster parent, and she's requested to have Marcus placed with her."

"I shouldn't be surprised, but I am." Beth missed the warmth and strength of Ty's hand, but his protective move felt comforting.

"And get this." Ty perked up and gave her an enthusiastic grin. "Marcus has some artistic talent. Robin showed me a few sketches that the kid had sent her, and he's good. What better mentor than Agatha?" Ty shook his head. "I was skeptical about her taking on parenting a boy who's been through what he has, but she's determined."

"Maybe they're what each other needs right now." *And maybe the same goes for you and me.*

"Maybe. I think I'd feel better if she wasn't going to be left on her own to handle what might come up. Marcus is twelve now, and before long, he'll be a teenager. I could help her out with him if . . ."

"If you were staying." The hard truth.

"Yeah."

What was that tone in his voice? Sadness? Regret? Why?

It had always been his plan to leave Meriside as soon as possible so he and Brandon could create their program for at-risk youth. She would never hold him back from following his dreams, but dare she hope that he might change his mind about Colorado and find his purpose here?

A year could bring a lot of change. Maybe he would fall in love with the community and see there were plenty of opportunities to help other kids like Marcus. And if those things didn't motivate him, could she be enough reason to stay?

"Look at both of us, on forced rest." Ty trailed his finger back and forth on her shoulder. "Two peas, eh?"

Beth ran a hand through her short dark hair. "After all that's happened in the past several days, maybe we do need to take a breath."

"As they say, easier said than done."

Twenty-Eight

"**W**elcome to the Hoh Rain Forest, the most carefully preserved rain forest in the northern hemisphere." Beth stretched her arms out to embrace the vast wooded area mentally and emotionally. A sanctuary from concrete, traffic, and stress.

Beth and Ty had taken a slower pace for close to a week after her hospital visit and his attack, but they both needed a little adventure before returning to work full-time.

He grabbed his backpack. "I've been eager to explore this area, so I'm glad you suggested coming."

"It's one of my favorite places in the Olympics." She locked the car. "Let's go. There's a large map of the trails at the visitor center. I have my favorites, but I'll let you decide which one we hike first."

Beth could have checked to see if lodging was available at the Kalaloch Lodge. She and Liam had a tradition of coming the night before and getting up first thing in the morning to hike several trails before they headed home at the end of the day. But it might have felt awkward for her to invite Tyler to do the same. And besides, some things were sacred, and those memories with her brother were precious.

So instead, she'd bribed Tyler with pancakes for breakfast if he'd get up early for the three-hour drive. She wanted to arrive before ten as the trails were popular with many regular hikers and tourists during the summer months.

"The two shorter trails, the Hall of Mosses and the Spruce Nature Trail, aren't strenuous." Beth pointed to the large map posted in front of them. "The other hikes will take us deeper into the wilderness."

"And your favorite?" He shifted his backpack.

"They're all special for various reasons, but the Hall of Mosses is a short, easy trail." She stepped away from the map to allow other visitors to look closer.

"I'm not opposed to hiking five miles or longer, but since we're both supposed to be taking it easy, let's start with that one."

Beth took a sip from her water bottle. "Don't play it safe on my account," she said, teasing. "I can handle it."

"Not at all. I'm not afraid for *you*. I'm worried about *me*. Agatha left a note."

"A note?"

"Yeah . . . and I'm terrified of the tongue-lashing we'll get if we arrive home dragging because we didn't listen to doctors' orders and overdid it."

Laughter burst from Beth. "All right then. Let's get started. The adventure begins." She led him to the trailhead. "A warning. I always carry a camera, and I stop often to take shots of anything and everything I find interesting."

"Wildlife?"

"There's a good chance we might come across some." She thought for a moment. "Roosevelt elk, black bears, and river otters have been spotted in the park during daylight. Bobcats and mountain lions are more active at night."

The trail was wide enough they could walk side by side,

and that made it easier to talk as they made their way deeper into the canopied forest. Curtains of moss hung from Sitka spruce and western hemlock towering over them.

Ty gazed up, seeming to take it all in. "This is incredible. Some of these trees must be over three hundred feet tall."

"It is amazing." Beth moved her camera lens until she had a close-up of a unique plant in focus. "The forest's ecosystem hasn't changed for thousands of years."

She took the shot and lowered the camera. "This place reminds me of illustrations in fantasy books. I'm always on the lookout for fairies or gnomes."

"I can understand that. The ground is thick with ferns." Ty studied the branches above them. "The trees are blanketed with moss. You'd think the branches would suffer from being covered heavily, but they seem healthy."

"Moss is an epiphyte, not a parasite. So, it's a plant that grows on other vegetation without harming it. Epiphytes get their moisture and nutrients from the air, rain, fog, and the debris that accumulates around them." Beth stopped walking and faced Tyler. "Sorry. I didn't mean for our outing to turn into a science field trip."

"No need to apologize at all. It's cool that you know this stuff. What else can you tell me?"

"Do you really want to know?" she asked with a hint of surprise. "Or are you just being nice?"

He placed his hand on his chest and feigned shock. "Me? Nice? Never!"

She gave him a gentle nudge.

"Ow!" Ty made an exaggerated jump back. "You trying to add more black and blue marks to my body?" He gave a nod toward a man and woman heading their way. "Do I need to ask for protection?"

They moved to the side of the path so the couple could go on ahead, greeting them as they passed by.

"You're pathetic," Beth teased after the other hikers were out of hearing range.

"I was wounded."

"Right . . ." She perched her hands on her hips and pursed her lips—her warning look. He was having way too much fun, but she enjoyed the banter, even if she wouldn't admit it. "Come on."

"I'm right there with you, and I *am* serious." He looked her in the eyes. "I'd like to learn more. Please."

She gave a left shoulder shrug. "Okay."

They took their time, stopping to take photos along the way. Beth shared bits of information on various forms of vegetation, careful not to overwhelm him with too many details. But Tyler seemed genuinely interested, and that touched her deeply. Beth had never spent time with a guy who cared even a smidgen about what fascinated her.

"These giant trees provide shade to the hundreds of mosses and ferns below. When a tree falls, the area now open to the sky provides not only sunlight, but also nutrition and new life to whatever grows on its fallen trunk."

"The circle of life."

"That's right." She took hold of a branch and placed her palm on the center of a huge leaf, twice the size of her hand. "Big-leaf maple."

He examined the foliage. "The name fits."

Beth spotted a wooden bench set back a few feet from the trail, out of the way, but not so far as to intrude upon the forest. "Would you mind if we sat for a while? I'd like to take a moment to soak in what's around us."

"Sure." Ty slipped off his pack and settled in next to her.

She leaned back and contemplated the covering overhead. Sunlight filtered through the delicate web created by moss draped over branches like a protective shawl. Beth inhaled the mulchy aroma rising from the forest floor.

Along the way, she'd picked up the familiar scent of cedar, the subtle hint of citrus from the western hemlock, and the fragrant Douglas fir. Birds shared their songs, and several insects buzzed as they zipped through the air.

Tyler took a long drink from his water bottle. "There hasn't been a drop of rain all day."

Beth chuckled. "You're assuming because it's a rain forest . . ."

"Bad assumption, huh?" He laughed at himself.

"I can understand why you'd expect at least a shower. But it's the middle of July, and the entire West Coast has experienced a hot, dry summer." Beth brushed a small black beetle from her arm. "This forest can get as much as fourteen feet of rain per year."

"Feet?"

"You heard right."

He whistled. "Wow. Maybe it was a good thing we didn't come during the rainy season."

"Oh, you've got that wrong." Special memories of her brother's laughter as they dodged water cascading off the forest vegetation filled her mind. "That's the best time to come. It's always thrilling to watch the Coho salmon in the middle of a spawning run."

She smiled. "Liam and I used to put on our rain gear and hike the trails every winter and spring, sometimes during a downpour. Showers and fog make the forest even more magical."

"I wish I could have met your brother. He must have been a great guy."

Beth released a sigh, but this one wasn't filled with pain. Instead, only appreciation for having Liam in her life. "He was the best."

"You've interned at the penitentiary for two and a half months. Only a few weeks to go before you're done."

"It's gone quickly and better than I expected." After wondering if she'd ever get a chance to pursue setting up her own business as a horticultural therapist, that possibility was now ahead. Her dream becoming a reality felt both exciting and surreal.

"And with Abbey? Has it been more difficult or easier than what you thought?"

"A lot of time has passed since the accident—and it *was* an accident." Beth moistened her lips. "But grief has a way of sneaking up on you. Sometimes it comes out sideways as anger, and other times . . . other times, the weeping is uncontrollable."

She rubbed the top of the bench, then clutched it. "But I don't think my anger is directed at Abbey anymore. It's focused on the situation. The *entire* situation, starting with what influenced Abbey to drink and drive." Beth looked into Tyler's eyes and drank in his understanding.

"Abbey and I have kept some distance these past months, but we've also shared some interaction. That's become easier as I've watched her become a role model for the other inmates." An image of Abbey smiling and chatting with prisoners in the gardens came to Beth. "She's been kind, empathetic, even a teacher. The women are drawn to her."

"I've seen changes in her too. Your willingness to work

beside her has made an impact." His voice grew tender. "You have no idea of the differences you've made for Abbey and the other inmates."

Ty believing in Beth and her ability to affect lives, even in small ways, touched her deeply. She attempted to swallow the lump in her throat, and a sheen of moisture covered her eyes, blurring her vision. "Thank you," she whispered. "'Let us not become weary in doing good, for at the proper time we will reap a harvest if we do not give up.'"

"Galatians 6:9."

"You remembered." For some reason, that pleased her. "Those words have helped me deal with my feelings about Abbey as well as my interactions with the other women at the prison." Beth wanted to explain. Of all people, Ty would understand, even if she wasn't eloquent.

"Every time I see a plant poking its way through a crack in a brick wall or between several rocks and it manages to bloom, I'm reminded of how God works. It only takes a smidgen of dirt and water for a seed to find a home and grow into something beautiful. I have to believe it's the same for one's heart."

"I like that image." Ty scratched his chin. "I can see how that fits in with what you're doing at the prison."

"I hope I've planted seeds there, but at the same time, I've been careful to not push my beliefs on anyone."

He nodded. "Most people don't like to be told what to believe, or judged if they have an opposing opinion."

"But I also don't want to be shy about talking about my faith." Beth raised her face toward the sky for a moment and absorbed the sun's rays filtering through the lacy veil covering the branches above them. "It can be tricky, finding that balance. Perhaps even more so in a prison setting where I need to keep

262 | DAWN KINZER

silent about my beliefs unless asked."

"In our professional positions, proselytizing is considered crossing boundaries, but I've found in my own life that actions speak louder than words," he said thoughtfully. That was something they agreed on. She'd always felt the same way. She lowered her gaze and fixed it on Ty's handsome, kind face. In this place and moment, Beth felt so close to him and understood. "Right! I think we can show the women at the prison who God is—his character—through relationship and treating them with patience and grace."

"I see that happening already, Beth." Ty shifted and relaxed against the back of the bench. "You know, not all prisons are constructed from physical bars."

"Then what?"

"People can be imprisoned emotionally, mentally, and spiritually. Sometimes by their own choosing. Other times because no matter how hard they try, they can't find the key that will release them."

These past months, Beth had witnessed how being restricted from some things and separated from others impacted human beings. "And when you add prison bars to that mix, any kind of freedom must sometimes feel out of reach—impossible, even."

"That's where we come in. What we do offers some hope." Ty reached over, grasped her hand, and didn't let go. "You're amazing." His bluish-green eyes were mesmerizing.

"I've never met anyone like you, Beth. You care deeply for people." He leaned in closer, and her heart quickened, anticipating his lips brushing against hers, but quiet chattering from people approaching from a distance broke the intimate connection. He straightened, and the kiss never came.

Crushed by his abrupt reaction, she slid a few inches down the bench. Was there more to his backing off than the other hikers? "There are those who think I care too much," she said softly.

He tilted his head and frowned as though questioning that possibility.

"My mom." Now she'd done it. Beth had opened the door, so he deserved an explanation. "She's been encouraging me to take a breath and step back. I think my time in the hospital brought her concerns to the forefront."

"Once a parent, always a parent, so says mine."

"Mine too." Beth smiled, still relishing the touch of his hand enveloping hers.

A gray-haired couple strolled down the path toward them. The lean man, wearing glasses and dressed in tan shorts and a light blue polo shirt, made gestures with both hands, as though telling his companion a wild story. They caught sight of Beth and Tyler, stopped briefly and talked, then proceeded until they reached them.

"Good morning, young people!" The gentleman's enthusiastic tone and sincere smile elicited grins from Ty and Beth. "Enjoying the trail?"

"We are!" Ty released her hand, and slid forward on the bench, as if waiting to hear what the hiker would say next. "I've never seen anything like this in person. And my friend here tells me it's even more spectacular during the rainy season."

"It is. I encourage you to return." The older man put his arm around the woman standing next to him dressed in beige capris and a pink short-sleeved shirt. Striking white hair framed the delicate face showing few wrinkles. Her bright blue eyes sparkled. "I'm Carl Bromstad, and this is my wife,

Helen."

"Nice to meet you." Beth stood, and Tyler followed her lead. "I'm Beth and this is Tyler. Were you hoping to rest here? We'd be happy to give you the bench and continue with our hike."

"Oh, no, dear." Helen put her arm through her husband's. "We're not tired. But we *are* hoping you might do us a favor."

Ty and Beth exchanged glances. He seemed game, so she shrugged and returned her attention to their fellow hikers.

"Five years ago, I asked Helen to marry me while sitting on this very bench." Carl pulled out a cell phone. "There's a pretty decent camera in this thing, and I'd like to get a photo of us together, but I'm not so good at taking selfies."

"I'd be honored to take your picture." Beth held out her hand and took the phone.

"Thanks so much." Helen sat on the bench and patted the space next to her. "Come on, dear."

While the couple got settled, Beth got a feel for the camera's settings and filters. The natural lighting in that spot was already perfect. She took numerous shots—some portraits which softened the background, which she preferred, but also a few from farther away to include the incredible surroundings. Carl and Helen were delighted with the results.

"Could we do the same for you?" Carl asked. "I'm not a pro, but I'll give it my best try."

Beth turned to Tyler to gauge his reaction.

"Sure!" He whipped out his cell phone before Beth had a chance to refuse, which she wouldn't have.

Several clicks later, the Bromstads were on their way, and Tyler had texted the photos to Beth. The pics had turned out remarkably well—something to help them remember the day and each other.

"That was fun—and interesting. They're nice people." He lounged on the bench.

"I hope you don't plan on staying here indefinitely." Beth laughed. "You know there's a lot more to explore."

"I know. But we didn't get a chance to finish our conversation." Ty raised his eyebrows.

"We didn't, did we?" Beth had been so distracted by the Bromstads, she'd forgotten. It was sweet that he remembered.

"We were talking about your mom and how she's worried about you. Are her feelings valid?"

"Maybe—probably." Beth paused. Could she be vulnerable with Ty and tell all? "Mom is convinced that I take on too much responsibility for other people's success and happiness. She believes I carry burdens that don't belong to me, and she feels that drive has become detrimental to my emotional and physical health."

"I don't think caring less is the answer."

"Good." He understood that she couldn't change her DNA and stop being the person God created.

"But maybe it's not up to you—or me—to do it alone." He paused. "We won't be as effective if we don't take time out for ourselves. We can't run on empty. And we can't do it all and be all things to all people."

Tyler moved closer to Beth and clasped her hand between his. "Scripture says if we're feeling weary and burdened, we should hand the weight over to God. He doesn't want us to carry everything on our own shoulders."

"And no better place to chat with him than in the middle of his creation." She always felt closer to her heavenly Father in the forest where she was no longer distracted by her long to-do list.

"Nothing stopping us," he said matter-of-factly.

They bowed their heads and prayed silently, and Beth asked for wisdom in knowing how to serve in a loving and healthy way.

She raised her head, slipped her hand from his, and studied her surroundings, inspired. "Ty, so many people hunger for peace and a refuge where they can find rest and community."

"And it's not always easy to find," he said quietly.

"Well . . . I may have come up with a solution that will solve that challenge and several others."

Twenty-Nine

B eth delivered the potato salad, a family favorite, to the picnic table in the backyard of her mother's home. Sunday's temperature was still comfortable for July and perfect for an evening meal outdoors. The light breeze carried floral scents from the gardens, and she stood still for a moment with her eyes closed, inhaling the fragrance.

She slipped her cell from the back pocket of her jean shorts and gazed at her favorite photo with Ty—for the hundredth time. For not being a pro, Carl Bromstad had captured a lovely image yesterday.

"Are you going to just stand there, fixated on your phone, and make us carry everything else out? Or are you going to help?" Harmony asked in a teasing tone, setting a small platter filled with cold ham and turkey slices next to a basket holding Kaylee's fresh whole wheat buns.

"What are you staring at, anyway?" Harmony peeked at the phone screen. "Nice pic! Easy to tell that you two enjoyed your time together."

"Oh, really?" Beth's face heated, and it wasn't from the sun's warmth.

Harmony chuckled, and her eyebrows knit together as though it was ridiculous to assume anything else. "Oh, come on! Admit it." She pointed to the photo. "You're into the guy, and he's obviously crazy about you. If you two beamed any brighter, you'd outshine the sun."

Beth made a funny face at her sister. "Man, a girl can't catch a break around here."

"You know," Harmony said, her tone becoming serious, "he texted me constantly while you were in the hospital."

"He did? I didn't know."

"Ty was really worried about you." Harmony gave a nod toward the picture. "The man cares for you."

Beth glanced over her shoulder. No one in earshot. "We almost kissed. It *felt* like he wanted to, but . . ." Oh, good grief. She sounded like a teenager—no, a tweenager.

Harmony perked up. "Where? When? What happened?"

"Yesterday on the trail. We were interrupted by a sweet, elderly couple. They wanted their photo taken, and then they offered to take ours." Beth held up her cell, indicating that's how she got the pic in the first place.

"Bummer! I mean, nice to have a memento of the day, but sad that the kiss didn't happen."

"I'm not so sure." Beth shrugged. "I mean, in the moment I was disappointed." *More* than disappointed. But what good would it do to dwell on what could have happened? "Maybe it was for the best."

Harmony cocked her head. "You don't really believe that."

"Okay, I admit that I have strong feelings for Ty." Beth stared at the photo again as though another look would provide answers to her dilemma. "But what if I'm setting myself up for hurt? His plans don't include Meriside."

"Plans can change. Ask him," Harmony said, as though she'd offered a simple solution. "He's got a good job, and his aunt is here."

"There's more to it. I can't be the reason for Ty giving up on his vision. He could have regrets later. And I don't want to stand in the way of what God wants for him. If—*when*—Ty and Brandon create their program, they'll have the potential to help a lot of kids."

"But what if you're supposed to be a part of that?" Harmony sucked in her bottom lip, and her eyebrows rose. "What if in God's view, there was purpose in you and Ty meeting and becoming involved in each other's lives?"

"I suppose that's possible." Beth dropped onto the bench attached to the picnic table. "And if it is, that purpose will have to be made undeniably clear."

"Because . . .?" Harmony drew out the word.

"Because . . ." Beth said, imitating her sister's tone. She smiled. "I believe I've been given a new direction for our family."

Harmony jolted. "What does that mean?"

"I'll spill when you, Mom, Kaylee, and I can all sit down together. But before I share anything, I want to give you the same consideration we're trying to give Kaylee."

"I don't understand." Harmony sat next to her and leaned back against the table.

Beth hesitated, then drew a deep breath. "When I was about eight years old, Mom got upset and yelled at me. I didn't understand why. I hadn't done anything wrong. But she was so angry, I ran out of the house sobbing and into the garage where Dad was tinkering on our car."

"That doesn't sound like Mom."

"I learned later that I wasn't the cause of her blowup, but she'd taken out her hurt and frustration on me. She apologized that night." Beth moistened her lips. "Anyway, Dad stopped what he was doing, wiped his hands, and set me on a stool. I told him what had happened, and he comforted me."

"That was Dad."

"Yeah." Beth smiled. "The point of the story is, that was the first time I understood what it felt like to be seen and heard. I learned how important it is to take time to listen." She reached over and placed her hand on her sister's. "I want you to feel seen and heard, Sis."

Harmony squinted. "I do."

"Good. But I need to ask. Do you ever feel like you're missing out on anything because of being so devoted to the family and the business?"

"So, *that's* what you were leading up to." Harmony's body relaxed, and she shot Beth a smile. "No, not at all. I love my job and the people I work with, including my family."

She crossed one leg over the other. "My friends are a bit scattered, but we make time for each other. It's only an hour by ferry to the Seattle waterfront, so it's easy to meet friends on that side of the Sound. And other times, they come over here to hike and kayak. I'm happy, Beth. *Really.* You don't need to worry about me."

"I just wanted to be sure." Her sister's words relieved Beth. Now she could move forward with confidence that her proposal for more upheaval wouldn't hold Harmony back from pursuing anything her heart desired.

A few more trips from the kitchen and they had everything in place for the meal. Beth, Mom, Harmony, and Kaylee all sat at the table, bowed their heads, and thanked the Lord for their blessings.

Conversations moved from what Kaylee was going to bake next to the challenges Beth had been encountering with the internship. Then Mom wanted to cover floral arrangements ordered for upcoming weddings.

Beth savored her bite of decadent chocolate and salted caramel cheesecake with a crunchy praline topping. Another Kaylee creation. She licked her lips and set her fork down. They were together, relaxed, and in a good mood. Now might be the perfect time to approach them with her concept. *Help me out here, Lord.*

"I have an idea I'd like to run by you." Beth glanced around the table. All eyes were on her. "I know that Your Secret Garden has been a wonderful place. It's served our family and the community well for many years. It's been a second home for us."

She reached for her glass and held it more for security than to quench her thirst. "But times have changed, and the business is struggling. I think we should adapt and modify."

Mom's chin tilted up, and her arms crossed over her chest. "So . . . what do you have in mind?"

Impressions of what could be created had come in waves over the last twenty-four hours, and Beth's enthusiasm had grown. "I'd like us to consider a renovation—a makeover—that would suit our needs and passions better."

"If we're struggling financially now, how could we possibly pull that off?" Harmony's eyebrows knit together. "And I don't understand how rearranging what we have now will help."

"What's the harm in hearing her out?" Kaylee asked in a meek voice.

"You have something more in mind than just sprucing things up, don't you?" Mom folded her hands on the table. "We're listening."

"Why should we follow the norm?" Beth asked with

confidence. "What if we created a small retreat area as part of our business? Kaylee could use part of the space for her café or tea shop, and I could use an area for horticultural therapy where individuals or groups could gather to work on projects."

Harmony frowned. "I don't want to be a spoilsport, but if I want to relax and have a little time out, I just head over to the waterfront or drive up into the mountains. We have access to so many beautiful spots in our area within a short distance."

"But that's *you*. Not everyone enjoys hiking or has the time. Others may not have the ability to tackle the trails." How could Beth get them to understand?

"I'm thinking about people who juggle responsibilities to jobs and families," she continued, "as well as those who have physical limitations. Wouldn't they love a peaceful place where they could escape for even an hour to relax and think? Connect with a friend in a pretty atmosphere where music wasn't blaring?" Beth's mind reeled with possibilities. "And there could be so many fun holiday projects we could help create with their kids without them worrying about the mess in their own homes."

Mom sighed. "It's a lovely concept, but with no extra funds to invest and no room to expand . . ."

"I know it sounds crazy." But still wonderful.

"Not crazy, just not realistic," Harmony said, now sounding empathetic to her sister's desire to try something new.

Beth sipped her water, then set the glass down. "Mom, you've always been passionate about floral arrangements and growing flowers." Maybe her proposal would make more sense if they were reminded of their reality. "The nursery part of our business—vegetable starts, shrubs, trees, and the rest were Dad's and Liam's responsibilities. Kaylee has no interest in helping someone pick out the right kind of mulch, and if I pursue my own career, I won't have time to manage that area alone."

Mom nodded. "I know, hon."

"I'm not asking to make drastic overhauls overnight." Inspiration flowed, as though God had turned on the faucet to possibilities that Beth had been too exhausted or distracted before to see. "We should take some time to work on our strategy. Lay down a foundation before we try to build something that will work for everyone. It might take a year to carry out a plan."

"That sounds reasonable." Harmony smiled. "And practical."

Beth felt encouraged. Her sister was coming around. "We're moving into summer now. What if we intentionally phase out the nursery and garden center by spring of next year? Maybe we should keep one greenhouse. I propose we take down the structure that houses the garden center and prepare to add Kaylee's café and tearoom in that space."

Kaylee's eyes lit up. "Could we really do that?"

"I could expand our current gift shop and incorporate items like fancy teacups and teas that would normally be expected in a shop connected to a tearoom." Harmony grinned and raised her upturned palms. "It could be a win-win. Every part of the business could be tastefully connected while still being separated."

They were catching on. Beth's chest felt pounds lighter, and her breathing came easier. "Your Secret Garden could become just that. A sanctuary where beautiful gardens surround the café and people could enjoy the atmosphere whether they spend time inside or out."

Excitement, like a shaken carbonated drink, fizzed within

Beth. "Mom, you could sell freshly picked flowers from the gardens, and I could use the space for therapy sessions. It would bring people in to see the gift shop and what we have to offer in terms of houseplants. Our quality is so much better than those offered by the chain store."

"You're right." Mom's shoulders eased. "People have other options to get what we offer in the garden center. Our regular customers would understand and adjust if we discontinued selling those items, and Meriside doesn't have anything like what you're suggesting."

"During fall and winter months, I could offer classes on making wreaths and dried arrangements. And I'd love to teach students how to create paper out of flower petals." Beth reached over and squeezed her mother's hand. "Mom, I have so many ideas. We could make special occasion seed-paper cards. They're more than greetings. Once the recipient plants the homemade paper with embedded seeds, the paper degrades, and the seeds germinate and grow plants like wildflowers. That's one project I have in mind for the women at the prison."

Kaylee cleared her throat. "I still have money saved from the insurance settlement." Her smile seemed genuine, but her eyes revealed remaining grief. "It's been five years since I graduated with a business degree. I never used what I learned because there wasn't a need."

"I know we didn't give you a chance with the family business, Kaylee, and that was a mistake," Mom said, regret filling her voice.

"That wasn't all your fault. I didn't ask." Kaylee wound strands of long hair around her finger. "But now that I know what direction I'd like to go, I should take some refresher courses and additional classes online pertaining to running a restaurant."

"That's wonderful!" Harmony said. "Liam would be proud of you."

Kaylee's smile widened at hearing Harmony's encouragement. "I'd also like to commit another part of the money toward the renovations, if we agree to move ahead on Beth's proposal."

Harmony raised her hand. "I'm in!"

"Okay." Mom nodded, then took a moment to look each one of them in the eyes. "I suggest we all give this some serious thought and make a list of what we need to research. We don't want to dive in headfirst without knowing what we're plunging into."

It was one thing to fantasize about potential success and another to make that dream a reality. But Mom, Harmony, and Kaylee were all onboard to do their part, and their individual gifts would be huge assets. Each would contribute their time and talents, and they'd work as a team.

Beth had opened her family up to exploring a new adventure, and the prospects excited her. They also terrified her. Would it be possible to finally let go and no longer feel responsible for her family's well-being?

Thirty

"**M**arcus still asleep?" Tyler was an early riser, and Agatha was a night owl, so he was usually the first one up, but since the boy's arrival four days ago, Tyler had been coming in second. "He's never slept past six."

"The poor kid had nightmares about Luke crawling through the window and carrying him off. He didn't get much rest, so I'm glad he's still conked out." Agatha placed scrambled eggs with onions, green pepper, and cheese in front of Ty. Two pieces of buttered whole wheat toast flanked the protein, and she set a jar of blackberry jam and a small ceramic pot filled with honey within his reach.

"He woke you?" Ty drizzled honey over one piece of toast, took a bite, then followed it with a gulp of strong, dark coffee.

"That's why I'm dragging a bit this morning. I sat with him until he dozed off." Agatha poured hazelnut creamer into her drink, inhaled the steam, and sipped. "It was kind of you to give up your room and sleep on the pull-out couch in the den."

"No problem." Ty set his cup down. "The plan is for Marcus to stay long-term, so it's only right that he settles in and has his own space. My house is done, except for some custom work, so I'll move my things out there today. I can sleep on a cot until the bedroom furniture I ordered is delivered."

"The social worker is coming by this morning to see

Marcus. She won't be visiting as often after today, but I understand wanting to make sure he's situated and comfortable." Concern filled Agatha's eyes, and she rubbed her hands together.

"You worried about the visit?"

"A little. After last night . . ."

"Auntie, it will be fine." Ty smiled, hoping to reassure her. "It's not unusual for kids who have experienced trauma to have nightmares and worse."

"I know. It's just—it's just that I want the best for him, and I want him to feel safe and secure here."

"From what I've witnessed these past few days, he does. Marcus couldn't have been placed in a better home."

"For now, it's considered temporary, but I hope he can find a permanent refuge here." Agatha's lips twitched into a hint of a smile. "I'm still hanging on to the possibility of bringing Robin into the fold when the time comes for her release. It wouldn't take much to move some things I've stored down here to the attic and clear out the side room for her. That space, with all the natural light that comes through the windows, would make a lovely bedroom."

"That would be extremely kind of you, but let's see how things go with her brother first."

"It was a blessing that after he confessed to dealing drugs and explained how Luke forced him, he was given leniency." Agatha picked up her fork and stirred the eggs on her plate. "It's also fortunate that he lived in Larksville and not in Meriside. Marcus can get a fresh start at the school here."

"Yeah, a new beginning." Ty bit into his toast and returned the remaining piece to his plate. He rubbed his forehead, then propped his elbow on the table and laid his head on his fist.

"Something else worrying you?"

He looked up and stared into his aunt's compassionate eyes. "I don't know how Beth will take my sudden change of plans."

"You got past keeping secrets from each other, and I know you care deeply about her." Agatha cupped her hands around the mug sitting on the table and massaged the side with one thumb. "She deserves to hear about it from you—not someone else."

"You're right." Ty drained his mug and stood. "This is her Saturday off from working at Your Secret Garden. She has one more week at the prison to complete her internship, but yesterday's meeting with Lisa must have gone well because Beth has an update to share." He assumed she had received a glowing report concerning her work, but he was still anxious to hear whatever there was to tell.

"She also mentioned wanting my input on some project, and I think it may have something to do with a brainstorm she had while at the rain forest. But she wasn't ready to divulge anything then." He carried his empty dishes to the sink, rinsed them, and placed them in the dishwasher. "I'm taking her out to lunch so we can talk."

"Doors may be opening for you both."

"It sounds that way." Would Beth be upset by his news? They'd grown close since the day he'd arrived and found her in Agatha's garden. More than close—he loved her and couldn't imagine leaving her behind.

Did she love *him*? Enough to uproot her entire life and put their relationship ahead of her family's needs? He prayed she'd have the courage to take a risk and let him prove they could have a great life together.

He and Beth had a lot to discuss, and there were questions that needed to be answered.

"I can imagine Brandon is pumped up."

"Not as much as you'd think, which is a little confusing."

"You're *confused*?" Agatha gave him the look that said she didn't believe him. "Maybe he's not convinced this life-changing decision is the best one for you."

"It's the opportunity we've both been hoping for since I got out of prison."

"You're sure it's the *right* one?" Agatha asked, her eyes locking on his.

Ty and Beth strolled Meriside's waterfront toward the restaurant. The sun's rays sparkled on the water like white glitter under a bright light, and the salty breeze coming off the Sound cooled the hot late July temperature. The Olympics rose in the distance, their white peaks stark against the clear blue sky.

"The mountains are brilliant today." Beth pulled out her phone and held it up. "Selfie to celebrate my internship coming to an end?"

"Sure, let's take one." He wouldn't need a photo to remember her, but it would be nice to add this one to the shot taken in the rain forest. Tyler's heart squeezed. He could lose her. It was a real possibility once he explained his job change and timeline. Agatha had challenged his decision. Was he doing the right thing?

Beth propped her sunglasses on her head. Then she stood next to Ty and turned her cell camera toward them. "Okay, you'll need to move in closer if we want to include the mountains in the background."

He drew behind her, put his arm around her waist, and leaned in. Her soft hair brushed against his face, and he inhaled the citrus scent left from her shampoo. He'd tuck this moment away.

"Smile and say *best day ever!*" They grinned, she clicked, and another moment in their relationship was documented— at least until she decided to delete the photo. And she might once she heard his plans had suddenly shifted.

"Oh, I love this one!" She held up her phone in front of him. "It's perfect."

Ty had yearned to kiss her in the forest the other day but feared she might believe he was leading her on. He never wanted to do anything that would hurt her. Now he viewed their beaming faces on the screen. They looked good together— happy. "Would you send that to me?"

If she ever dumped this image, he'd at least have a copy for himself.

Thirty-One

"The Seafood Shack makes the best crab rolls in the area." Beth took another bite and savored the sandwich made with fresh crabmeat tossed with mayo, lemon, celery, chives, and seasonings. The dressing on her Caesar salad was applied lightly enough to add flavor without drenching the crisp lettuce.

"No argument from me on that claim. The fries are pretty great too." Ty moved his plate in her direction. He'd eaten half the pile, but a large amount remained. "Help yourself."

"Thanks. I'll try a few." Beth bit into a crunchy piece, salty but not overbearing, and not greasy like some could get. "Good," she said as she wiped her hands on a napkin. She had several things she wanted to discuss with Ty, but where to start? A job possibility or her ideas for renovating Your Secret Garden?

"Hey, you've been keeping me in suspense long enough. You know—your good news?" Ty bit into his sandwich and wiped his mouth with a paper napkin.

She'd start by sharing the recent development at the prison. "Lisa pulled me into her office yesterday and told me that if I want to stay on, she'll do everything in her power to make a full-time paid position available."

"That proves how much you've impressed her." Ty reached

across the table, and grasping Beth's hand, wove his fingers between hers. "I'm proud of you."

"Thank you." Warmth flowed from his touch up through her arm and into her chest, where her heart captured his affection. "It would change the course I've been pursuing, so it doesn't feel like the right path for me, but I promised Lisa that I would give it serious consideration. Regardless, her offer has given me more confidence in my ability to step into new and uncomfortable situations."

"That's worth a lot." Ty's fingers slipped from hers. "I'm happy for you." His shoulders dropped, and his eyes grew serious. Just a second ago, he seemed relaxed and having a good time.

"What's going on? Something is bothering you."

He leaned back against the booth. "I asked you this before, but I need to bring it up again."

"Okay." Beth took another sip of her diet cola. His tone made her nervous. "The question?"

"Would you consider leaving Meriside?" He shook his head. "Not leaving *forever*. I mean, would you consider living anywhere else?"

Beth searched his eyes for answers as to why he asked such a bizarre question, and she found concern, fear, doubt, and desire. Her heart beat triple-time. "You know I can't move from here, right? My family needs me, more than ever."

"Because the business is struggling."

"Yes. And last Sunday, I—*we*—decided to make some changes concerning Your Secret Garden. I've wanted to get your input on some things related to construction, but we've both been so busy with work this past week, and then Marcus moved in . . ." How many times had Beth picked up the phone to call Ty or had headed in his direction only to be interrupted by someone else's needs?

"I agree. It's been crazy, and I've been focused on helping Marcus feel at home with Agatha." Ty leaned forward. "But I have time to listen now. So, please. Fill me in on your plans."

Beth believed in the vision, yet she desperately wanted his understanding and support. "We're not looking at making small modifications. More like major transformations. I can't ask Mom, my sister, and Kaylee to handle the huge undertaking by themselves. I'm the one pushing for a new direction, and I can't walk away from promises made to them."

Ty listened, his focus on her never wavering, and Beth explained closing the garden center and opening an indoor and outdoor tea garden space where people could relax and reflect. Another similar venue would allow small groups to gather for meetings or celebrations, and they'd also offer classes on gardening, floral design, nature crafts, and therapeutic activities.

"What do you think?" Why was she holding her breath? Beth exhaled slowly.

He on the other hand, took a deep breath. "Ah . . ." Ty cupped his chin in his hand and paused as if contemplating what to say next. He leaned forward with hands folded on the table. "It sounds amazing, Beth. *Really*, it does. But it's also an enormous undertaking. Are you sure you can handle what it will take to pull it off?"

How could he say that? After all she'd done to prove herself, he didn't trust her ability to make the project successful? Beth wasn't naïve. She knew professional help would be needed. Maybe she was wrong in thinking she could depend on him for some guidance. "Why are you doubting me and my family?"

"It's not that I'm questioning the concept, but didn't you

land in the hospital because you took on too much?" He reached across the table for her hand again, but this time she pulled back. "What happened to finding more balance instead of running yourself ragged?"

"I don't intend on doing it all on my own," she said quietly, not wanting to draw attention from other diners. "We'll work together on this, and we're aware that the entire product won't be completed overnight. It may take a year or more."

"It's good to hear that you don't have unrealistic expectations. Maybe take small steps, find good contractors and designers, and see what's manageable."

Really? Ty was talking to her as if she didn't know any-thing—and he didn't know *her.* And he was acting like they hadn't already worked together on a renovation—*his reno*—and that stung. It was a smaller project, but what she accom-plished there should have demonstrated that she wasn't clueless.

"And you?" She swallowed her pride and forced herself to look in his eyes. "Since you seem invested in how we forge ahead, are you willing to share your renovation knowledge with us? That is, if we need another opinion?"

Ty glanced to the side as if to delay his answer for even a moment. Then he returned his gaze and focused on her. "I won't be here," he whispered just loud enough for her to hear. "For any of it."

His words sucked the air from her lungs, and Beth blinked. What happened to a year or more? "When are you leaving?" she asked, her former irritation replaced by sadness and loss.

"Soon." Ty removed the straw from his empty glass and bent it between his fingers. There was a suppressed excitement about him in the way his body shifted in his seat, and his eyes lit up like a lighthouse on a dark evening. "I got a call three days ago offering me the job as the director of social services at the penitentiary in Colorado, and I accepted."

Her chest ached. It didn't matter that no promises had been made or declarations of love expressed. She wasn't prepared to watch him walk out of her life.

"I told Max right away but asked him to keep it quiet for a few days until details were confirmed." Ty crushed the straw held in his hand. "I didn't want rumors to spread at the prison here."

It was understandable his supervisor would be one of the first to know, but why had he waited three days to tell *her*? Had Beth been foolish to believe they were close, and she meant something special to him? "I thought that position wasn't going to open for at least a year."

"The man who held it was going to retire then, but he had a stroke, and there was a need to fill the role immediately. Because two other people were also considered, it took several video conference calls before I was offered the job." Ty paused and took a breath. "I'm expected to report in ten days, so I've given my notice at the prison here, but I'll be around long enough to see you finish your internship."

"And the house?" Beth's eyes stung from the tears gathering, and her throat felt raw. "You just finished the renovations."

"Aside from Brandon's special projects, and those will be completed soon."

All the love and work he'd put into the home and grounds, and now he wouldn't get the chance to enjoy the fruits of his labor.

He dropped the mutilated straw on his plate. "I'll have to sell the place—or rent it out." Ty seemed to hesitate. "Would you be interested? You've left your mark on the property too, and it would make me feel good to know it was being loved."

"No, Ty." Even if she could afford it, she couldn't imagine living there without him. Too many memories of him were attached to the home now, and they'd only make her miss him more.

"Because?" he asked with a gentle tone, and his tender gaze gave her courage.

"We said no more secrets, so here's the truth." *Just say it.* "With planning renovations for Your Secret Garden, personal finances might be tight for a while. And even if I could afford the rent, I couldn't live in that house and be tied to you." The lump in her throat almost choked her. "Not when I love you and . . ." Her voice hitched. She couldn't force the rest of her words out. A warm drop of moisture trickled down her face.

"Beth . . ." Ty reached for her hand, and his tender touch melted her insides like vanilla ice cream on a hot summer day. "I love you too."

She jolted. *He loves me?* Confusion filled every pore. Then why leave her? "I don't understand."

"I'm so sorry. It wasn't my intention to hurt or disappoint you." His eyes pooled, but with two brisk movements, he wiped the tears away. Ty cleared his throat. "If I had my way, you'd pack up and head to Colorado with me. I was going to ask you to do that very thing, but you reminded me again that your heart is with your family. And now that you have big plans for Your Secret Garden, I understand that you can't walk away."

She was too stunned to speak.

"It seems we're both unwilling to break commitments to those we care about." Ty released her hand, then reached for a clean napkin and swiped it beneath his nose.

"If you didn't keep your promises to Brandon, it would destroy something in you. I don't want that to happen."

He heaved a deep sigh. "So here we are."

"Here we are." Beth's throat felt raw from the emotion she fought to control.

"Neither of us can let our people down, so we put them ahead of ourselves."

"It's the right thing to do." Why couldn't she for once do the "wrong" thing and not feel overwhelming guilt?

Tyler's shoulders slumped. "Yeah, the right thing."

God had made a way for them to both achieve their professional dreams. But did it have to mean a personal loss? Must she and Ty sacrifice a potentially loving relationship for the good of others?

Should she feel this mix of resentment and sadness? Did it make her a bad and ungrateful person? She'd focused so hard on unselfishly meeting other people's needs and feelings, she'd neglected taking care of her own, and now instead of being free to love the man in front of her, she felt restrained—imprisoned.

Thirty-Two

B eth walked down the hall toward Lisa's office. This was the last Monday she would spend as an intern, and it was the first day staff and inmates would be aware that Tyler was soon leaving his position at the prison. The place wouldn't feel the same without him.

Gratitude filled her heart for his presence in her life. She would never have entertained the idea of having an internship at the prison if Ty hadn't encouraged it.

Although she grieved silently about him accepting the job in Colorado, she was also happy for him. Beth believed that when you love someone, you put their desires and needs ahead of your own.

Still, it hurt to think about his absence here, at Agatha's, the house they'd worked so hard to bring back to life . . . She'd miss him at every turn.

Sure, they would video chat, but it wouldn't be enough to sustain a relationship long-distance indefinitely. At some point, one of them would need to move to the other's location for them to continue growing together as a couple.

Was it wise to try? Or should they say goodbye now and not risk the deep pain and loss that could come with more time passing? Her head and heart hurt from pondering it.

Two raps, and Lisa opened the door to her office. "Beth,

please come in."

"Thank you." She took the chair offered. "I wanted to touch base on this week's schedule before I head out to the gardens."

"I printed the agenda for you." Lisa handed her a list with instructions for each day. "Have you given thought to applying here for a permanent job? With my recommendation, I'm confident you'd be hired quickly."

"I have given serious consideration to your proposal, and I'm honored that you would think me worthy of the position." This was more difficult than expected. Beth didn't want to let her new friend down. "I've learned so much, and I'm grateful for the experience, but I won't be returning after my internship."

"I'm sorry to hear that," Lisa said, her expression and tone filled with disappointment.

"You've been a wonderful mentor, and I'm thankful for all you, the volunteers, and the inmates have taught me. I'll never forget the time spent here. It's been invaluable, and I'll miss you and working alongside the women. But my place is with my family's business, and my dream has always been to develop my own therapy services."

Lisa offered an understanding smile. "I get it. But remember, my door is always open."

"Thanks." Beth let out a small sigh of relief.

A single question had continued to plague her mind. If she let go of her resentment and forgave Abbey completely, would that mean she'd discarded all loyalty to her dad and brother? She now felt confident of the answer. They'd want her to live a life filled with joy without *anything* holding her back.

"I'd like to talk about one more thing." Something she'd prayed about the past two days.

"Please, go ahead. I have time." Lisa folded her hands on her desk and gave Beth her full attention.

"It's about Abbey." Would she surprise Lisa with her request? Would Lisa approve?

"Okay." Her eyebrows furrowed. "Has she caused any problems for you?"

"No, not at all. We've been able to work and communicate well in the gardens when essential. Without forced direct interaction, the time spent around her has been easier than I expected." Beth had been pleasantly surprised as her comfort level increased slowly over the past weeks. "I've watched Abbey interact with the other prisoners, and she's become almost a role model for some of them. It's clear that many women respect her, and it's been interesting to observe."

"I agree, and to be honest, Beth, I think you've been a huge influence on her, even from a distance."

"Me?" Beth had barely spoken to Abbey and only when necessary.

"Whatever you said during the mediation meeting in Tyler's office that day had an impact on her. I believe she's been trying to prove to herself—and you—that she's worthy to participate in the program. The horticultural project means a lot to her, and you could have made it difficult for her to be involved, but you didn't."

When she first started the internship, Beth certainly didn't want Abbey to be anywhere near her. But each day, God had changed Beth's heart toward the inmate a little more. "Lisa, I only have until the end of the week before my time here comes to an end. With your permission, I'd like to talk to Abbey. I think it might be important for both of us."

"You're asking for another mediation?"

"No, just your consent to talk freely with her, if she's open to it." Beth wasn't sure what she'd say, but she'd trust the Holy Spirit to come through for her and provide the words.

"Yes, go ahead. It might be what you both need. But make sure Abbey doesn't feel forced into a conversation."

"Agreed. I just want to share my heart. She doesn't have to say anything or even listen if she doesn't want to."

Beth's towering shadow shielded Abbey from the sun's bright rays. "Okay if I join you?"

Abbey looked up, and the expression on her face relayed her surprise. She nodded. "Sure. I could use some help."

They worked quietly under the hot July sun, harvesting and dropping green beans into a cardboard box. *Lord, give me wisdom—when to speak—and what to say.*

"You don't know how many nights I lie awake, asking God why a horrible person like me is still alive when two good people were taken from this earth," Abbey said, breaking the silence, her voice oozing with pain. "I don't understand why he took them and left me here."

Beth turned toward her. Abbey had opened the door to talking about God, so Beth was free to share her faith, but she'd be careful to hold back and follow Abbey's lead.

"I know." Abbey nibbled on her lower lip. "They're gone because of my choices—my mistakes—but I'd take their place if I could."

A coppery butterfly with black markings flitting from one bloom to another landed on Beth's sleeve. This lovely creature was once a fuzzy caterpillar with limited travel. Incredible transformations were possible.

Her heart softened. "You're not a horrible person." Abbey was no more a sinner than she or anyone else. God loved her as much as he loved Beth, Harmony, or Kaylee. "I don't know what you are, but you're not bad. I know nothing about you, really."

Ask her.

"Abbey, I'd like to hear your story."

"My story? I don't understand."

"I'd like to learn more about you and what brought you to that night of the accident. But only what you feel comfortable talking about." Beth wanted to encourage Abbey to share what might be helpful to both, not push her into talking about her past if she didn't want to go there.

Abbey tugged on her long ponytail. "I . . ."

"I have an idea." Beth scanned the garden areas to see where the two of them might find a little privacy from the other inmates and volunteers. "Over there." She pointed to a small flower garden close to the fence, planted with colorful zinnias. "That plot needs weeding, and if you feel like talking while we work, I'll listen."

"Okay," she whispered.

They hauled trowels and two buckets to hold pulled weeds over there. Side by side, they dug in the rich, fertilized dirt. As they turned over soil and removed unwanted vegetation, earthworms surfaced, then wiggled their way back underground to safety.

Beth held a worm in her hand and watched it squirm across her palm. "Did you know that earthworms are one of the hardest working critters in the garden?"

"No." Abbey reached for one and examined it. "I thought

they were only good for fishing." She offered a half smile. "And for bird food."

"Oh, God made them for far more. They process organic material both in the soil and in our compost piles. And then they recycle the contents into nutrients." Beth returned the squiggling creature to the ground, and he escaped beneath the warm earth. "Earthworms and nightcrawlers create tunnels for air, water, and plant roots."

"Cool." Abbey dropped her worm, and it wiggled until it was buried beneath the dirt.

"Earthworms, bees, and butterflies were all created for a purpose. They each have an important role to carry out, and I believe the same thing goes for people."

Abbey leaned forward with her hands resting on her knees. "You think that's true for *everyone*?"

"I do."

Several minutes passed in silence. Beth waited patiently. Would Abbey disclose anything about her life? Was Beth ready to learn more about what had brought this inmate to cause tragedy, upheaval, and heartbreak? Was Beth prepared to experience possible empathy toward the woman kneeling next to her?

Abbey dumped a handful of weeds into her bucket. She sat back on her heels, laid her palms on her thighs, and stared at the ground. "I had a drinking problem." She shook her head. "Correction. I *have* a problem—a disease. Once an alcoholic . . ."

"Always an alcoholic," Beth said, finishing the woman's sentence. Should Beth set her trowel aside and sit beside her? Would that stop Abbey from spilling her truth, or would it convince her that she was being seen and heard? *Lord, help!*

Beth's hand stilled as though it was being held in place—

294 | DAWN KINZER

as though her heavenly Father had covered it with his own. *Okay, Lord.* She shoved her pail aside and sat cross-legged on the ground, hoping to prove that she was willing to listen.

Abbey wiped her brow with the back of her hand. "The disease runs in my family, and it was passed down to me through my dad. It wasn't his fault. He didn't understand why liquor had such a hold on him."

She took several deep breaths. "Seven years ago, I gave birth to a baby girl, and my dad made me give her up. I was only fifteen, so I didn't have any say. And I knew I couldn't raise her without help."

"What about your mom?"

"Ran off with another guy when I was three, and I haven't seen or heard from her since." Abbey's forehead furrowed. "I *think* I was three. It's hard to remember. Dad said she abandoned us because she didn't want to put up with me. Maybe that's true. Or maybe she couldn't deal with an angry drunk in the house."

"It's not your fault she left." Beth kicked into counselor mode and distanced herself internally so she could listen and be supportive without getting sucked in emotionally to Abbey's story or be affected by her own conflicted feelings about this woman.

"Maybe. I still don't get it. I haven't seen my own daughter since they took her away in the hospital, but I still miss her every day." Abbey gazed up at the sky, as though searching for her child. She dropped her head, and her shoulders slumped. "That's when I started drinking. I was hurting so bad."

"You were trying to cope with your grief." How did people survive that kind of loss without family or friends to support them? Without faith in a loving God who was always there to comfort? Without hope that he had something good planned for the future?

"My daughter is seven now, and I sometimes wonder if she looks like me. I wonder if she's happy."

"I'm sorry you've experienced so much pain." And that was the truth. "The father of your child?"

"He never accepted responsibility for the pregnancy, and I don't know what happened to him." Abbey moistened her lips. "I was drinking the night of the accident. I'd just lost my job as a waitress in a restaurant. I missed too many shifts because I was either drinking or hungover. My rent was due, and I didn't have enough money to pay all my bills, so of course, I spent what little I did have on booze," she said almost sarcastically, hinting that she realized her actions had been foolish and irresponsible.

Beth didn't know what to say, so she didn't say anything.

Abbey rubbed her eyes. "Ahh . . ." she said as she released a rush of air from her lungs. "I'm not making excuses! I'm just telling you how it was and how ashamed and sorry I am for the hurt I caused."

Breathe. Beth tried to swallow, but her mouth had gone dry. "I believe you," she whispered. She'd heard Abbey apologize before, but this time the sincere words touched Beth in an unexpected way, unlike before. She made a conscious decision to no longer remain in a supportive counseling position and allowed herself to feel genuine compassion toward Abbey.

"Thank you." Her sincere tone and tear-filled eyes relayed that Beth's simple response was meaningful. "After the accident I went through detox. That was like living hell. I thought I was going to die, and part of me wanted to."

"But you came through it."

"And now I'm in rehab and meet with a group of women in recovery here." Abbey's sad smile was filled with regret, and her eyes begged for Beth's understanding.

"I'm glad you're getting some help. I truly am, and I appreciate you being vulnerable with me."

"You deserve the truth, and so does your family."

"You're giving me permission to share your history with my mom and sisters?" The revelations had been helpful for Beth's perspective and heart, and she was confident that knowing more about Abbey would do the same for them.

"Yes. I want them to know." Abbey sniffed. "It's not that I believe anything I've told you will make you or them feel sorry for me. I don't even want that."

"What *do* you want?"

"For you all to believe that I would never hurt anyone intentionally."

"We already do, Abbey."

"I just—I just I don't understand why you don't hate me, or how you can stand to be around me."

No matter what Beth and her family said to Abbey—or how often—she would probably always be weighed down by guilt. Unless she came to know the One who could free her from that heavy burden.

Who else will tell her, if not you?

Of course God would turn things completely around. Beth had arrived at the prison months ago filled with anger toward the woman sitting next to her, and now she felt his presence and nudge to talk about love, forgiveness, and redemption.

Abbey was broken. That was clear.

Beth had always felt more comfortable with sharing her faith through relationship instead of beating a person over the head with Bible verses. Yes, Scripture carried power, but she liked to take things slow and develop trust. One of the things she and Ty had in common. They both believed actions spoke louder than words.

"Can I ask you a question?" Abbey asked, jolting Beth out of her private thoughts.

"Hmm? Oh, sure." Where was this going?

"Why do you do this?"

"By *this* do you mean why do I garden? Or why am I here working in the prison?"

"Both." Abbey rubbed her upper arms, then crossed them in front of her. "When you asked me to stay in the program, you talked about your dad giving you grace when you messed up and used your mom's nail polish. So I understand that you're trying to be like your dad, and you've forgiven me for causing the accident. But I still don't get why you choose to work here with us convicts."

Lord, you cracked the door open. Give me the words.

Beth folded her hands. If she couldn't pray out loud, she'd at least give a signal that she needed reinforcements from the heavenly hosts. "No one is perfect. It's impossible, no matter how hard we try. We all make mistakes. Some are small and easily dismissed, but others have potential to do damage, either to ourselves or other people."

"I guess . . ."

"I forgive others because God forgives me all the time—daily even. Sometimes by the minute." Beth grinned and relaxed at seeing the corners of Abbey's mouth twitch into a small smile.

"You believe in that stuff? That there's a God and a heaven?" Abbey sounded skeptical.

"With my whole heart." How could she explain? "I can feel his presence everywhere, but even more so when I'm enjoying his creation and the way he meant this world to exist. Beautiful and for our pleasure. I feel close to him when I spend time in the forest, at the ocean, or digging in a small patch of dirt."

"So that's why gardening is your thing."

"And that's why I want to share it with people both inside and outside of these walls. I believe spending time with nature is healing. Shutting out the chaos of the world for even a moment to feel the breeze, smell the wonderful scents, and observe wildlife gives us small glimpses of heaven. It draws us closer to God and reminds us that he is all powerful and has created this world. The other things . . . jobs, cities, technology . . . they're all temporary. They won't last forever. But God's love will."

Abbey seemed deep in thought. She twisted a small stick in her hands, and her face had turned a shade of pink, hinting that she was being affected emotionally as well. "I don't know how to . . ." Her face scrunched up.

"Find God?"

"You talk about him like you know him. Just like the lady who works with the prison ministry here. But if he's *God*, doesn't he have better things to do than pay attention to you or me?"

"You've been talking to a minister?" Did Beth's expression reveal her shock?

"Not a preacher—a woman who volunteers." Abbey picked up a handful of dirt, then watched it sift through her fingers. "She's kind, and I like talking to her. I've been invited to her Bible study, but I haven't gone. Maybe I will. I haven't decided."

God had worked a miracle, and Beth felt lighter than she

had in a very long time. By sharing a simple story from her childhood, a seed had been planted, and now the desire to understand faith was growing in Abbey. She wasn't solely responsible for Abbey experiencing God's love. Beth only needed to do her part, and he would take care of the rest.

"God wants nothing more than to have a relationship with us, but he won't force us into one. It's up to us to accept it." Inspiration hit at the right time—*God's* time. Beth shifted into a kneeling position, and with a raised palm, she made a sweeping gesture that took in everything around them. "Tell me, what do you see? What's surrounding you?"

Abbey scanned the prison yard. "Concrete walls, a fence, prisoners, volunteers, and guards."

"And . . . the most important thing?" Beth raised her eyebrows.

She smiled. "The gardens."

"And they're wonderful examples of what can bloom where love is planted." Beth touched the soil next to her. "As seeds are watered and nourished, they grow and provide beauty. God plants other types of seeds in our hearts. We water and feed them by reading our Bibles and spending time with him. Prayer is merely conversation with God." She held her hand over her heart. "I promise, the result can be wonderful, glorious gardens within, where we find peace, hope, and joy."

"It sounds nice but also kind of . . ." Abbey, sounding tentative, waved her hand in the air.

Beth laughed. "Like a bunch of hooey?"

"Yeah."

"I get it. The supernatural can seem unnatural until it isn't. And that can only come through learning more about what

God has to say about his love for us and what he wants for our lives." *Don't hold back now—ask.* "Abbey . . . would it be okay if I brought you a Bible?"

Thirty-Three

O nly three days left on the job and then another seven before Ty was expected in Colorado. He'd soon leave this place he'd come to love—the *woman* he loved. What was he doing? Why couldn't he have more of a free spirit like Aunt Agatha? What would be wrong with changing the original plan?

Nothing except breaking a promise to his best friend, disregarding what he believed was God's purpose for his life, and potentially losing the chance to gain his father's respect. Ty wasn't willing to give up on trying to have a relationship with Beth, but with them living so far apart, was it realistic?

Was there any way to resolve this and get what he wanted without hurting someone else? What *did* he want? To stay here with Beth and build a life with her. And to still help the people he believed God had called him to serve.

Lord, I could sure use some answers—some direction.

He pulled a pitcher of lemonade from the refrigerator in Agatha's kitchen, poured a glass, and downed the refreshing drink in a few gulps. Outside temps still showed eighty-three degrees at 7:35 p.m., and Agatha didn't have air-conditioning in her house. Sweat trickled down the back of his neck.

Ty opened the screen door and jumped. Brandon stood at the base of the steps. "What are you doing here? You weren't

302 | DAWN KINZER

supposed to make it back for two more days."

Brandon slacked his hip and raised one hand. "Thanks for the welcome." He relaxed and grinned. "We need to talk, buddy."

"Okay . . . when a woman says 'we need to talk,' it gives a guy the heads-up that he's in trouble." Ty rushed down the steps. "Or are *you* the one in trouble? Did something happen when you got home? Anything go wrong with the bookcases?"

"No, come see for yourself." Brandon gestured for Ty to follow him. He led the way to the front of Agatha's house, where a large moving truck sat on the side of the road.

Ty whistled. "Did you build enough furniture to fill the entire house?"

"No." Brandon gave him a pat on the back. "I have some news."

"What's going on?" Why didn't Brandon call and fill him in before showing up at the door?

"I had a long talk with my dad and brother, laid it all out, and told them the truth." Brandon wiped the beads of moisture from his brow. "I didn't hold back, but I tried to explain how I felt as respectfully as possible."

"Meaning?" Had his friend found the courage to speak up? Brandon, discontented, had wanted to step away from his dad's business for some time.

"I told them I loved them and appreciated the opportunity I've had all these years to learn, grow, and be a part of something we created together. But it was time for me to pursue new goals." Brandon rubbed the palms of his hands together. "Focus on making handcrafted furniture and using my skills to mentor kids."

Adrenaline raced through Ty's veins. Did this mean he and

Brandon could start developing their program for at-risk kids now? All the waiting had finally come to an end?

"Dad was disappointed, but he understood. My brother supports my decision." Brandon chuckled. "I don't know if that's because he believes in me, or he's thrilled to have me out of his way."

"I'm proud of you. I know standing up to your dad wasn't easy." Ty grinned. "I've met the guy, and he's no pushover!"

"Thanks."

"But you've left something out of the story." Ty gestured toward the vehicle. "The units you built must take up only a fraction of the space." He turned and faced Brandon. "Or is this about us taking a road trip together and you helping me move back to Colorado? I don't have that much to transport, but this will do the job."

Brandon flashed a satisfied grin. "Nope—didn't intend to haul your stuff anywhere."

"I'm confused. Why not?"

"Aside from the beautiful, custom woodwork that will blow you away, my own things take up the space."

"What?" Ty asked with a jolt. "You've packed up *everything*?"

Agatha came out the front door wearing a pale pink, sleeveless, flowing dress and strolled toward them. "Welcome home, Brandon!"

Home? What did she know that Ty didn't? Or was she merely wanting to make him *feel* at home?

"Thanks, Agatha!" Brandon met her halfway, they embraced briefly, then they joined Ty on the lawn.

His gaze pinged from one to the other. "What's going on? It feels like you two are in cahoots."

"Cahoots?" Agatha clapped her hands together. "I haven't heard that term in a long time, but yes, I guess we are."

"Like I spelled it out for my dad, I'm going to be honest with you." Brandon laid his hands on Ty's shoulders and looked him in the eyes. "I don't think you should take the job in Colorado. This is where your heart is, this is where you belong—where we *both* belong."

"Brandon! Why would you uproot yourself?" Was his friend suggesting they both settle here for Ty's sake, or was Brandon feeling pulled here too? "What about our plans?"

"I think it's time to deviate. Something better has come along—Meriside and the people here." Brandon removed his hands from Ty's shoulders. "I realize I sprung this whole thing on you without warning. Maybe I should have told you up front. But if I had, you would have tried to convince me to change my mind."

Although touched by his friend's generosity, Ty felt conflicted. How could he ask more of Brandon when all he'd ever done was put other people first? "I can't ask you to sacrifice anything more for me."

"You didn't ask, and I'm not giving up anything. My folks are a short flight away. And if I stayed there, my dad would eventually be tempted to pull me back into his business."

Brandon slipped his hands into the front pockets of his jeans. "And what about all the mountain trails and ocean beaches you promised to explore with me? I'm ready for new adventures."

"So you have this all figured out." It sounded like Brandon felt confident this decision was the best direction for them both.

"I had plenty of time to think on the drive here, and trust

me, I'm being selfish by asking you to stay." Brandon grinned. "I'll find a place of my own where I can live and set up shop. We can create a program for at-risk kids anywhere. It doesn't have to be in Colorado. Didn't you mention a juvenile detention center in the area?"

Ty was trying to grasp everything Brandon threw at him. His thoughts spun. Could they actually do this? Ty's heart raced from nervous excitement. Their decision could change kids' lives—*their* lives. It would give him a chance to love Beth the way he'd hoped—the way she deserved. "Why didn't you say anything when I told you about the job offer?"

"Look, if you still want to move and keep our initial plan, I'll turn this beast around without unpacking, and we'll head back over the pass." Brandon pulled keys from his pocket and brandished them in the air. "But you called after I'd already gotten on the road, and I wanted to talk to you in person and show you how serious I am about creating a life here. I thought I'd have more time to convince you *this* is home before you had to make a choice."

Agatha stepped forward. "Ty, see it for what it is . . . God moving in miraculous ways you didn't expect. Get out of his way and let him help you be successful."

Unexpected emotions made Ty's throat ache. "Why would God open the door to the prison job in Colorado if that's not his will for me?" he asked in a raspy voice.

"It seems to me that God is being generous by giving you a choice." Agatha's eyes sparkled with wisdom. "He's made the way and given you two options. He's letting you choose which is more important to you."

Ty scrubbed his face with his hands. "I don't know."

"Maybe your heavenly Father gave you the position in

Colorado, so you'd know he didn't let you down. He doesn't want you to carry regrets or doubt that he answers prayers." She fingered her long braid. "Sometimes we think we know what we want when we really desire and need something else. And we're often tempted to settle for what is *good* when he yearns to give us the *best*."

Agatha wrapped her arm around his waist and drew him to her side. "Tyler, you must decide which path to take."

His heart was here with Beth, people he'd come to care about, and his work at the prison.

Ty's cell rang, and he pulled it from his back pocket. *Dad.* Now? He didn't expect to hear from his parents for another week. "I need to take this." He stepped away, sat in the shade on the front steps to Agatha's house, and accepted the call.

"Hi, Dad." Ty checked his watch. It read 8:03 p.m. here, so it was 5:03 a.m. in Germany. "You're up early. Is everything okay?" Had something happened to Mom?

"Sure. Everything is fine." His dad sounded alert, despite the hour. "I won't keep you long. I just wanted to let you know that your mom and I got your message. Congratulations! Landing that job as director of social services is a big deal. Your hard work is paying off."

The joy Ty felt only minutes ago deflated like a popped balloon. His entire life, he'd waited for the day his father would express even a small amount of pride in him, and now he had to disappoint his dad one more time. But God had given Ty his own purpose to fulfill, and even if his dad's response to Ty's decision might hurt, it was more important to please God than anyone else.

"Thanks, Dad, but I've decided to not take it. I'm staying here." *I need your help, Lord.*

Silence.

"Dad?" Maybe it was better that they weren't on a video chat this call. A visual of his dad's reaction would be worse than waiting for him to speak. "I'm sorry if you're angry or if I've let you down again. But I believe God wants me here."

Silence.

His dad hadn't hung up, so at least he was listening. "I'm making a difference at the women's prison, even more than I believed possible. And Brandon has decided to move and get his woodworking business established in Meriside."

Ty would lay it all out. It was time for his parents to know the man he'd become. "I'll continue working at the women's prison, but Brandon and I are going to move ahead with creating a program that will help kids who are in danger of getting into trouble or who need direction after being released from juvie. We can also help youth whose parents are incarcerated. We want to support them and give them alternatives to getting into criminal activities themselves."

He'd never shared that information with his parents before, believing it was best to wait until he could follow through and prove he was serious about pursuing that dream.

"Tyler . . ." Dad cleared his throat. Silence.

He braced himself for a lecture. His dad would tell him he was making a mistake by turning down the prestigious job in Colorado. He'd question Ty's ability to get financial backing and his experience for running that kind of youth program.

"Ty . . ." Dad said quietly. "You don't need to be sorry. I'm the one who needs to apologize for making you feel that you've failed us."

He held his breath for a moment. His dad had never called him anything but Tyler. And he'd also never expressed any remorse for his words or actions concerning Ty.

"The truth is . . . I haven't treated you right, especially as a father who is supposed to be an example of a godly man. Although I've been understanding and ministered to people who have made far worse blunders and created a mess of their lives, I've held you to a higher standard. I made it more about me than you. After all, how could a chaplain lead other men when he couldn't keep his own son out of trouble? It was wrong to put that on you. Please forgive me."

"I—I . . ." Who was this man? Ty would never have anticipated this conversation. Only God could move his father to change. "I forgive you, Dad."

"Good. Thank you." A huge sigh came through the phone. "It's important that you follow God's leading, Ty. You're a strong, intelligent man, and your mom and I are proud of you." His dad paused. "I love you, Son."

His vision blurred. Ty couldn't remember any other time when his dad had expressed those feelings. He wanted to say the words back, but they stuck in his throat, and he couldn't force them through his lips.

"I need to get going here in a minute, but anything else you want to talk about, Son, before we hang up?"

"Ah . . . yeah. I met someone. She's special, Dad. Her name is Beth, and she's beautiful, kind, giving, and she's a woman of faith. She uses garden therapy to help people."

"She sounds wonderful, Ty."

"I love her, Dad." Confessing it to his father confirmed Ty's strong feelings. They weren't fleeting. They ran deep and true.

"I can hear it in your voice. I'm happy for you, and I'll look forward to meeting her someday."

"Dad?"

"Yes, Ty?"

"I love you too."

Thirty-Four

A lmost time to lock up Your Secret Garden for the night. Only two days remained before Beth's internship would end. She'd waited so long to accomplish this goal, and now mixed emotions gave rise to relief, accomplishment, exhilaration, and even sadness.

The job that initially felt overwhelming in an intimidating environment had become life-changing in the best way. Beth had grown in confidence. Even more important, she'd found peace and a new understanding working with the prisoners.

By listening to the women's stories, she'd learned to be more tolerant and compassionate. True, they were all there because they'd broken the law, but they were paying for their mistakes. And although not all were repentant and willing to change, many yearned to create a better life for themselves and their families. It felt rewarding to watch them respond to nature and bloom themselves through participation in the horticulture program.

And the biggest surprise and gift of all was finding the ability to not only forgive Abbey but also sincerely care about her and her future. With God's help, Beth had found the capacity to see Abbey through his eyes.

Beth and Ty had shared few words since he'd told her about his plans on Saturday to leave Meriside soon. They thought they were protecting each other as they prepared to say goodbye.

Instead of grabbing every free moment together, Beth had kept busy with her work, and he'd focused on helping Marcus get settled in Meriside. Although, Agatha was doing an amazing job making the boy feel at home herself. Ty had also spent one last evening playing checkers with Henry Middleton. But now Beth regretted wasting even a minute she could have shared with Ty.

Mom laid the shears she'd been using to cut flower stems on the counter. "We have visitors."

Beth peered up from the computer screen, but the rays from the setting sun blinded her. She moved around to the front of the desk to a spot blocked from direct light.

"What are Ty and Brandon doing here?" Harmony asked as she stepped to Beth's side.

"I don't know." She hadn't expected Brandon to show up for several more days.

The two men opened the door and stopped short at seeing the three women staring. Tyler and Brandon glanced at each other, then continued inside.

"Hi." Ty sounded guarded. "Did Agatha warn you we were coming?"

Beth shook her head. "No . . . was she supposed to?"

"The three of you—never mind." Ty shook his head and chuckled.

Brandon gave them one of his charismatic grins. "We'd like to talk."

"To all of you." Ty's stance relaxed. "I promise it won't take much time."

"Hi, guys!" Kaylee strolled in from the back room as

though the men's appearance that time of night wasn't unusual. "When did you get into town?" She shot a welcoming smile at Brandon.

Ty turned to Beth, his gaze penetrating hers, making her heart thump wildly. He stepped next to her and whispered, "Can we talk privately—about us? After we explain a few things to your mom and sisters?"

His familiar woodsy scent enticed her, but she fought the urge to move into his arms. Instead, she merely nodded. What was God up to? Beth believed she and Ty could find a solution to being together if they wanted it bad enough. She'd sent up silent prayers throughout the past few days, waiting for answers, but none had come. Did Ty's request for time alone mean something had changed?

"What's going on?" Mom asked, her brows furrowed.

Beth stole a glance at Ty, her heart aching to know what he was thinking—feeling.

The four Miller women stood in front of the counter, waiting for this apparent news flash that was so important Brandon and Ty wanted them all together. Beth's hands clenched in front of her. Why were they acting so mysterious?

Ty turned to Brandon. "Where do we start?"

"Anywhere." Beth wiped moist palms on her jeans. They were taking too long to explain, and it made her nervous.

"Yeah, okay." Brandon tilted his head and gave a nod. "To start, I got into town last night with custom pieces for Ty's house. But I also brought pretty much everything else I own."

"You're moving here?" Beth grabbed Harmony's upper arm.

"Oww!"

"Sorry!" Beth released her grip, and her focus flitted

between the two guys. "Really? That's amazing, but if Tyler is relocating to Colorado, how does that make sense?"

Tyler perched his hand on his buddy's shoulder. "We're both making Meriside our home."

Beth gasped quietly, and her heart pounded in rapid rhythm like a musician in a snare drum competition. Ty was staying. She wouldn't need to say goodbye. Liquid pooled in her eyes, and she tried to blink back the tears of gratitude before they escaped. God had made a way when there seemed to be no way.

"I went into work this morning and retracted my resignation. Luckily for me, my supervisor is thrilled he doesn't need to break in a new social worker." Ty wiped his forehead with an exaggerated motion. "Then Brandon and I spent several hours this evening working on a new plan. We still have a lot to figure out, but we've got a good start."

"I'll find my own place to live, but for now, I'll bunk out at Ty's house. Once I secure a spot big enough for me to set up my woodworking shop, I'll get my business up and running." Brandon eyed Ty and grinned. "And my partner here and I will develop the program for kids we've talked about for years."

Beth glanced at Kaylee, whose face glowed at the announcement. Had she taken her eyes off Brandon since he'd arrived?

"It won't happen overnight, but we have to start somewhere, and we can implement some initial steps." Ty's gaze swept the four women but returned to Beth. "But we also wanted to let you know that if you're open to it, we'd like to help with the renovation and see your own dream come true for Your Secret Garden."

Beth's jaw dropped. "Ty!" This was an answer to many

314 | DAWN KINZER

prayers. She'd been learning to set down the weight associated with taking care of her family, and Ty's announcement allowed her to breathe even more freely. She didn't need to carry full responsibility. They were in this together, and Beth would accept all the help she could get in making Your Secret Garden a success.

"It's impossible for us to do all the work," Ty said. "We're not qualified or licensed for everything involved, like electricity and plumbing, and realistically, we won't have the time."

Brandon dropped his hand on Ty's shoulder and smiled at the women. "Right, and you don't want the reno to drag on indefinitely. But we'll do what we can, and we want to ensure that what we can't accomplish ourselves will be done well and for a reasonable price."

"Tyler—Brandon—we don't know how to thank you . . ." Mom's voice hitched, and she wiped her eyes.

Brandon shook his head. "No need to thank us. I couldn't stop thinking about the project on my drive here from Colorado, especially about the tearoom and garden, and I'd like to run some ideas by you when you're ready to move forward."

"I'd love to hear them!" Kaylee's cheeks flushed, and her tone bubbled with excitement.

Watching Kaylee, Beth's heart sighed with joy. Her sister-in-law was healing from her grief. Maybe now she could begin to embrace a new future.

"Let's celebrate!" Kaylee lifted both hands into the air. "I brought peach tortes, chocolate chip cookies, and lemon bars in this afternoon for the employees, but plenty are left in the kitchenette."

"I'm in! Don't need to ask me twice." Brandon made a sweeping gesture. "Lead the way."

Mom and Harmony followed, but Tyler held Beth back.

"Can we talk now—just the two of us?"

"I'd like that," she said, nodding. "Let's go out to the greenhouse. We'll have more privacy there." Now that Ty staying in Meriside was becoming reality, had he realized his feelings for her weren't as strong as he'd claimed? Was that why he didn't rush to tell her about the change of plans as soon as they were made?

He followed her into the area that housed benches of potted plants and hanging floral baskets. They were surrounded by a rainbow of color, and lovely fragrances filled the air. A beautiful red, orange, and pink sky could be seen through the glass ceiling.

Ty took Beth's hands and enfolded them within his own. "I want to talk about us—you and me."

"Is there an *us*?" Beth couldn't look at him. Instead, she focused on the ground. Was he attempting to let her down easily? He hadn't been willing to remain in Meriside for her, but now that his friend wanted to move, Ty had changed his plans. "If you're staying because of Brandon, that's okay."

"I know it looked like I was putting my friend ahead of you and our relationship." His voice carried a hint of desperation. "But I didn't know what to do. It felt like no matter what choice I made, I was going to disappoint someone I loved and lose out on something wonderful that could change my life."

Ty squeezed her hands. "You know that when I was arrested, my dad was so hurt and angry, he wouldn't talk to me—for months. He eventually forgave me for letting him down, and we moved on the best we could." Ty stared to the left. "But Brandon . . . he showed up that first visitors' day. He told me it didn't matter what I'd done or what I'd do in the future, he'd always love me as a friend and brother."

316 | DAWN KINZER

Beth had heard all of this before. She understood his loyalty to Brandon, so where was Ty going with this?

"He gave me the gift of unconditional love, Beth. After experiencing my dad's rejection, I didn't realize how much I needed what Brandon offered until then, and it took everything I had in that moment to not break down and cry like a baby." Ty's intense gaze held her. "I'd do anything for him."

"I know." She pulled her eyes away from his. "Although it hurt to think I wasn't important enough for you to change your plans, it was wrong to put everything on you when I was unwilling to make similar sacrifices. I'm sorry."

"The truth is, we've wanted the same thing. We just didn't know how to get it." Ty wrapped his arms around her and drew her close.

He kissed the top of her head tenderly. "I finally realized that a big part of my drive to get that position in Colorado was wanting to prove to my dad that I was worthy of his respect. I was trying hard to please him when I should have been more concerned about following the journey God had chosen for me, knowing that the greatest blessings would come with that path."

"And now? Are you no longer concerned about your relationship with your dad?" What could have brought such a drastic change?

"I'll always want his approval, but we talked last night and were honest with each other. Things are different—*better*—between us now." Ty tightened his embrace. "I filled him in on everything, including how I feel about you."

"Me?" Beth whispered. Dare she hope that he wanted a serious relationship? Ty wouldn't mention her to his dad unless he cared deeply, would he?

"I was a fool before. Please forgive me." He caressed her cheek, sending waves of warmth through her body. "I didn't change my mind about the job because Brandon decided to move here. He offered to return to Colorado with me, but I didn't want to leave Meriside, my job, or my aunt. More importantly, I didn't want to leave *you*."

Beth tilted her head back, and he held her face between his hands. Ty searched her eyes, and she revealed her heart. She felt his warm breath on her lips, and she parted them slightly, anticipating his touch.

Her arms wrapped around his shoulders, her fingers massaging the nape of his neck as his lips brushed hers with several tender kisses. She drew him closer, letting him know she was ready for more, and the kisses deepened.

They pulled away, as if both recognized in unison the heat ignited between them needed to be controlled. Beth attempted to slow her breathing and smiled.

Ty grinned in return, tousled her short hair, and holding the back of her neck, kissed her forehead. "Can you believe it? God has offered us everything we've wanted—rewarding jobs, family, friends—and each other."

Should she believe it? During her life there had always been another crisis—another storm. Could she trust there wouldn't be another? What could she do to prevent tragedy from happening again?

"What's wrong?" His thumb trailed her jaw gently.

"I struggled for so long, wondering why God hadn't fulfilled my desires. Now that everything is falling into place, I'm afraid it's all too good to be true and none of it will last."

"Agatha reminded me today that sometimes we need to get out of God's way. We don't earn his favor by proving that we're worthy of his blessings." Ty wrapped his arm around her shoulder and drew her to his side.

He stroked her arm, soothing her. "God loves us unconditionally and wants the best for us. And when challenges show up in the future—and they will—we won't have to face them alone. The Lord is always standing with us, and we have each other, not to mention those people in the other room chowing down on dessert."

She stood on tiptoe and kissed his cheek. It had taken her a long time to accept the truth that she didn't need to carry any responsibility, burden, or concerns alone.

"I love you, Beth."

"And I love *you*." She did—completely.

"We make a great team." He held her hand over his heart, and she felt it beating beneath her palm. "And I believe we can build a wonderful life together."

"One that thrives and helps others to flourish too."

"Remember what you told me after we first met?" Ty lifted her chin and kissed her lightly on the lips. His touch sent warm waves through her body, and he whispered near her ear, "Where love is planted . . ."

"Surely something beautiful will grow."

Discussion Questions

1. Now that you've read *Where Love is Planted*, do you think the title relates to the story? If so, in what ways?

2. Beth feels responsible for her family's well-being to the point of putting her dreams on hold indefinitely. Why is she willing to do this?

3. What do you think draws Beth to Agatha and their friendship?

4. What are the motivations behind Tyler's goals and his willingness to pursue them even at a possible loss to personal happiness? Do you agree with his decision to move to Colorado, regardless of what he may leave behind?

5. At the beginning of the story, Beth and Ty refrain from sharing information regarding their personal pasts. Why?

6. What did you think when Tyler purchased the home Beth had her eyes on? Would you have dealt with the situation the same way as Beth?

7. Are the ways Beth handles grief and facing Abbey Ward realistic? Relatable?

8. How does Tyler's relationship with his parents affect his decisions? His goals?

9. What do you think of Beth's ideas to recreate Your Secret Garden and the family business?

10. Which character do you relate to the most and why?

Dear Reader,

Where Love is Planted has been a labor of love. The anecdotes Beth shares about her father are my own. Although I tweaked them slightly to fit the setting, I experienced similar moments with my dad, and they've influenced how I've lived my life and raised my daughters.

The fictional town, Meriside, was inspired by the port town where I reside in Washington State. Yes, there is a woman's prison located only sixteen miles from our town, and a county juvenile detention facility is located nearby. While this story is fiction, the information included concerning Corrections Hope Gardens and the Sustainability in Prisons Project is factual. The Olympic Mountains and the national park are only a drive away, and there are many hiking trails to explore in our area. Please visit my author website at www.dawnkinzer.com to see some of the photos I've taken on my outdoor adventures.

When I started brainstorming this story, I searched for a profession I hadn't seen included in fiction before. I was thrilled to learn about horticultural therapists. If you visited my home, you'd see real indoor plants, a yard full of flowers, and a backyard with a view of the woods. Although I love the ocean and mountains, the forest is truly my happy place.

Spending time in nature and gardening brings me peace, and it's always been a way for me to feel closer to God than anywhere else. I sense his presence in the stillness, in the growing things around me, and in the amazing beauty he offers us. We only need to look!

God bless! Dawn

Acknowledgements

Readers . . . You're the reason I share my stories, and your encouragement and support inspire me to continue pouring words onto the page.

Annette Irby . . . My dear friend and editor. I'm so grateful that we share this writing journey.

Jessica Snell . . . You've become more than a proofreader. While pointing out my errors, you've also become a friend and partner in the publishing process. I'm thankful!

Sarah Holt . . . Your input on autistic children was so valuable. Thank you for sharing some of your experiences!

Sonny Kinzer, my husband . . . We're a team in all the best ways. I couldn't do this without you.

God, my Father . . . My stories and their messages come from you. I'm only the vessel, trying to do the best job possible in relaying them.

Meet the Author

Dawn Kinzer, a mom and grandmother, lives with her husband in the beautiful Pacific Northwest. Favorite things include dark chocolate, cinnamon, popcorn, strong coffee, good wine, the mountains, family time, and *Masterpiece Theatre*.

You can find out more about Dawn and her books by visiting www.dawnkinzer.com.

She loves to hear from her readers. You may contact her at dawnkinzer2940@gmail.com.

Other places to connect: Facebook, Goodreads, Pinterest, BookBub, Amazon Author Page, and Instagram

FREEBIE! Download "Maggie's Miracle"—a short story—as a gift when you visit www.dawnkinzer.com and sign up to receive Dawn's author newsletter sharing interesting tidbits about her books, photos, and other fun stuff about her writing world. Also available for purchase on Kindle.

The Daughters of Riverton

Historical Romance Series

Take a trip back to the early 1900s and spend time in the small farming community of Riverton, Wisconsin, where people find the courage to forgive, pursue their dreams—and love.

Book 1 – ***Sarah's Smile***

Book 2 – ***Hope's Design***

Book 3 – ***Rebecca's Song***

Though they follow a time sequence with some characters playing a role in every story, each book is a stand-alone romance featuring a different couple.

Questions that can be used for self-reflection or discussion are included at the end of each story.

Available in ebook and paperback on Amazon.
Available in paperback on Barnes & Noble.com
and Books-A- Million. com

By All Appearances

Contemporary Romance

*An attractive special events planner
is determined to keep her distance.
A disfigured musician struggles to guard his heart.
By all appearances, both are destined to fail.*

Available in ebook and paperback on Amazon.
Available in paperback on Barnes & Noble.com
and Books-A- Million.com

A Night Divine

Contemporary Christmas Romance

A popular model eager to find purpose.
An outreach minister with a hidden past.
A tragedy bound them together.
But will the truth tear them apart?

With a Trusting Heart

Historical Romance

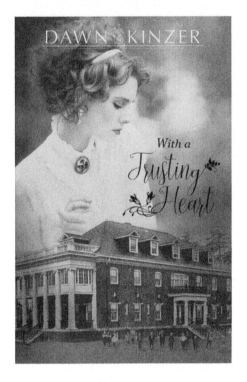

*Will trust be the winning ticket
to mending two wounded hearts?*

This story was inspired by events that took place at the 1909
Alaska-Yukon-Pacific Expo—Seattle's first world's fair.

Available in ebook and paperback on Amazon.
Available in paperback on Barnes & Noble.com
and Books-A- Million.com

Made in the USA
Monee, IL
18 September 2023

42943573R00184